This is a work of fiction. Names, characters, places, and incidents are either the product of the author's imagination or used fictitiously. Any resemblance to actual persons, living or dead, events, or locales is entirely coincidental.

RIGHT OF FIRST REFUSAL

Cover design: Maggie Hall
Interior formatting: Cait Greer

ISBN-10: 0-9909168-2-0 (e-book)
ISBN-13: 978-0-9909168-2-6

ISBN-10: 0-9909168-4-7 (paperback)
ISBN-13: 978-0-9909168-4-0

Other books by Dahlia Adler

The Radleigh University Series
Last Will and Testament

The Daylight Falls Series
Behind the Scenes
Under the Lights

Just Visiting

To Lindsay, who refuses to let me give up,
and to Yoni, for a second chance when it mattered most

chapter one

The stream of profanity that rings through my dorm room is made a thousand times funnier by the fact that it's in French. Inexplicably so, since my Filipina-American former roommate is the one yelping it. It's hard to run and help her when all I wanna do is laugh, *but*, it is my stuff I'm pretty sure she just dropped on her foot, so.

"You all right there, Queen B?" I slide off my bed, where I got distracted trying to decide where to store my shin guards now that I have to go back to taking up only half my room. Not sure how I used to do this back when Lizzie and I were cohabitating, but right now, it seems impossible to store my stuff in the allotted space.

"How do you have so much *crap*, Cait?" Lizzie calls back from where she's buried in what used to be her closet. As of today, that closet now belongs to one Andrea Nelson, a girl I've never met but who's apparently a sophomore—same as me and Lizzie—who was thrilled to get in off the Radleigh University housing waitlist. My suite was a no-brainer, given it had not one but two open spots, since Lizzie not only ditched me for an off-campus apartment, but took our best friend and suitemate, Frankie Bellisario, with her.

"I know, right?" As if on cue, Frankie pops up in the doorway, cracking a piece of gum so huge I can smell the artificial watermelon flavor from here. "You'd think I'd be the mess around here, but my room's alllll clean and ready for Samantha What's-her-face."

"I'm pretty sure it's Samara," says Lizzie, climbing over the heap of clothing she dropped and hopping onto her old bed to nurse her foot. Such a drama queen. "But sounds like you'll be making a great first impression."

"Hey, I have no impression to make," Frankie reminds us, perching on Lizzie's old desk, which is unfortunately still piled high with my old notebooks and test papers from last semester. "These newbies are Cait's problem."

She grins, flipping her blue-streaked mane, and I glare at her. "Sure. Make light of the fact that you two ditched me. Bitches."

"You were invited to join us," says Lizzie, picking up a pair of gym shorts between her fingers and wrinkling her nose. "Though I don't know how the hell we thought we were ever gonna have room for your stuff."

"Ha ha." There's no point in rehashing the conversation. Lizzie only got the new apartment in the first place because she'd gotten custody of her little brothers when her parents were killed in an accident a few weeks into the school year. She'd relinquished custody to her godmother after a few months, but that didn't relieve her of the apartment. Her brothers leaving meant the room they shared was now free, but my lacrosse scholarship requires me to stay in campus housing. Frankie, on the other hand, had no such ties, and is a total whore for a little outdoor space.

That leaves me, my generally absentee suitemate—a pre-med named Stamatina—and two new strangers who are likely arriving today, given classes start tomorrow and neither's shown up yet.

God, I hope they don't suck.

"You need to either throw some of this shit out," says Lizzie, holding up a handful of…I'm actually not sure what, "or ship it back to your Mom's, because that new girl is gonna drown in here."

I sigh and join Lizzie in the closet, and we spend the next half hour splitting my stuff up by playing "Fuck/Marry/Kill."

"Definitely marry that sequin top," Frankie says authoritatively, blowing a bubble. "I love that thing."

"That's because it's *yours*." Lizzie plucks it off the pile and tosses it at her. "Guess you were only actually fucking it."

I snort with laughter at that, at least until both Lizzie and Frankie declare that I need to Kill my favorite Celtics T-shirt.

"Are you kidding me?" I hug it to my chest and inhale, somehow expecting it to carry the scent of the games I used to go to with my dad and older brother, a billion years pre-divorce. But it doesn't smell like hot dogs or beer, just the dust it's been gathering for months. "No. This stays."

"There is no *way* that thing fits you, you Amazon," says Lizzie. "It's at least two sizes too small. How many years pre-growth spurt is that thing, anyway?"

"The shirt stays!"

"I think she wants to fuck the shirt," Frankie stage-whispers to Lizzie.

"Are you kidding? Did you hear that determination in her voice? *That's* marriage, Frank. Cait is going to *marry* that shirt. And we are going to wear some hot-as-fuck co-maid of honor dresses. It'll be glorious."

"Does this mean she's gonna finally get some ass?" Frankie gasps. "Hell, I'll wear a gown made out of that nasty-ass shirt if it does."

"Fuck you both," I sing-song, snapping the shirt at Frankie's ass. She cracks up and whips me back with the sequined thing, and in no more than ten seconds, we've spread out in an all-out war, with my clothing as the weapons. I nearly twist my ankle on my desk chair dodging the wrath of the button-down Lizzie's wielding—a shirt I'm pretty sure I've worn exactly zero times in the year and a half I've been at Radleigh—but quickly recover and nail her on the leg with my Celtic Pride.

We're having so much fun being back together like this, just the three of us, that we're all startled as hell when an unfamiliar fourth voice cuts in.

"Um, am I in the right place?"

Immediately, I toss the shirt onto my bed and dust my hands off on my sweats. "Andrea?"

"Andi," she says quickly. "Are you Caitlin?"

"Cait." She looks so terrified of the three of us, I almost laugh again, but I'm pretty sure laughing in your roommate's face on her first day in a new room isn't considered polite. "This is Lizzie and Frankie. They used to live here. They don't anymore."

"Oh." She glances at her new bed and desk, both of which are still piled high with my crap. "Um, am I…I mean, are these…?"

"Right, sorry!" I start snatching the piles and tossing them onto my own bed and desk, feeling a little like an asshole now. "They were just helping me clear space for you."

She glances from closet to closet, both of which are obviously busting at the seams with my stuff. "Uh huh."

Frankie snort-laughs, and then Lizzie's phone pings with a text. "Ooh, it's Connor. We're grabbing dinner at the Mexican place that opened up over break. You guys wanna join?"

I'm kinda desperate to say yes—I'm sick of the inside of these walls, and I'm *starving*—but I need to clean this place up, and leaving Andi alone on her first day seems like kind of a dick move. I open my mouth to tell them to go on ahead, when another new voice—this one much deeper and decidedly male—floats into the room. "Andi, which one is it?"

"On the right!" she calls over her shoulder.

A moment later, the source of the voice steps into the doorway, and any words that might've formed in my brain disintegrate completely. Just…vaporize into nothing.

My roommate may be new to me, but her boyfriend isn't.

In fact, I know Lawrence Mason quite well. Or at least I did when we were teenagers at athletic camp.

But I left him behind—along with my virginity. And trust me when I say I expected to see the former again about as realistically as the latter.

Holy. Shit.

"Mexican sounds perfect," I squeak back to Lizzie. "Let's go." Before anyone can say another word, I'm out of the suite like a bat out of hell.

I can always pick up shoes from Lizzie's on the way.

• • •

"What the hell was that?" Lizzie demands as soon as we're all seated. "I wish you would've seen that poor girl's face when you bolted out of there."

"Not to mention the guy's!" Frankie laughs. "Christ, I thought he was gonna pass out from, like, proximity to your insanity."

"I said I'd explain later," I mutter, mentally begging a waitress to come over so I can hide my burning face in a menu. As the member of our trio—well, quartet, I guess, now that Lizzie's boyfriend Connor's a permanent fixture—who *doesn't* thrive on drama, I'm not enjoying this nearly as much as they are. At least Connor has the grace not to ask what the hell we're all talking about.

"Yeah, and it's later," says Lizzie. "So spill."

"You'd think you'd wanna spend more time around that guy," Frankie adds. "He was pretty hot, no? I mean, taken, obviously, but…" She whistles. Badly.

A waiter does indeed come over then to distribute menus and drop off a basket of tortilla chips, but it doesn't distract anyone for a second. Not even when

Connor pointedly says, “Hey, will you look at how many kinds of burritos there are on the menu that have nothing to do with harassing Cait about her private life!”

Connor may be twenty-freaking-five and waaaay too old to be dating my best friend— especially considering he used to be her TA—but right now, he’s my favorite person at this table.

“Connor,” says Lizzie, squeezing his hand on the table. “You don’t understand. Cait *never* has drama. Cait’s favorite thing in life is giving *us* shit for our drama. I basically need whatever information she’s withholding in order to live. And I need to live in order for you to get laid tonight, so, take that into consideration.”

Connor pauses, nabs a chip from the basket, and takes a thoughtful bite. “So, Cait, are you gonna spill, or…?”

Men. Such traitors the second sex becomes part of the equation.

I sigh. A year and a half of living with these girls is long enough to know they won’t be shaking this anytime soon. “Fine.” I take a long sip from my water glass. “Let’s just say that wasn’t the first time I’ve met Andrea’s—Andi’s—boyfriend.”

Three pairs of eyebrows shoot up. Well, two pairs; Connor’s not quite as skilled in eyebrow acrobatics as the girls are. "Do tell." Frankie props her chin up on her hands, dark eyes shining.

"We went to camp together, like, a billion years ago. Sports camp. He's a basketball guy, I think." I don't know why I add the "I think" part. Of course Lawrence Mason is a basketball guy. At Stone Lake, he was *the* basketball guy. And I was *the* lacrosse girl. We made one hell of a power couple, as far as those things went.

"So that's it?" Connor asks. "You know the guy from summer camp?"

"Hmm." Now Lizzie pops a chip into her mouth with one hand, using the other to twirl a long black strand of hair around her finger. "I think she more than 'knows' him. I think maybe she knows him…biblically. Am I getting warmer, Caitlin?"

If I ate tortilla chips, I'd be stuffing a handful into my face right now. As it is, I really wish they'd brought some healthier foods out to snack on. *Some* of us are in training year round.

"Wait, what was his name again?" asks Frankie.

"Lawrence…something, I think," Lizzie answers before I can get in a word. "I don't remember hearing about a Lawrence, though. Do you, Frank?"

"I do not." Frankie taps her fingers on the table in a pattern I'm guessing is a Rihanna song—they always are. "Let's see. Cait's prom date was definitely not a Lawrence; it was…Mike?"

"Matt," says Lizzie, making clear I've told these girls way too much about my life. "And the guy from the boat was Hector—definitely not Lawrence."

"We *have* heard about a guy from sports camp, though—"

"Oh my God," I blurt. "Just stop. It's Mase, okay? The name you're thinking of is Mase. His last name's Mason, and kids in camp used to call him Mase."

Both of their mouths drop open, and suddenly, I want to crawl under the table and die. "Mase!" they say excitedly in unison. "Mase!"

"So, we know the name Mase?" Connor asks.

Lizzie smirks. "We *definitely* know the name Mase. Mase took Cait's ladyflower under the stars during a *very* romantic evening."

"Good job, Cait-Cait!" Frankie throws an arm around my shoulders. "I had no idea Star Boy was so hot!"

"Star Boy?" With every word out of Connor's mouth, he sounds more and more confused, and I want to disappear that much more.

"He charmed her with his knowledge of the constellations," Frankie says dreamily. "Man—athletic skills, brainy, *and* that ass! No wonder you gave it up."

Fuck it. I grab a handful of greasy, fatty chips and stuff them in my face; I'll run it off in laps tomorrow anyway. "I hate you guys. So much."

"You love us and you know it." Lizzie reaches across the table and squeezes my hand. "So that's Mase! He *is* hot. And I don't remember things ending really badly, so why'd you run out?"

"Are you kidding me? What part of 'My new roommate is dating the guy I lost my virginity to' sounds like I should've stuck around?"

"She has a point," says Connor.

"It's in the past!" Frankie argues. "Have a good laugh, reminisce for five minutes, done."

"I…think that's more your style than Cait's, Frank," says Lizzie. "Some people get a little more…attached."

"Attached" is one word for it. One might also say that I didn't get over him quite as quickly as I'd thought I would when we mutually parted with the understanding it was our last summer at camp and it'd be too hard to try to make it work.

One might say it was kinda startling to see that I found him even more attractive now, in the two seconds I saw him, than I had back then. And I'd found him *quite* attractive then.

One might say I suspected it would be a very, very slippery slope back into wanting him—liking him—if I spent more than two seconds alone with him.

One might say that for all the details I'd shared with Lizzie and Frankie about my love life, the one I hadn't was this: I'd been in love with Lawrence Mason.

And I'm pretty sure he'd been in love with me, too.

But before I can utter any of this to them—before I can even decide if I want to—the waiter reappears.

"Have you made any decisions yet?"

So far, only bad ones. Really, really bad ones.

chapter two

The best thing about Mexican restaurants is that they have tequila when you desperately need it.

It's not even ten o'clock when I get back to the dorm, but I creep in quietly anyway, hoping maybe Andi's exhausted enough to have passed out. Or maybe I've really scared her off, and she'll just spend the night at Mase's…wherever that is. He can't possibly go here; there's no way I wouldn't have seen him at some point over the past year and a half. He's not exactly easy to miss.

I can't even imagine what he's doing here now, unless he's somehow come to torture me. Tall, dark, and handsome torture. With my *roommate*. As if I weren't pissed enough about losing Lizzie, now she gets replaced by—

Ugh, I can't even think about it.

Before I can even shut the door behind me, it becomes obvious there was no point in trying to be silent; not only is Andi awake and present, but she's sitting at the table with another girl—my new suitemate, I'm guessing.

"Hey," I say, inwardly cringing at how awkward I sound. I have no idea how I'm gonna explain to Andi why I ran out, and now I get to make a bad impression on yet another newbie. "You must be…" I realize I'm about to say "Samantha What's-Her-Face," and I can't recall any other name, so I just let the words fall off my tongue.

"Samara," she says, her voice like honey. Her skin's smooth and golden too—darker than my Nordic pale, exaggerated in the dead of winter, and closer to Andi's beautiful bronze. Bronze that probably looks warm and gorgeous with Mase's rich, deep brown. I can't help tallying what feels like another strike against me with him, further proof that a contrast I've always thought was beautiful is actually just clashing.

"Are you Cait?" Samara prods in a lilting southern accent, and I realize I've just been standing there, spacing out.

"Oh, yeah, sorry. I'm Cait. I met Andi earlier, but…"

Lord, please let me crawl into my bed and die.

"I'm sorry about that," Andi says, the words coming out in a rush like she's been holding them back for hours. "I didn't even think before bringing my boyfriend in before. If you have a trigger thing with guys in your space—"

"No!" I blurt, then instantly regret it. I sound crazy. I feel a little crazy. But as much as I want to take the excuse she's offering to have him banned from my room, at least without prior warning, I can't let her think she hurt me like that. "I mean, you're sweet to be considerate, but no. Nothing like that. I was just a little stir-crazy after spending the day cleaning. Must've inhaled too many fumes or something." As if I busted out a single cleaning supply today.

"Oh, okay, phew." She laughs. "He just transferred here this semester, and he doesn't know anyone, so he'll probably be around a decent amount until he makes friends, if that's okay. I mean, he's not a complete loser or anything," she adds quickly. "He's just new."

This conversation is completely surreal. Thank you, girl I don't even know, for telling me that my hot-as-fuck ex-boyfriend is not a complete loser. I wasn't sure.

Of course, that still leaves the question: What the hell is Lawrence Mason doing here?

Mase was *good* at basketball in high school. Good enough to get scouted by the best of the best. Good enough to end up at Indiana. I stopped following his career once I started on lacrosse; my own college sport is the only one I track like a hawk. I can't imagine what could send him from a major Division-I team to one that's barely D-III. Lax is the *only* D-I team at Radleigh, and it's why I came here in the first place.

So why did he?

Did he come here for *Andi*?

Not that I can ask her any of those things. And Samara's kind of staring at me as if I've grown another head. I'm guessing my cheeks are tequila-bright, as they tend to get. I should just go to bed. Make a better impression tomorrow. Or not. I have enough friends, between my traitorous former suitemates and the lax team. I should just go to bed.

Yes. Bed. That sounds good.

"I'm gonna go to bed," I announce. "Big day tomorrow." Not that I have class before noon, but I do have practice in the morning—at the gym, thanks to the snow on the field. "So, uh, nice to meet you guys. G'night."

Not my smoothest exit, but it does the trick. The other girls murmur, "Good night," and I feel their eyes on my back as I let myself into my room.

Inside, Andi's stuff is perfectly neat, from her pristine sheets to the color-coordinated drawers next to her bed. I can already tell she's gonna hate living with me, and the feeling will probably be mutual. It's exactly the opposite of the feeling I had from when I walked into my freshman dorm the first day of orientation and saw a pair of brown legs emerging from an oversized T-shirt—and nothing else—as Lizzie repeatedly jumped up to try to hang her Idris Elba poster on the wall.

I walk over to her desk, above which hangs a picture-frame trio. The top picture is obviously her family, and the bottom one looks like a group of friends, but it's the middle one I can't stop staring at. The one of her and Mase, smiling at the camera, her pretty brown curls cascading over her shoulders, his perfect teeth bright against his dark skin. I wonder how long ago it was taken, how long they've been together. I wonder if they went to high school together. I wonder if she knew him back when I did, and what made them get together.

I wonder if she's ever heard the story of the girl he lost his virginity to under the stars at summer camp.

I wonder if I'm mildly deranged and torturing myself for no good reason.

At least that one, I know the answer to.

I change into my T-shirt and sweats and get under the covers, feeling gross for not brushing my teeth but deciding it's worth not having to go back out there.

And then I lie awake, praying for sleep that won't come, far too many memories filling my brain.

• • •

Waking up at five is basically like breathing for me at this point, and the fact that Andi's still asleep with no sign of moving is just a bonus. I slip out of bed as quietly as I can and jump into the shower, relishing the calming feeling of the water on my skin. I feel like shit, both from the tequila and a lousy, way-too-short night's sleep, but I need to get the semester off to a good start. I have a real shot at being named captain this spring for next year, but only if I keep my grades up and stay in shape.

A prospect that sounded like a complete no-brainer, back when Radleigh held zero distractions.

Mase is not a distraction, I remind myself as I rub shampoo into my hair. *Mase is your roommate's boyfriend, and a guy you used to know. That's it.* I try to focus on something else—my first practice back from break, my afternoon stats class, the fact that I have to officially declare this semester—but I know that's all stuff I can handle.

Mase's existence on this campus is a brand-new problem.

I quickly finish up, throw on my practice sweats, and then bundle up to face the Upstate New York cold. At least trudging through the snow to the gym takes my mind off of Mase for a few minutes while I place the focus on not falling on my ass. By the time I step into the building and head toward the mats for my dynamic warmup, I'm finally feeling a little more clearheaded.

Which is, of course, exactly when that familiar deep voice rumbles, "Caitlin Johannssen."

"Mase." I say it without even thinking, before I even turn around. And when I do turn, he's smiling. But not the kind that shows off his teeth. It's simultaneously amused and pained, and gives me the feeling I don't wanna hear the next words out of his mouth.

"Mase. Shit. No one's called me that in years."

I pull off my sweatshirt; it's a billion degrees in here. "People call you Lawrence?"

"Law, mostly."

"Oh." Law. I don't know Law. I guess it fits.

"I suppose I shouldn't be surprised to see you here," he says, and I wonder if I'm imagining the way his dark eyes flicker down my legs. "Still an athlete, obviously."

Did you think I wouldn't be? I wanna ask, but that would suggest he's been thinking about me at all. "Yup. Still lacrosse. Are you…here to play basketball?"

"Nope."

I wait for him to elaborate. He doesn't.

"You're here, though," I say after a minute. "You go to Radleigh now?"

"Yup. Just transferred." He scratches the back of his shaved head. "Small world, huh?"

Tiny. Too tiny. So tiny it's suffocating me right now. I'm standing here in the gym at a fairly small university in upstate New York, talking to a guy I haven't seen in almost four years, who also happens to be one of three men in the entire universe who knows exactly where I have a café au lait birthmark shaped like a cruise ship.

"So, you're Andi's new roommate. That's… weird."

"I was there first," I point out.

This time, when he smiles, there are teeth. "Ever competitive, huh, Johannssen?"

The unintended double-meaning behind my words brings a flush to my cheeks. "I *meant* to the suite."

He raises his eyebrows innocently. "And what'd you think *I* meant?"

I huff out a sigh, but it breaks into a laugh. "This isn't gonna be really weird, is it?"

"Not if we don't let it." He nods decisively. "We shouldn't let it."

"Did you tell Andi? After I left yesterday, I mean?"

He reaches up to squeeze the back of his neck, and it's so familiar as his nervous gesture that I feel a nostalgic pang at the sight.

It also makes his biceps look really, really good.

"No," he admits, his voice dripping with regret. "It felt too weird. That was probably a dumb move, but I don't want shit to be awkward."

"Agreed," I say quickly, relieved. There's just nothing good to be gained from learning your new roommate used to bang your boyfriend. *Just like there's nothing good to be gained from thinking about that you used to bang your roommate's boyfriend.*

"So…okay then." He glances down at his watch. "I should go. But I guess I'll be seeing you around."

That's it? That's the great Cait-and-Mase reunion? "Yeah, I guess." The words taste bitter in my mouth, though I'm not sure why. "See you around, Mase." I purse my lips as I remember that's not him anymore. "Sorry. Law."

He smiles again. Teeth, again. "See you around, Jo."

I debate telling him no one's called me that in years either, but for some reason, I don't, and then he's gone.

• • •

I linger at the gym for a while after practice, drying my hair completely after my shower so it won't freeze outdoors. Every now and again I question my wisdom at staying in the northeast and continuing to subject myself to this weather. But I prefer having actual seasons to year-round sun, and more importantly, my dad's just an hour bus ride away, right outside Syracuse.

There are still a few hours before my first class, so I make my way toward the coffee shop, not allowing myself to glance around to see if Mase is still present. I don't make it far before I feel my phone vibrate in the back pocket of my jeans. I slide it out and check the screen, then pick it up. "Hey, Dad. Please tell me this is a surprise 'I have tickets to the Celtics game this weekend' call. You know those are my favorites."

He laughs, but it sounds…nervous? I have *never* heard my dad sound nervous when it wasn't about having money on a team that was up or down by only a couple of points with ten seconds to go. "Alas, not one of those calls, Caity-Cat, but I hope you'll think it's good news. You remember Abigail, don't you?"

"Your receptionist, right? The one who made us that awful dinner a couple of weeks ago?"

He coughs. "Yeah, that's her, though that's not quite the most flattering way to be remembered. Anyway, she and I…we're, uh…"

We're? No. I think about the dainty little blonde only a few years older than I am—probably about the same age as my big sister, Cammie—who served us raw pork chops with overcooked green beans and burnt rice. Who asked if lacrosse was "the one with the stick." Who spent half of dinner texting at the table, even though "no phones at dinner" has always been my father's number one rule.

I mean, it's not like I couldn't guess they were hooking up—serving us dinner isn't exactly in the job description of a receptionist at a local paper—but I spent two weeks of my winter break at my dad's house and that was the only time I saw her. Whatever he's about to say is *not* going to sit well.

"You're...dating?" I try to fill in. In fairness to him, this is a pretty new conversation for us. My parents divorced when I was in high school—to no one's surprise—but while my mom's semi-seriously dated a few men since then, my dad has been living the bachelor lifestyle he was obviously meant for. Being a small town sports editor who has Heineken and pretzels for dinner more often than not doesn't exactly scream Relationship Guy. "Is your boss okay with that?"

"We're getting married, Caity," he says in a rush. "Abigail and I. We're getting married."

I freeze in my tracks. "You have got to be kidding me."

"Cait—"

"I don't even know her! And neither do Matt and Cammie! We just met her last month and now you're bringing her into the family? Why the hell—oh, no."

"Caitlin."

My head is swimming. It's a billion degrees below zero outside but I am sweating through my clothes. This can't be happening. "Tell me she's not pregnant, Dad. Tell me you did not get some random woman pregnant."

"She's not some random woman, young lady, and she's going to be your stepmother, so I hope you'll learn to treat her with more respect. And you'll have plenty of chances to meet her before we move—"

"Move? Move where?"

"Abigail wants to be closer to her mother when the baby comes, which is perfectly reasonable, Cait."

Nothing about this mess is "reasonable." I can't even believe this is my life right now. I can't believe my father is talking about a new wife and a new child and all of this is happening in a random phone call before the season has even started. "Where's her mother?" I ask, though I'm sure I don't want to know.

There's a long silence, and my stomach drops. "San Diego, honey," he says in a low voice. "You and Matt are already off to college, and Cammie's living on her own in Brookline; you don't need me around here."

I don't need him. Right. Because who cares that he used to come to my biggest games but hasn't even acknowledged them since this new chick came into his life? Who cares that he won't be a bus ride away for a weekend? Who cares that I'm about to have a new baby brother or sister, and he or she will be living three thousand miles away? Yeah, I definitely don't need that.

"How do Matt and Cammie feel about this?" I ask, because there's no way they're on board. There's *no* way.

"I wanted to tell you first, Caity-Cat. We've always had a special bond, and—"

I cut him off with a snort. “Yeah, it’s so special that you’re running off to California with your child bride. Okay. Why don’t you give Cammie a call and see how she feels about your happy news, Dad.” It’s uber bitchy of me and I know it—he and Cammie barely even talked when he and my mom were still married—but right now I don’t give a shit. “I have to go. It’s freezing outside and I’ve just been standing here, and I have to go to class.”

“At least let me tell you details about—”

“Later,” I bite out.

“Fine. I’ll call you during my dinner break.”

“Fine.” He usually eats around six. I can always arrange to be back at the gym at six.

Not my fault it has shitty cell service.

chapter three

I'm dying to skip class and wallow, but that doesn't really seem like an option for the first day. Instead, I wolf down a turkey sandwich and make my way to the Econ building. The nice thing about a class like Advanced Microeconomic Theory is that I know I'm already gonna know pretty much everyone in it; we'll all have been in Intro and Intermediate together too.

It also means I definitely won't be bumping into Mase or Andi.

I spot Vindra Swami almost immediately and smile when she waves me over. She and I have been buddying our way through Micro ever since we were paired up for an assignment the first week of Intro and completely kicked everyone else's asses. "How was your break?" she asks as soon as I slide in next to her.

Just a prelude to a total shitshow, apparently. "Pretty good, though I had a couple of nightmares that Professor Stein would be back to teach Advanced."

She laughs. "Oh, good—it wasn't just me. I still consider pulling off an A last semester to be a minor miracle."

"Totally." I'd gotten an A-minus, which I'd classify as miraculous too, though it did require studying for the final at such absurd hours to work around my lax schedule that I'd learned to survive on three hours of sleep a night. "How was your break?"

"Glorious," she says dreamily, an instant reminder that she'd spent half of it on a trip to Jamaica with her boyfriend, Jeff, who goes to…one of the SUNYs—I forget whether it's Albany or Binghamton. "It's so depressing to be back up here in the freezing cold."

We chat for a bit while the rest of the class fills in with familiar faces, pausing every now and again to respond to someone saying hi. There are only two other athletes in the class besides me—Jake Moss, who's a point guard on the basketball team, and Quentin Russell, the second-string wide receiver—and they both slap me five as they pass on their way to seats in the back. We in the athletic community at Radleigh aren't quite the rock stars we might be at a bigger school, especially with all the other sports being D-III, but we're tight-knit. Other than Lizzie and Frankie, they're my favorite people here, and in classes, we tend to cling to each other, since we all know the pain of working around practice and game schedules.

It's nice to have people who get you. I used to think my dad was one of those people. But if he were, he never would've made a decision like that without talking to me, without at least pretending what I wanted mattered.

Just thinking about my father puts a scowl back on my face just as Professor Arnold walks into the room. I've never had him before, but the Econ department at Radleigh's relatively small, and every professor's face is a familiar one. Rumor has it he's a huge sports fan and has a special place in his heart—and grade book—for athletes, but I'm definitely not relying on that.

"All right, everybody—settle down." Professor Arnold watches us with hawk eyes as everyone shifts in their seats and grows quiet. "Welcome to Advanced Microeconomic Theory. If you have not taken Intermediate Microeconomics, you are in the wrong room. Please see the registrar about being put in another class." He waits, as if half of us are going to suddenly file out. When no one does, he coughs and speaks again.

"In-class participation is going to be worth ten percent of your grade, so if you're feeling shy, or unable to rise to the challenge of delivering critical analysis, again, this is not the class for you." My gut churns a little bit at that, not because I'm nervous I'm not up to the task—I can do pretty much anything involving numbers in my sleep—but because I truly hate public speaking. Thankfully, Vindra loves it—she does theater, too—and I know she'll have me covered for any presentations.

"Thirty percent of your grade will depend on in-class presentations, and the materials you provide with said presentations," he continues, as if reading my mind. "You'll be required to deliver these presentations in pairs." Vindra and I exchange smiles, but they quickly fall with Professor Arnold's next words. "I know most if not all of you have been in class together before, and many of you have probably been working in the same pairs for multiple semesters. As it is extremely important that you open your minds to different ways of thinking, for this class you'll be required to work with a new partner. And don't think I can't easily find out who you've partnered with in the past, by the way."

Is it my imagination, or do his eyes laser in on me and Vindra?

"This blows," I mutter as soon as his gaze shifts. "I don't wanna find a new partner."

"Me neither. We're a total dream team."

I chew on my lip as I glance around the room, trying to figure out a reasonable replacement. Andrew Tucker's a misogynistic asshole who doesn't seem to grasp that women can do math too, so he's out. I can see Melanie Aziz and Justin Lieb have already paired up. Hmm, maybe—

A wadded up piece of paper lands precisely in the middle of my desk, and I smile. Only one person in the class has that perfect a toss. As I unfold it, I already know I'm gonna say yes to Jake Moss, even though I suspect the only reason he and Quentin have gotten this far is because their frat's rumored to keep old tests on file.

An hour and a half later, class is over, and Jake and I walk out together to plan our first meet-up. "He's kind of a hardass, isn't he?"

"No worse than Stein," I point out, pulling on my gloves. "This is definitely not gonna be an easy A."

"Shit, I'll take a not-so-easy B-minus," Jake says with a laugh. "I just need to keep my ass on the team, and speaking of hardasses, the new assistant coach is…yeah. Makes Arnold and Stein look like chumps. And he's a student, too, which is extra fucked-up."

"Yikes. I didn't realize you guys were getting someone new." I walk through the door Jake holds open, and immediately wince against the cold. "What happened to Sturmer?"

"Got an offer at FSU over break. Kind of a no-brainer move. Who wants to fuck around with us lame D-IIIs, right?"

I smile wryly and say nothing. Lacrosse obviously isn't one of the NCAA's top priority sports, but being the school's only D-I team does have its perks. Coach Brady's a hardass too, but he's one of the best of the best, and unlike my father, he isn't going anywhere.

"Where's this guy from?"

"Indiana. He was a rising star there or some shit, but he got a nasty concussion and bailed—on the team, the school…everything."

My entire body grows cold. There's only one guy he can possibly be talking about, and it explains a whole lot. A concussion or two is by no means a career-ender, but Mase has been playing ball since he could walk; he's racked up his fair share. When all the crazy shit started coming out about chronic traumatic encephalopathy in athletes, I made him promise he'd never let that happen to him, but it wasn't necessary—he was plenty spooked on his own.

I guess that last hit spooked him for good.

Fuck.

"Good thing we have this whole Econ backup plan, just in case," Jake says with a grin, oblivious to my horror. "I can meet up this weekend, but we've got a home game Saturday. You coming?"

I hadn't planned to, but I haven't been to a game in a while, and it sounds like fun. I used to love watching Mase play, and not just because his arms look great in a jersey. Not that there's any reason for me to be thinking about Lawrence Mason; he's certainly *not* why I'm interested in going. "Yeah, sure. I can hit that up."

"And bring your friend Frankie?" he adds, waggling his eyebrows.

"God, you boys are all so predictable."

"What? She's hot."

"She is," I agree. "I'll see what I can do. *If* you make time to study afterward. Deal?"

"Deal." We exchange numbers, then say goodbye and part ways—him for his frat house, and me for my dorm. It's only as I near my room that I realize Mase might be in there—that he might always drop by, that it may be impossible to stay out of his way, or keep him out of mine.

I take a sharp turn away from the dorm and head off to Lizzie and Frankie's place instead, despite the bitter cold.

• • •

No one's home over there—Frankie's probably at her art studio and Lizzie's probably underneath Connor somewhere—so I just wander for a while, trying to clear my head. Instead, all that time alone has the opposite effect, and thoughts of Mase collide with thoughts of my father, who apparently couldn't wait to reach out, because I have three missed calls from him.

I still can't bring myself to call him back.

Instead, I call Cammie, knowing my sister will be a welcome voice of sanity in this whole shitshow. She picks up after three rings, and skips all possible pleasantries. "If you're calling to convince me to talk to Dad about this ridiculous wedding—"

"Please, Cam, you're preaching to the choir. Trust me. I've been ignoring him since I spoke to him this morning."

"Oh. I just assumed…"

She doesn't finish her sentence, but she doesn't have to. Dad and I have always been a team, bonded by our love of endorphins, competition, and Monday Night Football. Throughout high school, he was my biggest cheerleader on the lacrosse sidelines, and even in college, he's kept it up as much as he can. Cammie's passions, on the other hand, include ballet and criminology, neither of which our father has ever been inclined to indulge.

It's what makes this whole thing feel like that many more daggers in my back.

"Yeah, no. I support Dad, but not about bringing some woman we barely know into the family, and *not* about moving across the country. Like, does he even give a shit that this means we won't even know our new sibling?"

There's silence on the other end, and then, "Our what?"

Oh, fuck. Fuck fuck fuck. "Dad didn't tell you that part?"

"I didn't pick up when he called the first time around; he left me a voice mail telling me he's marrying that woman who can't cook or communicate with other human beings around a dinner table. Though his language might've been a little different than mine. That woman is *pregnant*?" She laughs, so bitterly it ices my veins even more harshly than the snow I'm trudging in back to my dorm as we talk. "Of fucking course."

"Yeah, so, a little hard to be on Team Dad right now."

"Welcome to my life."

I opt to sidestep that one. "Yeah, well, we're gonna have to deal with him eventually. Any idea what you're gonna say?"

"To him? Nothing. Same as I've been saying to him for years. There's no chance in hell I'm standing up at that wedding as if he and I have any kind of relationship."

I exhale, watching my breath turn to clouds in the cold. The problem is, he and I *do* have a relationship, which means it's a whole lot easier for Cammie to avoid this mess than it is for me. I know I can't avoid him forever, but with classes just starting, Mase showing up out of nowhere, and the new class partnership rules throwing me off my game, I can't deal with him any more today. "Fair enough," I say, "but what about the baby? Don't you care to know our new brother or sister?"

"Well, I haven't exactly had a whole lot of time to factor that into my thoughts," she grumbles, "but no, frankly, I don't really. I already have a sister and brother who share much better DNA with me. I'm set, thanks."

I don't really know how to respond to that, so I'm grateful when my dorm finally comes into view…for five seconds, until I remember why I'd been avoiding it in the first place. I tell Cammie I'll keep her apprised of any new developments, but that I have to go, and then I say a silent prayer that Mase doesn't wanna see me in my room any more than I wanna see him.

Thankfully, no one's home but Samara, who's sitting at the communal table, sipping tea and reading from a paperback. "Hey," I greet her, tossing off all my outerwear the second I'm inside. The suite, of course, is boiling hot.

"Hey. Still brutally cold out there?"

"Yup." I pull my sweater over my head, careful not to yank my tank top up with it, and toss it onto the couch. Only when I notice her eyes following the movements do I realize she's not as used to my messiness as Lizzie and Frankie were, and I quickly gather up all my stuff and put it away as if that were my plan all long. "You have class yet today?"

"Two this morning," she drawls, then takes another sip of her tea. "There's more hot water in the kettle, if you want, and teabags in one of the middle cabinets."

After all that wandering in the cold, tea does sound pretty good right now. "Great, thank you." I pour myself a cup and wonder whether I should take it into my room or sit down and get to know Samara. It's weird, having new people in the suite, but I decide to make an effort and sit down. "So, where'd you transfer from?"

"Clemson."

"You left the warm south for this?" I raise an eyebrow and take a sip. "Why?"

Her mouth twitches, like she's trying to decide just how much to say. "I needed a little more space between me and my family. I thought a thousand miles would probably cover it."

"And has it?"

Now it twitches into a smile. "Still remains to be seen. But so far, so good."

We drink for another minute in silence, and I realize I like this girl. She's not loud and brash like Lizzie or Frankie, but she's clearly got her own edge under that sweet-as-pie drawl. Maybe having new girls in the suite won't be all that bad.

"Is your family close by?" she asks.

Or maybe it will be.

"My dad is." I tap my fingers against the side of the mug, relishing its warmth, trying not to think about the fact that that won't be true much longer. "My mom's in Vermont, sister's in Massachusetts, and brother's at school in Ohio. We're kinda spread out all over the place."

"Ah, divorce. Is it weird that I'm jealous?"

I'm glad I hadn't started drinking my tea again, or I probably would've spit it out. "Jealous?"

She rolls her eyes. "Let's just say my parents aren't the most functional unit."

"Oh, I feel you there." I take a sip of the hot liquid. It's sweet, peach-flavored. "My dad just called me today to tell me that he's getting married to a woman I've met exactly once. Oh, and she's having their baby. And moving them to San Diego."

One of her perfectly arched eyebrows rises upward. "Hmm. Okay. You might win."

As I trace the lacrosse logo on my mug, it occurs to me that Samara's the first person I've told, even before Lizzie or Frankie. That feels really weird, but now that the words are out, I need to talk about them. "I just don't really know how to deal with it yet. I called my sister, and ended up accidentally being the one to break the news to her about the baby, so that sucked."

"That sounds like an understatement. And how'd your conversation go with your dad?"

"It didn't, really. I've been ignoring him. He'll be calling again tonight. I plan on ignoring that call, too."

She snorts. "Sounds like my kind of strategy."

"I don't think I saw your parents here, actually. Did they move you in?"

"Nope. Haven't really spoken to them since I got here," she says flatly. "Trust me, it's for the best."

I look down sourly into the contents of the mug. “Parents suck sometimes.” All of a sudden, I feel impossibly exhausted from this day. “Thank you for the tea. I think I’m gonna lie down for a little bit before my next class.” I take one more sip, then get up and wash out the mug. Just before I lock myself in my room for the next hour, though, I turn back. “Hey, Samara?”

She glances up from her book. “Yeah?”

“You wanna go to a basketball game with me on Saturday?”

Surprise flashes across her face, but she hides it quickly. “Sure, why not?”

Feeling a little less like a jerk for my not-so-warm welcome last night, I smile. “Great. I think it’s at one, but I’ll double-check and let you know.”

Then I close the door back up so I can get in some solid wallowing time.

chapter four

"So, are you doing this Jake kid, or what?" Frankie asks as we pick our way through the crowd in the bleachers to find where Samara is saving us seats. We're ten minutes late because I had to make Frankie change into something that wouldn't result in frostbite on our way to the gym, and the place is packed. When it's this brutally cold outside, on-campus events tend to get a whole lot more popular.

"No, I'm not *doing* Jake—we're friends, and we're partnering up for a class presentation." I crane my neck and finally spot Samara's thick, honey-colored twist of hair up toward the back corner of the room. "There she is," I say, nodding in her direction. "Come on."

But Frankie stops short. "*That's* your suitemate? The blonde in the pink sweater?"

"Yeah, why? You know her?"

"Uh, no, but I'd sure as hell like to. How did you not tell me she's obscenely gorgeous?"

Uh oh. "Frankie," I say with a sigh. "Come on. I have to live with her. This would be worse than you screwing one of my teammates."

"But…but…" She gestures at Samara. "*Cait.* Come *on.*"

"Keep walking, Bellisario," I grunt at her. "And don't even think about it."

"You suck, Johannssen," she grunts back, but she does keep walking, and I roll my eyes at the back of her colorfully streaked head. I love that Frankie sees sexual possibility everywhere she goes, but she has a knack for seeing it in some extremely inconvenient places. After she hooked up with not one but two of the lax girls last year, I had to institute some major ground rules. That was *not* a fun locker room fight.

"Maybe *you* should hook up with Jake," I suggest, sweeping a hand toward the court. "Hell, hook up with as many of the basketball guys as you want. Just not—"

I lose the ability to form words when I see Mase standing on the sidelines. Seeing him on the court triggers something so familiar in me that a smile creeps onto my lips, but at the same time, the fact that he's wearing a suit and not a jersey twists my heart.

"Is that your roommate's boyfriend?" Frankie asks, following my eye line. "I mean, uhh…"

I elbow her in the arm. "Yes, it is. Now shut up." I shuffle over to Samara with Frankie in tow. "Samara, this is Frankie. Frankie, Samara."

Frankie's eyes light up as she enthusiastically reaches out a hand to grip Samara's, and I resist the urge to mutter, "Down, girl."

"So you're my replacement," says Frankie. "How are you finding the bed?"

Good Lord. I leave Frankie to her flirting and focus my concentration back on Mase. It's so strange to see him just standing there, tugging his sleeves and pacing the sidelines. Of course, I imagine he must feel the same way.

The whistle blows, and the players gather back toward the bench. I see Mase wave Jake over, and what looks to be some light correction of his shooting stance. Lordy, this is weird, and probably not gonna help with Jake thinking he's a pain in the ass. But if that were me—if I'd lost the ability to play, and all I could do was watch other people do a subpar job at something I know I could crush…

"You okay?" Samara asks. "You look a little…sick."

"I'm good," I lie, feeling my heart ache as I watch Mase talk to different players in turn. This is why he's here. This is what he's doing. This is *all* he can do, now, forever. The idea of Mase not being able to play ball anymore is impossible to comprehend. And if it's that hard for me, who hasn't seen him play in years, I can only imagine how he's been processing it. "Just trying to catch up on what I've missed."

"Well, don't ask me," she says with a grin. "I know absolutely nothing about basketball. It's just nice to get out of the dorm. I'm not used to the crazy cold. I feel like I've been hiding indoors every spare moment possible."

"Where are you from?" Frankie asks.

"A small town near Charleston, South Carolina. Not that it's exactly beach weather down there right now, but it's a whole lot warmer than this."

Next to me, I can feel Frankie melting, though whether it's from the accent or from picturing Samara lying on the sand in a bikini, I'm not sure. "That sounds gorgeous," Frankie says dreamily. "Wouldn't mind pretending I'm there right now, frolicking in the waves in a teeny tiny bathing suit."

Subtlety: not Frankie's strong suit.

"You do make it sound a whole lot better than I remember it," Samara drawls, and both girls laugh.

Good Lord—it's mutual. This is so gonna be trouble.

Still, Frankie's one of my best friends, and by extension, I'm required to be her wingman whenever possible. "Frankie's a very talented artist," I confide to Samara. "Painting gorgeous pictures is kind of her specialty."

“Is that so?” Samara sounds suitably impressed.

“It is. I don’t know a thing about art, but I know she’s damn good at it.”

Frankie blushes, which makes me smile. Girl is never lacking for confidence, but she always, always blushes if you compliment her on the art front. Never mind that she’s absurdly talented and has been told she has an extremely promising future by every teacher she’s ever had. “I dabble,” she mumbles.

I roll my eyes. “She does way more than dabble. You should totally check out her art sometime. They have a few pieces up in the Art Department.”

Frankie pinches me through my jeans. “Okay, fangirl, you’ve earned your twenty bucks. Quit it.”

Samara laughs. “She’s certainly a compelling agent. I’ll have to come check it out sometime.”

The whistle blows again, diverting my attention back to the court while the two of them continue flirting over my lap. Jake plays point, but right now my eyes are on Darrell Watkins, the center. Center was Mase’s position—one I know he had to fight to keep at Indiana, since being just shy of 6’10” put him on the shorter side. I wonder if watching Darrell pains him, if he’s overly critical of the height of his dribble, the way he moves just a half-step too slow. I know when I’m on the sidelines watching my second-string, Christina Coville, I can’t stop myself from mentally correcting every step she takes.

I can't even imagine what I'd do if I had to watch her take my place in every single game.

I sure as hell wouldn't sit on the sidelines and watch it. Especially not without a flask handy.

"You need to stop obsessing over him," Frankie murmurs in my ear, startling me. I hadn't realized she and Samara had stopped talking. "It's getting really obvious, and I don't think you want your suitemate to notice."

I blink and look away. "I'm not obsessing," I lie, heat rising into my cheeks. "I'm just...sad for him. He's supposed to be playing. Apparently he got sidelined by an injury, permanently. I'm sympathizing."

"You're sympathizing a little too hard, considering he's banging your roommate."

"Are y'all talking about Law?" Samara asks.

Law. God. "We just…uh…"

"He's really tall," says Frankie smoothly, a born bullshitter. "We were just noticing."

Samara gives us a funny look but doesn't push it. "So, where's your third Musketeer tonight?" she asks, and I love her for changing the subject. "I've heard y'all usually travel in a pack."

Frankie laughs. "Ooh, our reputation precedes us? Nice!"

"Our third is currently in a nauseatingly happy new relationship with her former TA," I say, turning back just in time to see Jake sink a three from the top of the key. I jump up and cheer with everyone else, and sit back just in time to hear Frankie end her elaboration on my statement with "…fuck like rabid bunnies."

Which is a pretty accurate description.

Of course, it's nice to see Lizzie happy, and I'm a big Connor fan, too. But between her being off with him tonight and all the electricity crackling between Frankie and Samara right now, I can't help feeling a little lonely.

Not that I'm dying to be in a relationship, or even to hook up; lacrosse and Econ take up pretty much every waking hour of every day. But every now and again I do miss that feeling of having someone at my side, of feeling fingers wrap themselves around mine. I miss frantically tearing at someone's clothing because you just can't wait to see what's underneath, even if you've seen it a hundred times. I miss sinking my teeth into someone's broad shoulder, my nails into a hard, toned back.

I miss having a guy show me stars.

Yelling explodes from the court, disrupting my totally inappropriate thoughts, and I straighten up to see a fight breaking out. I see at least two of our white home jerseys and three of the Panthers' black ones, but from this distance, I can't tell exactly who's involved. I do know that if Jake's in there, and he's dumb enough to throw a punch, I'll kill him.

"Whaaaat the heck is happening here?" Samara murmurs.

"I don't know, but it's kinda hot," Frankie says gleefully, craning her neck to see over the crowd. "There's just something about sweaty men with cut biceps throwing punches…"

A quick glance at Samara makes it pretty clear she doesn't agree with Frankie's assessment, but before I have a second to read any further into that, I hear someone calling my name. Searching for the source of the voice, I lock nervous eyes with Jamie Ferrara, one of my lacrosse teammates and girlfriend of Ryan Pfeffer, a bench-riding small forward. I'm guessing from her expression that Ryan's butt isn't on the pine at this moment. "I'll be right back," I say to Frankie and Samara, then make my way down to where Jamie's nervously yanking on the cuffs of her sweater while the refs fruitlessly try to break up the rapidly growing cluster of sweaty ballers.

"He won't listen to me," Jamie says, stepping back to avoid an elbow to the shoulder. "I don't even know what happened. There was a foul, and then—"

"Fuck you, motherfucker!"

I yank Jamie back as a fist flies in our direction, aiming for Ryan's face, and thankfully missing. I don't know how this game has gotten so completely out of control, but Jamie's right to be freaked out. On the court, Coach Williams is fighting with the Panthers' coach, ignoring the players, and Mase…is completely frozen.

I open my mouth to yell out his name, and then remember that isn't his name anymore. "Law!" I yell instead. "Do something!"

If he hears me, he gives no indication, just keeps gaping at the mess on the court as if unsure where to begin.

This is beyond fucked up. "Mase!"

His head jerks up and he turns, his dark eyes narrowing into a glare as he spots me. The anger that flashes across his face throws me off balance, but it's only trained on me for a moment before he turns back to the court. And then, like lightning, he springs into action, pulling players off each other and making threats I can only half make out from this distance.

"Huh." Jamie clutches my arm. "So that's the new assistant coach, huh? That was weird."

I don't say anything. I don't even know what to say. This night got really weird, really fast. Or maybe it was weird the whole time.

"What'd you call him? Mase?"

"Just…nothing." I shake her off gently. "I gotta go back up to my friends, but Ryan's gonna be okay. I'll see you at practice in the morning."

I head back to Frankie and Samara, and I don't look back—not at Jamie, and most definitely not at Mase.

• • •

By the time the game ends, though, I haven't been able to get him—and all his weird behavior since coming to Radleigh—out of my head. Frankie's never been the world's most perceptive friend, but apparently, Samara has Obsession Radar. "You gonna to talk to him or what?" she asks as we get up and start gathering our things.

"Who?" Playing dumb's worth a shot, right?

Her lips twitch. "I'm starving. Anyone up for a bite to eat?"

"Yes, definitely," says Frankie, patting her tummy. "Well. You coming, Cait?"

"No," Samara answers for me. "Cait's sticking around here for a while. She'll meet us there. Or text you that she isn't."

Wow—Samara is one bossy bitch. I *do* like her. And, judging by the appreciative way Frankie grins, so does she.

Only my eyes aren't dropping to her V-neck.

I sigh. "Fine. I'll meet you there. Diner?"

"I thought we'd go to Tate's," says Frankie. "The diner's too far. It's fucking freezing."

"Tate's will be packed after a game. Brave the cold if you want a table. I'll call you when I'm on my way out."

She grumbles for all of two seconds before realizing she's got a walk with the newest object of her affections lying ahead of her, and knowing Frankie, she'll figure out a way to get warmed up by the time they hit the diner. While I don't actually know that Samara's into girls, I do know Frankie's pretty great at getting women to forget they aren't for a night.

I watch them leave, then turn back to Mase, who's talking to each Radleigh Renegade before he heads out. I keep my eyes on him while he gets his stuff together, and everyone else files out of the room. Soon, there are just a few stragglers. And him. And me.

I head down the bleachers and stand in his way before he can avoid me any further.

"What the hell are you doing here, Cait?"

"What am *I* doing here?" I stand up to my full five foot eleven, though I still barely hit his shoulder. "I go here, *Lawrence.* I've been going here for a year and a half. I go to these games. I have friends on the team. *I'm* not the surprise here."

He doesn't respond, just lets his eyes flash with anger, as if that'll make me back down—a sure sign he doesn't know me anymore. That maybe he never did.

"I asked you about basketball."

"You asked if I was here to play," he snaps. "I'm not."

"And you should've told me that, too. You should've told me all of it. Why didn't you, Mase? We used to tell each other things."

"We used to fuck, Cait."

The harsh words feel like a punch to the gut, but that's what he was going for, and I won't let him know he succeeded. Yeah, we used to fuck, but that doesn't negate that we were close friends, too. That we had conversations late into the night for weeks before we even kissed, let alone took it further.

Enough relationships and truths are being rewritten in my life right now, and I'm not letting him have this one, too.

"We used to do a lot more than fuck, Mase, and you know it. You sat with me in the hospital for hours when I was so dehydrated I needed an IV, remember? And I was the one holding you when your grandfather died. I know you hate spiders. I know the scar on your forehead's from when you tripped in the Stone Creek 10K, trying to avoid a frog that'd jumped in your path."

"You know little-kid shit about me, Cait. You have no idea who I am now."

"I know you got injured and can't play," I say firmly. "I know that must suck harder than anything. I *get* sports being your life, Mase. You know I do."

"You still play lacrosse?"

"You know I do."

"You still love it?"

"Yes."

"You plan to do it at least until you graduate?"

"Yes."

"Then you don't know shit."

He grabs his bag from the bench and stalks off, the slightest defeated slump of his shoulders the only thing marring his otherwise confident, angry stride.

chapter five

"He was such a dick," I grumble to Lizzie and Frankie the next morning over breakfast at the main dining hall. "Like no one in the world's ever had shit happen to them before."

"Want me to make him feel like a real asshole?" Lizzie offers wryly.

"Kind of," I mutter, though even Mase doesn't deserve Lizzie's Dead Parents Card. Not yet, anyway. "I just don't understand why he's pushing me away so hard. We used to be able to talk about things. If you suddenly found yourself in school with someone you used to be close to, and you were having a hard time, wouldn't you wanna talk to her?"

"Not to rub salt in any wounds," Frankie says delicately, plucking a couple of blueberries from my fruit parfait to make a face out of her waffle with a smile of syrup, "but he's kind of already got that here.

Maybe he's already set on the confiding front with his *current* girlfriend."

She's right, of course, but it doesn't stop the words from stinging. "Whatever," I mutter, swatting her hand away so I can take a bite of my breakfast. "There's still a huge gap between not confiding in me and being a total dick."

"Why don't you sniff out from Andi what his deal is?" Lizzie asks. "If you're so curious."

"Because that's super awkward? And a little pathetic. And she'll probably tell him, on top of that. Let's remember that I have to live with her. Like, close-quarters live with her, as you'll recall from before you two ditched me. Mase and I never even told her we know each other."

Frankie snorts. "Well that's brilliant. How long do you think she can possibly go without finding that out?"

"I'm certainly not telling her. And I'm not telling Samara, either." I narrow my eyes at her. "Speaking of which, are you seriously gonna try to bang my suitemate?"

"Wait." Lizzie puts down her fork and folds her arms across her chest as she smirks at Frankie. "You're trying to fuck your own replacement in the suite? I'm impressed, Frank. That is literally the most narcissistic thing I've ever heard."

Frankie does a little bow over the table. "Not that it's working. Girl's a little uptight. Also, possibly straight. For now."

"For now," Lizzie and I echo, rolling our eyes at each other.

"What happened to you last night, anyway?" Frankie spears a piece of waffle. "I thought you were gonna come after you talked to He Who Shall Not Be Named."

"I was too pissed," I admit, dragging my spoon through the yogurt. Despite a lengthy practice this morning, after which I'm usually starving, the sick feeling in my stomach I get thinking about my fight with Mase last night makes everything look unappealing. "I went straight to bed. Well, no," I add, recalling that my dad called yet again while I was doing my nighttime stretches, "I got into a fight with my dad, too, and *then* I went to bed."

"About what? Don't you and your dad have the perfect father-daughter relationship, or whatever?" asks Lizzie. "You guys are a Hallmark movie."

"Not when he's getting remarried to a woman expecting his baby and moving across the country," I say sourly. Just pushing the words out in the open makes me nauseated, and I drop my spoon with a clatter.

"Oh, Cait—" Lizzie starts, but I hold up my hand and cut her off. The truth is, I don't want to talk about any of it.

"Okay," says Frankie. "So, apparently Cait's Do-Not-Discuss list has quintupled in length overnight. I'm not feeling at my smoothest since last night's non-date. How about you, Lizzie B.? How's married life?"

"Bite your tongue, Francesca," says Lizzie, narrowing her eyes as she butters a piece of toast. Her lips are curving up, though, totally betraying her.

Frankie's not fooled either. "Please, I saw you two snuggled on the couch when I got home last night, watching a movie like an old married couple. If I hadn't heard two orgasms through the wall before I fell asleep, I'd be extremely worried about you."

"God, Frankie!" Lizzie tosses a packet of Splenda at her. "I told you—stop listening!"

She snorts. "Pretty sure they can hear you guys in Canada, Lizard. Just be glad I don't mind."

"Don't mind?" I ask, eyebrows raised. "Or take advantage of it?"

Frankie wiggles her fingers in the air before wrapping them around her coffee and taking a long sip. "I plead the fifth," she says with a grin.

"My Life as My Roommate's Jack-Off Fodder: the Lizzie Brandt Story," Lizzie says with a sigh. She rips off a piece of toast and pops it in her mouth. "But, since you asked, things with Connor are quite lovely, thank you."

"Meaning you guys are still boning fifty times a day?" I ask, shaking a little more sugar into my coffee.

"Precisely." Lizzie smiles smugly before chomping off another bite of toast. "And I should *not* be the only one here getting regular ass. Are you *sure* you don't wanna talk about this guy?"

"Very sure." Or maybe that's not exactly true. What I want is to know *what* to say. And right now, I have no clue. "I don't wanna talk about Mase, I don't wanna talk about my dad, and…yeah, I could probably do without talking about all the sex you're having and all the sex Frank thinks she's *gonna* have with my new suitemate."

"Well then," Frankie says, putting down her mug. "How 'bout them Yankees?"

• • •

The next day doesn't go very far in clearing all the drama from my head, and the stress throws me totally off my game so that lax practice kicks my ass. "You sure you're all right?" Tessa Young asks me for the third time that hour as the team files into the locker room after a particularly grueling hour of drills. "I don't think you've ever let me whack you that hard before."

"I didn't 'let' you," I utter, but I guess effectively I did. I'm a fucking slug out there right now. I know I can't just fight with my dad forever, and now I'm ignoring calls from Matt and Cammie, because I don't wanna hear Cammie's self-righteous rage *or* Matt's pleas for me to just suck it up, when he's so far away from all of us that this barely affects him. I clearly can't keep Mase out of my brain, especially when I hear Andi flirting with him on the phone at night, or see him staring at me from the picture of the two of them over her desk. And the stress of fucking up play after play and lagging on my run times is just a vicious cycle of misery at practice. "And yeah, I'm fine, thanks. Just some stupid shit on my mind."

She shrugs. "If you insist." She slips away then, which of course gives Coach Brady the perfect opportunity to slide right in, take me aside, and try to have the exact same conversation with me.

"Seriously, Coach, I'm fine. I'm sorry I've been playing like shit this week. It's just a little personal stuff."

"You need to get it sorted before this weekend," he says firmly but kindly. "You can't scrimmage like this. Cortes will you destroy you."

"I know, I know." I wipe sweat off my brow with my forearm, though I'm not sure what's causing it more—the practice or this stare-down. "I'll be better, Coach. I promise."

He nods and tells me to hit the showers, and I do so gratefully, anxious for the pounding pulse of the water on my skin. The water pressure in the Radleigh Athletic Center could take an eye out at the wrong angle, but I've always loved it that way. It has exactly the cleansing effect I need.

By the time I get out, most of the girls are gone, but Tessa and a couple of others are still lingering, blow-drying their hair or applying makeup. I take my time, waiting for everyone else to file out so I can have a little time alone in the quiet before I have to head back to my suite, but though Nora and Latisha and Jamie eventually leave, I get the distinct sense Tessa is actually waiting for me.

I sigh. "I told you, Tessa. I'm fine."

"I know you're fine," she says mildly. "I was just hoping for some company on the way back to east campus. No one else lives the same way."

"Kendra does."

"Kendra went straight to a date with Robbie. Must be nice, huh? To be so familiar with someone you can just roll out of the locker room and meet them at a movie? No worrying about your hair being frizzy or the billion ways your outfit is all wrong. I can't even imagine what that's like."

Funny how different priorities can be. I don't give much of a shit how I look on any given night. My skin's thankfully clear and my hair dries stick straight, so admittedly those aren't big concerns, and being an Amazon doesn't leave me with a ton of cute clothing options anyway. But it *does* sound nice to have that comfort with someone. It certainly was nice when I did, once upon a time. "Yeah."

"You seeing anyone these days?" she asks as I twist my hair up beneath my Patriots cap. I should probably blow dry it before leaving the gym, but now that Tessa's clearly waited for me, I feel bad taking any longer.

"Nope." I pull on my coat and scarf. "Not lately." *If by lately you mean in the least two years or so.* "You?"

As we make our way out of the gym, Tessa chatters on about a guy in Omega Nu she's hoping will ask her to some party or other this weekend, but I'm only half listening. Being in a five-block radius of the gym, I can't help my eyes darting all around, keeping an eye out for Mase's standout height. Tessa's distraction efforts are sweet, but they're not working. Nothing's working. I hate this, and I don't know how to fix it.

I don't even understand how it—how *I*—got so broken.

• • •

Oddly, it isn't the last I hear of the Omega Nu party that week. Jake and I hit the library the following night to talk about our project and get some homework done, since neither my room—which now contains a violin player, I learned upon returning to the suite last night—nor Jake's frat house makes for particularly ideal study conditions. We've been reading silently side by side for maybe twenty minutes when he says, "Hey, any chance you wanna come to this fraternity thing Friday night?"

I glance over at him. "With you?"

He laughs. "Yeah, with me. Does that make the offer more or less enticing?"

"Oh, hush." I whack him on the arm. "Sure, I should be free." A funny little feeling churns in my stomach as I say it, though. Usually when I go to parties, it's with Lizzie and Frankie or a couple of the lax girls on my arm, and I feel the need to make sure we're on the same page. "As friends, right?" Jake's cute, but—

"Yes, as friends. Man, you are tough, girl. Would you believe there are plenty of other ladies on campus who'd love a piece of the Moss Man?"

"Actually, I would, which is why I'm confused as to why you're not taking one of them. Hell, I'm surprised you didn't ask me about Frankie."

He raises his eyebrows. "Do you think she'd come?"

"Depends how talented you are."

It takes him a few seconds to get the double entendre, and then he bursts out laughing. Everyone in the library turns to glare at us as I clamp my hand over his mouth. But then I start laughing too, and people are not pleased. We force ourselves to calm down, and I shake my head. "God, I've been spending too much time with Lizzie Brandt."

"I approve," he says with a grin, blue eyes twinkling. "But would she? Come to the party, I mean."

"It's possible. Though she's working pretty hard on my suitemate right now."

"Your suitemate?"

"Samara. She's new." I pause. "You did know Frankie's pan, right?"

"Pan?"

"Pansexual." He blinks. "Attracted to all genders," I add.

"Isn't that just bi? What makes her pan?"

"The fact that she spent three weeks last year fucking a non-binary kid in her Italian class?" I shrug. "Loudly, I might add."

He shakes his head. "Okay, I didn't really follow any of that."

"Spend more time with Frankie," I suggest. "You learn a lot."

"Good to know. But I think I'll stick with you this time around, if you're still up for it."

"Super flattered that you'll settle for me." I smile so he knows I'm kidding. "Yeah, I'm still up for it." Why not, right? Free booze and a night off from thinking about my family and Mase sounds like exactly what I need. Plus, Jake and I are just friends, which makes things gloriously uncomplicated.

"Cool." He turns back to his book, twirling his pen through his fingers.

Cool. We get back to work and push through for another hour, but after that, we both start burning out so fast, there's no point in going on. We agree to call it a night, and start packing up our stuff. "Do you wanna meet up again on Sunday?" I ask. "Get it over with bright and early over breakfast at the diner."

"Can't," Jake says sourly, stuffing his notebook in his backpack. "Gotta head to church."

"Oh! I didn't know you were religious."

"I'm not; Mason's new rule—we've all gotta do community service with their pee wee basketball team once a month. Now I've gotta spend my Sunday morning teaching a bunch of little kids how to shoot a ball. Fucking pain in my ass."

I hide my smile behind my own notebooks as I tuck them back in my bag. This is another Mase-ism I know from the good ol' days. He grew up on basketball at his church community center in West Philly; they actually helped sponsor him for Stone Creek. He always said he wanted to give back someday. Go figure he'd take the entire team with him.

It sounds like fun, honestly. I haven't played basketball in forever, though I used to love to. When you're a 5'11" girl, you hear a *lot* of people guessing it'll be your sport, but I knew the instant I first grabbed a crosse in gym class that I wanted to be on the field, not the court. Still, I was pretty decent, and a little runtime on the hardwood plus some good karma points sound like exactly what I need. "How 'bout I join you, and then we can work on this stuff afterward?"

He shrugs. "Sure. Hell, maybe you can distract Mason so he can stop being such a pain in my ass."

My eyebrows shoot up before I can stop them. "He'll be there?"

"Pretty sure he's there every Sunday morning," says Jake. "That's what I hear, anyway."

Huh. I'm guessing he won't be quite as glad for company as Jake, but for better or for worse, I'm joining the boys on Sunday. And if it forces Mase to talk to me, all the better.

chapter six

Tessa never manages to wrangle that invite to the party, so when Jake and I show up at Gilded, the club where it's being held, I'm not sure who I'll know inside. I *do* know that the underwire of my strapless bra is digging into my boob, and there'd better be some top-shelf liquor inside to make up for the fact that I had to wear an actual dress to this thing.

"I can't believe you didn't tell me when you invited me that this was a fancy event," I mutter at Jake as he holds the door open for me. "A girl needs so much more warning when dressing up is involved. Especially a tall girl with a limited collection of both dresses and heels."

"Yeah, but I actually wanted you to show up," he says with a grin.

"You suck."

"Oh come on. This'll be fun."

I roll my eyes but let him take my arm and pull me inside. It's not that I don't like going out, but I'm more of a dive bar kinda girl—I'm not crazy about going anywhere I can't wear jeans.

This is definitely not a jeans kind of party.

Omega Nu is the athletes' frat, which means I do know a bunch of these guys, but they aren't all as decent as Jake. Some of them see the female athletes on campus as part of the group, and some of them think we're a joke. Naturally, I think the latter group can go fuck themselves, and I think it double when I see their ringleader, Carlton Hamp, leering at me as he gets himself a drink.

There's no escaping him; he makes his way over to us as soon as he slaps a tip on the bar. I brace myself for what's sure to be an obnoxious greeting. "Hey, Moss," he says with a nod at Jake. Then he turns to me, leering. "Lax Girl. I already told you—Omega Nu is for *athletes*; girls just built like NBA players need not apply." He looks me up and down. "You do clean up pretty good though."

"Carlton, step away from me before I throw your own drink in your face."

He laughs, and Jake curls an arm around my shoulders. "Dude, she's my date. Fuck off." He says it like he's kidding, though—like "Do not be the reason I don't get laid tonight"—and it makes me flinch out of his grip.

"I think it's time to get drinks, don't you?" I ask Jake.

Carlton snorts. "Good luck with that one, Moss."

I don't bother watching them to see what kind of glance they exchange; my eyes are already on the liquid prize.

As Jake gets me a vodka tonic and himself a Jack and Coke, I survey the room, checking to see who I know. Quentin from Econ is there, and he nods a hello when I catch his eye across the room, though I don't know his date. There are a couple of guys from the tennis team I've hung out with before, and a football player I went on a date with my first semester that could not have ended quickly enough.

Then I catch a glimpse of a dark-brown head above the rest of the crowd, and my heart thuds. *Mase*.

The guy turns. It isn't Mase—it's Xavier Thomas, last year's captain of the basketball team.

I let out a breath that's equal parts relief and disappointment.

"Here you go, milady." Jake hands me my glass, and I take a long sip of the cold, clear, bitter drink. "Whoa there. Don't you have your season opener tomorrow?"

"Don't remind me." I take another sip. Mase. Lax. So many things to drink away.

"Aye aye, captain." He drinks from his own glass, then says, "Come on, let's go say hi to Q."

We do, and from Quentin I get introduced to a couple other guys, and by the next time I glance at my watch, an entire hour has passed and it's actually been pretty fun. Even though my date's brain seems to be somewhere else.

"Remember that, Moss?" Darrell Watkins is saying, gesturing with a bottle of Heineken. "Fuck, that was hilarious."

But it's obvious looking at Jake that he's totally spaced out on this conversation, and it isn't the first time tonight. "I'm sure Jake would *never* be involved in something as juvenile as drawing a dick on a mascot's head," I tease, trying to help bring him back.

It takes a second before it clicks, and then he cracks up. "Oh, shit, yeah, man. Fucking UConn. Those assholes deserved it, though."

"For real." Jake's moved on to beer too now, and he clicks his Stella against Darrell's Heineken. Darrell keeps talking, but I watch as Jake's eyes drift off again. And this time, I follow them.

I don't know who he's staring at; all I see is a flash of long brown hair disappearing around the corner, presumably to go to the bathroom. I only know a couple of the girls at the party, but if Jake's got his eye on another guy's date, that's probably not gonna go over too well.

When he declares, “I gotta go piss—I’ll be right back,” I have the sinking feeling that he’s about to do something dumb. But there’s nothing I can do or say about it, so I just say, “Okay, cool,” and reach out a hand to take his beer to hold.

He doesn’t give it over, though. Instead, he tosses it back and drains it, even though there was half the bottle left. Then he walks off in the direction I just saw the brunette going, putting the empty bottle on a table along the way.

No one else seems to notice anything strange, so I just stick around, talking to Darrell, Quentin, their dates, and the other guys and girls who wander in and out.

Eventually, inevitably, the conversation turns to the new assistant coach.

“He’s such a fucking hardass,” Greg Parsons complains. “I know he’s bitter ’n shit about not being able to play anymore, but he doesn’t have to be such a fucking dickwad.”

I brace myself on Mase’s behalf, stifling the urge to defend him, especially since I know it’s the last thing he’d want from me.

“You deserved him calling you out on your runtimes, dude,” says Darrell. “Time to lay off the enchiladas.”

While the guys continue making fun of each other and talking shit about Mase, I excuse myself to go look for Jake. Not that I really want to go looking for him, but I wanna hear about my ex-boyfriend even less, and I have nothing else to do at this party right now. But when I walk down the same hallway he turned, all I see are closed bathroom doors.

Seems weird to linger outside the bathroom, waiting for him, but I'm not really sure how else to occupy myself. I pull my phone out of the clutch I borrowed from Frankie, but before I can even light up the screen, the door to one of the bathrooms opens, and a flash of long brown braids catch my eye.

And they aren't attached to a girl.

"Uh, hey." The guy glances behind him as he pulls the door shut. "I, uh…" He scratches his head, and I try to figure out why he looks so familiar. Then it hits me—he's a Radleigh running back. Troy something. I've never met him, but he's looking at me like he knows who I am.

Then his eyes dart back to the door, and I realize why.

"Let me guess," I say, trying to keep my voice even. "Still occupied?"

Troy swallows. He's a pretty hulking guy—at least 6'4", 240—but he's not even making eye contact with me right now.

"Get back to the party," I tell him with a sigh. "Your secret's plenty safe with me. I'd just like a minute with my 'date.'"

He gives me a jerky nod, and then bolts.

I rap on the door with the back of my hand. "I'm coming in, so your pants better be on, Moss." I push it open without waiting for a response.

Thankfully, they are, but it doesn't make him look any happier to see me. His face drains of color. "Cait. Fuck."

"Nice to see you too." I lock the door and lean back against it. "You could've told me I'm here to be your beard, Jake."

"It's not what you think."

I roll my eyes. "Of course it's what I think. For fuck's sake, do you really think you need to lie to me about this? Not to pull the 'I have a queer friend' card, but you realize Frankie is practically a sister to me, right?"

His shoulders slump. "Yeah, that's kinda why I was hoping you'd hook me up with her. I thought it'd be cool to…I don't know what. Have a buddy, I guess. But you really can't tell anyone, Cait. Please. Not just for me but—"

"I would *never*," I say firmly. "I would never, ever out a friend, Jake. Or even a guy I just met for three seconds in the hallway. I prom—"

A knock at the door snaps both of us to wide-eyed attention. "I gotta piss!" a drunken male voice yells from the other. "Hurry up!"

"Oh, shit." I didn't think Jake could look any more terrified, but I swear he's gone translucent. "What do we do?"

I take one look at Jake and I know there's only one answer to that question. I turn to the mirror, allow myself one brief moment to appreciate the meticulous curls Samara styled with her curling iron, and then muss the hell out of my hair. Then I rub my thumb across my red lipstick and turn back to Jake, swiping it across his lower lip. I glance at his outfit and decide it doesn't need any more rumpling; Troy did a pretty good job there.

Then, while Jake's mouth is still hanging open, I unlock and yank open the door. "Sorry about that," I say sweetly to the yeller, who turns out to be none other than Carlton. "Bathroom's free now."

Jake follows me out, and when I glance back, I see he's got a completely believable "Just got nailed" smile pasted on. I bite my tongue as he accepts high fives from random guys as we make our way back through the party, and as soon as we get to a slightly less crowded area, I feel hands grasp my waist. "Thank you," Jake whispers in my ear. "I owe you one."

I nod toward the bar. "I think I know how you can pay up."

"Deal." One hand remains on my waist as we make our way through the partiers, and I can't help noticing how nice it feels. I've fooled around a little here and there, but lately I keep feeling…partnership pangs, or something.

Just as quickly as the thought pops into my head, I feel like an idiot. I haven't given a shit about that in years. I'm clearly getting screwed up by all the coupling going on around me—Lizzie and Connor, Jake and Troy…and then there's Mase.

No, there is *actually* Mase, reaching the bar a second before we do, wearing a dark-blue shirt that looks annoyingly good on him. Though he's still an undergrad—presumably a junior, since he's a year older than I am—the fact that he's a student coach makes him a weird hybrid authority figure that means there's no way he's a candidate for Omega Nu. And considering the guys don't seem to appreciate how hard he's riding them (if only they knew quite how good he is at that), it's hard to imagine he was invited.

And yet, there he is.

"Hey, Mason," Jake says cheerfully upon spotting him. He sounds genuine, and for some reason, I like the fact that Jake's not among the contingent that wants Mase dead. "Didn't expect to see you here." He extends the hand that isn't around my waist to slap Mase's, and Mase reciprocates.

"Moss," he says with a nod. "And—" He turns to me, and whatever he was gonna say dies on his tongue. His eyes flicker downward for only a fraction of a moment, just enough to take in Jake's arm wrapped around me, and then he regains himself so quickly that I know no one would've noticed the slip if they hadn't been looking for it.

I was definitely looking for it.

"Cait Johannssen," he says with a slow smile. An *of fucking course you're here* smile. "Should've guessed."

"You guys know each other?" Jake looks between us.

"I know her roommate very well," he says smoothly.

"Pretty sure everyone knows her roommate very well," Jake replies with a smirk.

I turn to glare at Jake. "A) Frankie isn't my roommate, or even my suitemate anymore, and B) you say a bad word about her and I will cut off your fucking tongue."

He holds up both hands in surrender. "Kidding, kidding. You know I'm a Frankie fan."

Ugh. The sleaze he's trying to project now in the name of hetero-showmanship is just annoying me, and if he thinks he needs to do it for Mase's benefit, he should probably meet the super-gay little brother Mase adores. “Just get me that drink you promised, will you?”

“Yes, ma’am. Any requests?”

“Surprise me.”

Jake nods and pushes into the crowd.

Mase raises an eyebrow at me once Jake is out of earshot. “You trust a frat guy with your drink?”

I know he’s trying to sound disdainful, but a genuine note of concern slips in. “Despite projecting being kind of a dick right now, Jake is one of the decent ones,” I assure him. “Usually.” I glance around to see if Andi’s behind Mase somewhere, but he seems to be alone. “And what are you doing here? Slumming it? Spying on your underlings?”

“Just trying to have a good time, same as everybody else.”

“Everyone else might have a better time without their hardass coach here, watching them get plastered.”

He shrugs. “I’m not here to give anyone shit. We don’t have a game tomorrow. Which is more than I can say for you.”

Now it’s my eyebrows that shoot skyward. “And how do you know I have a game tomorrow? Lawrence Mason, are you checking out my schedule?”

“Should’ve seen that question coming,” he says, shaking his head. “And no—I had dinner with a couple of other student coaches, including Larissa Williams. She had a lot to say about her star sophomore, in fact.

The one who's apparently on track for captain and destined to break some Radleigh records, but also keeps up the highest GPA on the team."

"This player sounds pretty great."

"Doesn't she?"

We lock gazes, neither of us saying a word, and I can't imagine what he's thinking—whether it's admiration or hate I'm seeing, or a twisted combination of both. The longer our standoff continues, the more it feels like he's stripping me down to my soul. It's different from the silent staring contests we used to have, the ones that ranged anywhere from "I want you so badly right now" to "I'm going to unnerve you until you finally tell me what's bothering you," but…also not that different.

I'm just about to break when Jake returns with my drink. "Rum and Coke for the lady," he says, handing me a red plastic cup filled three-fourths of the way with bubbling brown liquid. "You want the same, Coach?"

"Just looking for water, but I'll get it. You two enjoy yourselves." He steps around us and moves through the crowd with panther-like grace that shouldn't turn me on as much as it does. It's hard not to watch him, and not just because he's tall. He walks like he's in control of every cell of his body.

He does a lot of things that way, if I recall correctly.

I wonder where Andi is tonight, whether she's in our room right now or meeting him here later or what. It seems so strange that I barely know the girl, barely know their relationship, even though she and I sleep just a few feet apart. But I do know she's in her bed every night, and he's not with her, so whatever their relationship is, I guess they're taking it slow.

Which, I remind myself for the millionth time, is none of my business.

"So, I'm not the only one who wants someone they can't have right now, huh?" Jake's voice and subsequent laughter are low in my ears.

God, I am *awful* at this whole subtlety thing. "Just shut up," I mutter, turning away and taking a long drink.

"Coach? Really?" Jake strokes his chin thoughtfully. "I wouldn't have picked him for you, but I'm not gonna lie—I've been pretty disappointed he doesn't join us in the showers."

I whack Jake on the chest and take another drink while the not-at-all unpleasant image of Mase sudsing up fills my brain. Funny thing about hooking up at summer camp—you get a certain kind of creative with your options. I've had sex with Mase in sleeping bags under the stars, in a gazebo, in the lake, in the backseat of a van, and in an empty bunk, but alas, never in a shower or a bed actually meant to fit two people.

"Holy shit." Jake cracks up, startling me out of my reverie. "You should see your face right now. You wanna ride that pine *hard*."

"One more word and I will destroy you, Moss," I snap. Then I drain the rest of the drink in three quick swallows. There's no point in lying to him now, and there's no need, either. "I keep your secret, and you keep mine. Understood?"

He nods. "Yes'm."

"Good." I hand him my empty cup. "Now get me another. I have some thoughts to obliterate."

chapter seven

I'm up bright and early on Sunday, and I realize I've gotten accustomed to getting dressed in the dark. When I used to live with Lizzie, she could sleep through pretty much anything, including when I turned on every light in the place looking for my lax gear. But Andi's far more sensitive to light and noise, and I'm pretty sure living with an early riser is already driving her completely nuts.

It doesn't help that I accidentally knock a textbook onto the floor when I reach into my desk drawer for a sweatband, jolting her awake. "What the—"

"Sorry!" I whisper. "I'm just on my way out. Go back to sleep."

She glances at the clock on her nightstand and yawns. "I thought you don't have practice on Sundays. Didn't you just have a game yesterday?"

We did, and we won, barely thanks to me. I only narrowly made my only goal, and I'm still cringing thinking about a sloppy pass I made to Tish in the second quarter. "Yeah, not practice; I'm going to play basketball. With Jake." I'm not sure why I add this last part, as if she would've assumed I was going to play with Mase and I needed to make it "safe" by turning it into a date with a different guy. Never mind that said date is interested in entirely different balls. Or that she'd have no reason to assume I was seeing Mase at all. Now I feel guilty, as if I'm lying, which makes no sense at all.

Still, my guilty conscience speaks, as it's so fond of doing. "He's volunteering at the community center, and I asked if I could come along. It's been a while since I've played, and it sounded like fun."

"Oh!" She smiles sleepily in recognition. "Law will be there. He loves that place. Tell him I say hi."

Law. It still jars me, but I need to internalize it, to make sure I use it. "Do you wanna come?" I offer. It occurs to me then that I have no idea if Andi actually plays sports at all. "I'm sure he'd be glad to see you."

She laughs. "Definitely not, thank you. I need more sleep, and playing ball with a bunch of kids does not sound like my idea of fun."

"Okay, well, I'll leave you to it. Sorry again for waking you up." I grab my coat from over my chair and head out.

I'm surprised to see Samara already sitting at the kitchen table when I close the bedroom door behind me, her hands cupping a steaming mug of fragrant tea, her long hair grazing the pages of a book. "Hey, didn't realize you were up," I greet her, taking care to keep my voice down.

"Couldn't sleep," she says, closing the paperback around her index finger. "What's your excuse?"

I explain about the youth group, and she nods. "That's cool that you're helping out. I used to be involved in my church youth group for a couple of years. It's really big where I'm from."

"Are you involved here?"

An expression I can't read flits across her face. "Nope. Done with that. Have fun, though." Then she pastes a smile back on, and I kind of like that she's the worst liar I've ever seen. "I can't believe it starts this early."

"It doesn't," I tell her. "I figured I'd leave myself some time to jog there. It's a couple miles."

She laughs, genuinely now, and shakes her head. "I don't understand how on earth you have the energy for this stuff. You make me feel so incredibly sluglike."

"Hey, you do yoga."

"Yeah, for a half an hour in the morning, a few times a week. That's a total joke to you."

"Lizzie and Frankie's idea of exercise is throwing popcorn at the TV when they don't like who wins showdowns on *The Voice*, so." I slide on my jacket and fill up my water bottle. "I'll see you later."

"Have fun," she trills, already looking back into her book.

Here's hoping.

• • •

It's a nice jog to the church, which looks especially pretty with the vestiges of last week's snowfall still dusting the dark slate roof. I take my time, even detouring a little, just enjoying the quiet. According to the sign out front, services don't start until eleven, so even on its busiest day of the week, the church is silent and peaceful right now.

Jake told me he'd be driving, but I know he has an Audi; the only car in the parking lot right now is a busted Pontiac that looks like it's been sitting there for a while, accumulating snow and dust. For a moment, I'm worried the building will be locked, but a quick check of the side door by the community center sign reveals it's open.

As soon as I enter, I hear the familiar sound of a basketball pounding the hardwood. There's a few seconds of slow dribbling followed by a swoosh. Then again. And again. Clearly some kid in this neighborhood is already a little basketball superstar. I follow the sound of the bouncing, assuming it'll take me to the gym, and I'm not wrong.

The problem is that once I find the open doorway, I see that the guy hitting nothin' but net is none other than Mase himself.

I'm tempted to turn and jog the two miles home, but he turns before I can even contemplate it. "Cait. What are you doing here?"

"Jake invited me. Sort of." It's warm in the gym, and I shrug off my jacket and unzip my hoodie. "Is it okay that I'm here?"

"You tell me." He tosses the ball to me, a little harder than necessary, and I grunt as it smacks me in the chest. "When's the last time you played something that didn't involve a stick and a bunch of girls?"

I smirk thinking about all the dirty jokes Lizzie could work with that statement, then break away and take a shot before Mase can react. It banks in neatly, and my smirk widens into a full-blown smile. "I think I might be all right, but if you need a game of Horse to prove it to you, I'm in."

He scoops up the ball and tosses it back, and I position myself a couple of feet inside the three-point line and take a shot, sinking it.

"All right, Johannssen, not bad. I may have underestimated you *slightly*, but you're still gonna eat my dust." He nudges me out of the way and takes the same shot, making it easily with barely a flick of his wrist. "You wanna take down a former D-I baller?

You're not gonna do it with weak-ass jump shots. Let's see a real challenge."

"You talk so damn big, Mason." I move off to the side, behind the three-point line, knowing that his weakest spot is just inside bounds. He snorts, no doubt realizing I'm playing off that old intel, but unfortunately, it's a weak spot for me, too, and it bounces off the rim.

He recovers it in one graceful leap, then lays it up out of habit. "Oh, shit," he says the second it leaves his fingertips. "I didn't mean for that to be my shot."

"Sucks for you!" I sing, replicating the layup easily.

"So damn cheap."

"Hey, ninety percent of the game is mental." I push the ball back at his chest. "Can't handle it?"

"Oh, I can handle anything," he says smoothly, taking the ball to the foul line. "Including a foul shot. Backward."

He makes it. I don't.

H.

"Show-off," I mutter, and he laughs and scoops the ball back up.

"You always were a sore loser."

"If you're talking about that two-on-two with Scheck and Braitway, Scheck was a fucking cheater. He traveled."

"He did not travel!" Mase calls his next shot—a fifteen-foot jumper with a bank required—and easily sinks it. "You're just a ridiculous hardass."

"Funny, that's exactly what I hear about you as a coach," I taunt, catching the ball and dribbling over to his spot. I make the same shot, bank and all. "Is this a reality show for you, *Law*? Not here to make friends?"

"It's a job," he replies, holding up his hands for the ball. "So no, I'm not here to make friends. I'm here to make those guys win occasionally."

My loyalty to my school—and to Jake—makes those words sting, and now it's my turn to "pass" the ball a little harder than necessary. But then I remember it's Mase's school now, too. He's not just working; he's a student. "How is it for you?" I ask as he tries his own side shot and, of course, nails it. "School, I mean. Not the coaching part. Are you liking Radleigh?"

"It's all right," he says, shrugging. "Cold as balls. Actually learning some shit, though, I think. And all my credits transferred, so I'm just here one more year after this."

I realize I don't even know what he's studying. I've always loved numbers, and I'd known I wanted to major in Math or Econ since I was a freshman in high school, maybe earlier. But Mase had been so set on a career in the NBA that he never gave it much thought. It made sense at the time, but he's a junior now, which means he must've picked something last year. "What's your major?"

He doesn't get a chance to answer before the door flies open and kids come running in, calling his name. It takes me a few seconds to realize they're swarming past a befuddled Jake and Quentin, who are twice some of their size but clearly out of their element surrounded by kids. I laugh and call out a greeting, and Jake's face relaxes into a smile.

"Hey, you made it." He wraps an arm around my shoulder and kisses me on the cheek. "Getting warmed up without the rest of us?"

"Just a little game of Horse, which I probably would've won if you guys hadn't shown up."

Mase snorts. "You do know you were losing, right?"

"Yeah, by one letter." I roll my eyes. "Anyway, let's get to this."

I quickly learn it's Mase's third week there, and though his team at Radleigh may not adore him, these kids clearly do. A young one named Peter is definitely his favorite, because Peter has the same kind of unbridled enthusiasm for the sport Mase once did. An older, taller one named Carlos is obviously the most talented, followed closely by Jerome, but we do our best to tend to all the kids equally, calling out when arms aren't bent quite right, the bounce of a dribble is too high, or footwork is sloppy.

I'm almost amazed it takes a full twenty minutes before a skinny, pimple-faced boy actually says, "Dude, why are we taking advice from a girl?"

"Because that girl can shoot you under the table," Mase responds without missing a beat. "Trust me."

He doesn't look at me when he says it, and he quickly changes the subject by having them all line up at the foul line, but it sparks a little warmth in me just the same. Unfortunately, Jake isn't oblivious to it.

"So what exactly did I miss this morning?" he murmurs at me as we go to the back of the line, leaving Mase to give each kid one-on-one instructions. "He's pretty confident in you for one morning of Horse."

Do I tell him about our history? It seems wrong to share something with him that even Andi doesn't know. But Jake can be trusted; he has to be, given the secret I'm keeping for him. And yet…

"I think he's just trying to inspire confidence in the hired help," I tell Jake, watching as Mase demonstrates a perfectly precise foul shot. "Or the volunteer help, I guess."

"If you say so, but for what it's worth, he did not look thrilled when I showed up. Or when I kissed you."

"Oh, hush. You're just seeing what you wanna see." *And maybe what* I *wanna see.*

"You keep telling yourself that, Johannssen." He shoots me a grin, then jogs up to join Mase.

The kids take foul shots one by one, and Jake, Quentin, and I all take cues from Mase on how to correct their form clearly and patiently. You'd think he'd been working with kids for years. It's a kinder, gentler side to him than I've ever seen, and for some reason it's not helping in my quest to keep things friendly.

"Hey," I break in just before the guys are about to start the next round. "How about we split up so everyone can get more shots in? Jake and I can take half the guys on the other side."

Mase's dark eyes flash from me to Jake, who's got a goofy grin on, and back to me. "Fine." He directs half the line to join us on the other side and promptly shuts up any of the whining about playing with "the girl," and for the rest of the time, Jake and I work through foul shots and layups while I work double-time not to let my gaze drift over to the other half of the court.

When the hour ends, though, and Mase gathers everyone together for a five-on-five, the guys protest that they wanna play us instead—five of them on the four of us.

"Then you won't all get to play," Mase protests.

"We'll rotate," Peter says authoritatively. "Come on. You afraid you old folks can't hack it?"

Jake narrows his eyes. "Who you calling old, punk?"

"So, that's a yes, then," says Carlos.

"Hoooo, burn," says Quentin. "All right, kids. Let's do this."

"You in, lady?" Peter asks. "Or you afraid to break a nail?"

"Man, kids these days still don't have better material than that?" I shoot back. "Depressing. In my day, we walked uphill to school both ways *and* had more clever insults."

Out of the corner of my eye, I see Mase biting his lip to keep it from quirking up, and I have to do the same.

But there's no avoiding him now that I've got a point to prove.

The kids decide to start off with Carlos, Peter, Jerome, Vince—speaker of the first sexist comment—and a small but fast kid named Oliver. We agree that I'll do the tipoff, because at least the kids somewhat approach my height. "Don't go easy on them, Jo…hannssen," Mase stumbles as he realizes he just called me by his old nickname for me.

It's *really* hard to contain my smirk, then. "I never do."

I win the tipoff and immediately pass to Mase; it's just instinct. We used to play together for fun all the time, pairing off against a couple of other guys, and we were a killer team. As he dribbles down the court, fending off Carlos in a way that's definitely going a little easy himself, I remind myself that Jake's the one who's supposed to be my "teammate" here, and not to let myself get carried away in old habits. Judging by the way Mase gravitates toward Quentin after that, I'm guessing he's made a similar calculation.

But still, there are a few points at which we can't help working together, and it feels like clockwork when we do. The way we anticipate each other's bodies, our awareness of the other's forms…it's made us very good at a lot of things in the past. But of course, I'm not thinking about anything other than basketball. Not when he slaps me five after I sink a beautiful three and an obnoxious little tingle trails down my arm. Not when he hoots proudly after I steal off Carlos, the same proud way he used to the super occasional times I'd manage it off one of the other basketball players in camp.

I'm not noticing any of that at all.

We play until we've had the chance to cycle all the kids in, and by the end, we've all gotten a good workout. When Jake slaps me five, he's glistening with sweat. Somewhere along the way he tossed off his shirt, and the sleeveless undershirt he's wearing does an admittedly nice job of showing off sculpted biceps. "Nice job, girl," he says, startling me with a showy kiss, followed by a wink.

My instinct is to whack him right in the chest for that little display, but I can't resist glancing in Mase's direction…and noticing that Jake may have had a method to his madness after all. Iciness practically radiates off Mase, and my lips twitch with the effort required not to smile at the set of his jaw.

Mase thinks Jake and I are together.

And he is so. Fucking. Jealous.

"Off to the showers?" I say to Jake brightly.

"I like the way you think," he says with a warm grin, waggling his eyebrows, exactly as I knew he would. Then his eyes dart to Mase. "I'm kidding, Coach. I'm always well behaved around kids." He flashes me a conspiratorial smile I'm only too happy to return. "I'll meet you out front and drive you home." He jogs off to the bench with his stuff, and I move to do the same.

"Jake Moss?" Mase asks, keeping his voice low. "Really?"

I shrug my gym bag onto my shoulder. "What can I say? I've always liked basketball players."

And then I leave him behind.

• • •

It's a little childish to let Mase believe I'm hooking up with Jake, but whatthefuckever; he has a girlfriend, and for some reason I give a shit, and if this makes me feel the tiniest bit better about it, then I'm gonna go with it. Doesn't hurt that it helps Jake, too.

But back in my dorm, poking at a grilled chicken wrap and looking at the reading for my Communications seminar without really seeing the words, all I can really think about is how good it felt to be back on the court with him.

I remember so well the first time I saw him. I was chilling on the bleachers with the other lax girls the summer after my freshman year of high school, talking and laughing about a game we'd just won against a rival camp. I was chugging a bottle of blue Gatorade with one hand while wiping the sweat from my forehead with the other when the guys a year ahead of us rolled out on the court. A couple of the guys were as tall as Mase—well over six feet even though they were only sixteen—but he stood out so strongly I nearly choked mid-drink.

He was on the team that'd drawn skins, and he looked like a fucking onyx statue. It was ridiculous. There wasn't a single guy in my high school class of four hundred kids cut to look like him, and it was obvious from the reverent silence that came over the lax girls that I wasn't the only one who noticed. For the next half hour, we snuck glances at the game—at him—without acknowledging we were doing it; for the hour after that, we dropped the pretense.

By the time the game ended—with Mase as the high scorer—landing the new guy became *the* goal of the summer. For the next few weeks, we showed up religiously at his games, lurked around their year's parties...basically, we nailed the teen girl stereotype. But I had the benefit of an older brother who'd taught me everything from how to open a beer with my teeth to how to take a beautiful jump shot. I had Cammie, who was both a master flirt and master pool player. Eventually, I started to stand out in the crowd, and one night, after a co-ed game played just for fun under the bright lights of the court by the lake, Mase brought me a cup of water and asked my name.

We ended up talking for hours afterward—about Philly and Burlington, about basketball and lacrosse, about being away from home, about his secret affinity for Reba McIntyre and mine for Elton John. And though we didn't so much as kiss goodnight, the next day, he was on the sidelines at my lacrosse game, whistling when I scored once, twice, three times.

That night, there were fireworks, and we made out below them until the last spark fizzled from the sky.

I don't realize I've drifted off somewhere during my reminiscing until the sound of my phone ringing jolts me awake. I'm having dinner tonight with Lizzie and Frankie, so I assume it's one of them when I hit the "Talk" button with my thumb, seeing a moment too late that I've just answered a call from the very person I've been avoiding the hardest. I debate hanging up, but it's not like I can avoid him forever.

"Hey, Dad. What's up?"

"I wanted to talk to you about something. Do you have a minute?"

I glance at Andi's bed; it's empty. "Yeah, I can talk."

"Good. I've been thinking about what you were saying, and you're right. This was all very sudden, and it's very far away to move, and it's not fair to keep you across the country from your new little brother or sister."

I breathe a sigh of relief. It's not "I realized it was absurd to marry a woman you don't even know and that I barely do either," or "Whoops, turns out she's not pregnant after all! So much for that," but it's a start. "I'm so glad to hear that, Dad. It just wouldn't be the same if you guys weren't here, and I'd never get to know Abigail—"

"No, sweetheart, we *are* moving, but great news—you can join us! I've looked into UCSD and I think it'll be perfect for you. They have lacrosse—"

"Not D-I, they don't."

"And just about all of your credits will transfer," he continues as if I haven't spoken. "We'll only be twenty minutes from campus, and just think of how close we'll be to the beach, and how great your tan will be."

As if I have *ever* given a fuck about my tan, but that's not even the most perplexing part of this whole arrangement. "I'm here on a lax scholarship, Dad. You know, that thing I needed to get in order to be able to afford college at all?"

"That's for me to worry about, Cait."

"Actually, being that I'm the student, that's for me to worry about, too. If we couldn't afford Radleigh, how can we suddenly afford UCSD, especially when you have a baby coming?"

"Can't you just trust me?"

"No."

He does *not* like that. "Caitlin, for your information, Abigail's grandfather is on the board. It's taken care of."

Oh my God, that's just perfect. His child bride's rich family is the solution to all our problems. Only the fact that I possess any respect for my father keeps me from sharing my thoughts right now. Instead, I just say, "It really doesn't matter. I'm not going anywhere."

"You aren't even going to consider it?"

"What's to consider? My lax team is here. My best friends are here. Mom is *way* closer to here, and so are Cammie and Matt. I'm not following you at the expense of everyone else in my life."

"Actually, Matt will be joining us here for his senior year next year," Dad says, trying and failing to keep an edge of smugness out of his voice. Clearly he'd been saving that particular trump card for last.

I shouldn't be surprised Matt wants to go—he's always loved the beach, and was likely gonna move to Florida or California after graduation anyway—but I am. Who transfers for just senior year? Especially if doing so comes with living with Dad, Abigail, and a new baby?

Then I realize: someone who's been working for years and taking out loans to go to Ohio, but wouldn't have to for UCSD. I may be in school on scholarship, but Matt is not, and it's hard to argue how awesome it would be for him to finally give up waiting tables after five years of busting his ass.

How much money does Abigail's family *have*, anyway? Or is the tuition discount if you're board-spawn just that good?

Either way, this isn't gonna make me give in. It's just manipulation. Matt can still spend as much of winter break at our mom's house with me as he always did. He can still come in for the lax finals if we make it, like he did last year.

But your baby brother or sister will know him and not you, an obnoxious little voice nags at my brain.

The call-waiting beep is perfectly timed to save me from having to respond. "That's Lizzie on the other line," I tell him after a quick glance at the screen. "We're making dinner plans. I have to go."

"Just think about it some more, Cait," he says, voice softening. "We can all go visit together for your spring break. Get nice and tan for the wedding."

"I'll go to a tanning salon when you pick a date," I say flatly as the phone beeps again. I picture Lizzie huffing with annoyance on the other end; patience is so not her virtue. Sure enough, she hangs up a second later.

"We *have* picked a date," my father says. "May twenty-sixth. In San Diego."

All thoughts of Lizzie fly out of my brain.

May twenty-sixth.

He must be fucking kidding me. That is the only possibility.

"Dad—"

"Honey, I know it's your lacrosse finals—"

"Championships, Dad. It's the fucking championships."

"It's also Abigail's grandparents' anniversary, and it would mean a lot to them—and to her—if we made it ours as well."

"Would those be the UCSD-funding grandparents?"

"Don't be snide, Caitlin."

"What else should I be? Did you really think I was gonna be okay with this?"

"I'm your father. This is my *wedding*. That is a *game*."

"It's the game that allowed me to go to a good college years before Abigail's rich family came along," I remind him. "It's a game you used to care a *lot* about me playing."

"I still do—of course I do—but honestly, we're talking about the championships. Am I supposed to say no to the date on the small chance your team makes it there?"

"You're supposed to think there's better than a small chance, for one, especially since we got pretty close last year," I spit. "You're also supposed to recognize that when your daughter is up for captain, nothing will kill her tenuous chances like 'Hey, guys, just FYI, I decided the odds of us making it to the championships are so low that I'm gonna bail to watch my dad make it legal with his spoiled child bride."

"That's enough, Caitlin Rebecca."

I exhale sharply. "Yeah, Dad, you know what? It really, really is. Good luck with your tan."

I slam End Call so hard, I nearly bruise my thumb.

chapter eight

My dad has the nerve to email me that night while I'm with Frankie and Lizzie, just as we'd finally moved on to a different subject after half an hour of my ranting over takeout at their apartment. The subject line is Wedding Details, which is enough to make me want to puke without even opening the missive.

I try to put my phone back down, but Lizzie grabs it from me. "Dude, you can't ignore this. It's ridiculous. You're not actually skipping your father's wedding and you know it, so you may as well see what you're in for."

"I am too skipping it," I declare childishly, gnawing at a drumstick. "Just put the phone away. I want to hear more about Frankie's new tattoo plans."

"Give her a few minutes to let her brain be free of her dad," says Frankie, and Lizzie reluctantly hands it back. I slip it into my pocket with a grateful smile, even though I suspect half the reason Frankie's backing me up right now is because she really does want to talk about her tattoo plans more than anything else.

Fine by me.

Frankie drags two fingers over the inside of her forearm to indicate where the two lines of poetry will go in a font she apparently spent hours picking out. "I think it's gonna look awesome," she declares. "I just need to sell a few more sketches online and it's all mine."

She has a pretty thriving website of drawings, and her specialty when she's really short on cash—which is pretty often—is recreating any photograph you send her in pencil. It's pretty awesome, and I kinda miss watching her do it like I used to when we lay around the dorm room in our pajamas on lazy Saturday afternoons I didn't have games.

"It doesn't strike you as a little creepy to steal lines from a classmate's poem and permanently embed them in your skin?" Lizzie asks.

"I asked her permission," says Frankie with a sniff. "I'll have you know she was honored."

"What are the lines again?" I ask, looking at the exposed skin of Frankie's arm to imagine them.

"'This is the story of a woman who had done it all wrong,'" she recites. "'She couldn't do it over, but she could do it differently.'"

"*That's* what you want on your arm?"

She shrugs. “I like it.”

“I do too, actually,” Lizzie says thoughtfully. “It’s honest.”

“Wanna get matching ones?” Frankie asks.

Lizzie laughs, spraying crumbs of jalapeno cornbread. “Pass. I am not a glutton for pain. The second hole in my ear is about as dramatic as I get. Take Cait with you.”

“What do you say, Cait? You wanna get matching tats?”

“If I *were* going to get a tattoo, it wouldn’t be that,” I say, taking a bite of my grilled chicken salad.

“Oh? What would you get?” Lizzie asks.

“Probably the lacrosse logo, on my foot or the underside of my wrist or something,” I say with a shrug. “We did all agree that if we ever won the championships, we’d do it.” Just mentioning the championships turns my stomach back into a ball of lead, and I push the salad away.

“Boring,” says Frankie, reaching for a pork rib. “Come on—you never thought of getting a more interesting tattoo than that?”

I don’t know if it’s any more interesting, but back when I used to lie on Mase’s chest in the grass, staring at the stars, I used to think I wanted to get one of those constellations tattooed on me somewhere—a way to make those memories indelible, permanent.

Turns out, they were; we just weren’t.

"Maybe a 12, for Tom Brady," I say with a shrug.

"There are certainly less hot men you could've chosen to brand yourself with," Lizzie concedes.

I know she means Tom Brady, but when I say, "no kidding," I don't.

"No ink for you, Lizzie B.?" I ask.

"Connor's name on your ass in gothic letters?" Frankie suggests.

She throws back her head and laughs. "God, can you imagine? 'What *is* that, Elizabeth?' Followed by a half-hour lecture on the history of the Goths."

"You guys have the most fucked-up foreplay," says Frankie. "Speaking of which, Cait, how's it going with that basketball guy?"

I open my mouth to insist there's nothing going on between me and Mase, but then I realize she means Jake. I'm not sure how word spread around campus that Jake Moss and Cait Johannssen are the newest jock It couple (though I suspect it involves some locker room talk I'd rather not know), but somehow it got back to Double Trouble over here. I hate lying to my friends so much, especially given how upset I was when Lizzie hid her hooking up with Connor from us last semester, but this is Jake's secret to tell.

"Fine," I mumble, the lie like dust on my tongue.

"When are you guys going out again?" Lizzie asks. She pops the last piece of cornbread into her mouth and follows it with a long swallow of beer. "I assume there's a thank-you date coming in exchange for your livening up this morning at church."

"It wasn't actually at church, and he doesn't owe me a thank-you," I say, eyeing her beer enviously while I sip my own glass of water. After my less than stellar performance lately, I'm taking a break from all reflex-slowing and hangover-inducing libations. "It was fun. I'm thinking about going back next week."

"I thought you said the guys only had to do it one weekend a month." Lizzie eyes me suspiciously. "Did you talk him into going back?"

Shit. I forgot I'd told them that part. Before I can figure out how to recover, Frankie stabs a rib sauce-stained finger in my face. "You're about to lie. You are wearing your fucking 'I'm about to lie' face. Don't even think about it. Out with it, Caitlin."

I sigh. "Mase was there, okay? It's nothing. We just played a little basketball and had fun, and I thought it'd be nice to do it again."

"With your ex-boyfriend," says Frankie. "Who's dating your roommate."

"Man, after all the shit you gave me for hooking up with Trevor when he was dating Sophie," Lizzie muses.

"This is so not the same thing. I'm *not* hooking up with Mase; I'm just trying to rekindle our friendship. Guys and girls can be friends, you know."

"They can," Lizzie agrees. "You two just can't."

"Watch me prove you wrong."

"Watch you get in way over your head with a guy you should be distancing yourself from," she counters. "Jake seems like a nice guy; why don't you just focus on him? Trust me from experience—messing with another girl's boyfriend is so not worth it."

"I'm not doing that," I argue. "I know he's with Andi. I just want to be friends."

"Why?" asks Frankie. "You're friends with a bunch of guys on campus. Why do you need one more? Why do you *need* to be friends with him?"

"And why would you risk screwing things up with a guy who's actually single?" Lizzie adds. "Stick with Jake. And if you're not really into him? Look for someone else. But don't make that someone else Mase. It just cannot end well."

In theory I know they're right, but of course they don't know why Jake is a non-starter. And I can't explain why I feel such a pull to have Mase back in my life, but I do. I'd never make a move on him—I know that. I am not the kind of girl who goes for another girl's boyfriend, and certainly not my roommate's. I trust myself.

Don't I?

This conversation is unsettling me, and even though continuing the lie about Jake makes me cringe, it feels like the only way to maintain my sanity right now. "You're right," I reply, ignoring the twinge in my gut. "I'm seeing Jake Tuesday night, to meet up for our project."

"Perfect!" Lizzie drains the last of her beer. "Trust me, sex in the library is something everyone should be trying at least once, anyway."

"Far, far too much information," I say at the same moment Frankie says, "Truth."

As they shift into talking about the best places to hook up on campus, I sit back and just listen, trying and failing not to remember when Mase and I used to contemplate the exact same thing—whether the gazebo was hidden enough (it was, except that one time it wasn't), whether we were brave enough to skinny dip in the lake at night (we were), whether it was safe to get each other off in the back seat of the bus during away games (as if anyone *wasn't* doing this).

Fuck. They're right. I need to stay away from him. And though obviously Jake's not the solution, if I don't find another guy to focus on, my brain is going to travel down the dangerous path of full-on coveting my roommate's boyfriend.

Plus, if I *do* end up going to my dad's wedding, I sure as hell don't want to do it alone.

The question is, who on earth do I want on my arm, and where on this campus do I find him?

• • •

I don't find any answers to my question in practice the next morning, but channeling all my aggression at the various shitty situations in my life sure does make me kick ass. "Nice hustle, Johannssen," Coach Brady praises me as we rip off our goggles and jog off the field—frozen but miraculously snow-free for the first time in a while—and toward the showers. "That was some first class ball-handling."

"Thanks, Coach."

"You play like that in our scrimmage against Stansbury this weekend, you just might fill Rivera's shoes," he says, referring to our captain in a voice low enough that only I can hear.

Not when everyone finds out I might have to bail on the championships, I think, but I don't say anything out loud, just nod firmly at Coach and keep jogging.

"Way to kick my ass today," Nora grunts at me as soon as I enter the locker room. I don't miss the admiration in her voice, even through her griping. As a goalie, she's used to anticipating plenty of shots from the attack line, but I've been more about posting assists to Tish and Tessa than shooting myself. Expert cradling is kinda my thing, and a big part of that is learning how to restrain your own power for accurate passing.

Today wasn't a day for restraint. I shot the shit out of the goal, and only now do I see the resulting welts on Nora's arms and abs. "Sorry, Price," I say sheepishly.

"You're lucky I'm a pain slut," she says with a wink as she strips down to nothing and steps into the shower. "Seriously, though, killer practice."

"Thanks." I strip down too and get in, the water's heat and pressure amazing on my sweaty skin. "Felt good." Especially after finally reading my dad's email from the day before, which ignored every word I said about not going to his wedding and instead provided me with a full schedule of events, ending with a PS that Abigail would be in touch to ask me a "very special favor."

If I could pre-emptively block Abigail from my phone and email, I would do it in a fucking heartbeat.

I finish my shower and towel off, and only when I overhear Nora and the second-string goalie, Janet, gossiping about how hot the Stansbury goalie is do I remember my resolution from the night before. I drift over to Tessa, who's rubbing lotion into her arms, and take the seat next to her on the bench. "Hey, can I ask you a weird question?"

"Always," she says without looking up.

Keeping my voice low so as not to be overheard by anyone else on the team—especially Nora, who'd probably die of laughter—I ask, "You don't have any friends you could set me up with, do you?"

She turns to me, her eyebrows shooting up to the sky. "*You* want to be set up?"

Immediately, my face heats up. "Never mind. It was stupid—" I start to stand, but she pulls me back down.

"No, crap, I'm sorry. It's just…I thought you were with Jake Moss."

I resist the urge to sigh, knowing I'm gonna have to lie again. "We're not exclusive," I say, which at least has plenty of truth to it too. "Honestly, I'd like to meet someone who's not on the basketball team. Maybe someone who's not an athlete at all." *The better the chance of avoiding Mase.*

Tessa laughs. "Join the club. Between lacrosse and Kinesiology, I can't even remember the last time I met a decent guy who wasn't an athlete. If you figure out where they dwell, feel free to hand out my number."

She makes a good point; Communications is full of athletes too, because it's full of easy-A classes, and I can't exactly pick up a guy in Econ now that Jake is my fake boyfriend.

God dammit.

A new guy isn't so likely, which means all I can do is work with the one I've got. Much as I fucking *hate* the idea of being a beard, at least the pretense will keep me honest when it comes to my roommate's boyfriend.

Time to kick this fauxmance into high gear.

chapter nine

Turns out, I don't even need to convince Jake keep our ruse going; he asks me first. "It's Troy's birthday this weekend," he confides to me quietly in the library the following night. "There's an Omega party Friday, and he's dying to do pretty much *anything* that isn't going to it."

"So…don't go."

Jake snorts. "Easier said than done. The only way to get out of going to an Omega party if you're a brother is basically to have a girlfriend insist on dragging your ass to something else."

"That is the most sexist piece of shit I've ever heard."

"You're talking to a basketball-playing frat boy who likes cock, Johannssen," he mutters under his breath. "You don't need to tell me how shitty the 'rules' are."

“Fair point.”

“Can you help me out?”

“What do you want me to do?”

“I don’t know yet,” he admits, “but I’m sure between the two of us we can come up with something. What do you want me to do for you?”

“I don’t know either,” I say with a grin, “but someday, I will call upon you for a favor, and when that day comes…”

“I’m in.” We fist-bump in agreement, then get back to work on our project.

By seven thirty, both our stomachs are rumbling, and we agree to adjourn to the dining hall with our books. We all but float in on the delicious scents of hash browns, burgers, and pizza as we brainstorm ways to make Troy’s birthday a good one, but my appetite and our plans drift into smoke when we enter the dining hall and immediately spot Mase and Andi sitting at a table in the center. They’re not being particularly touchy or even flirty from what I can see, but having not seen them together since that first day, I’m surprised at how hard the image of them hits me in the gut.

“You wanna go to Tate’s?” Jake asks, but the second the words are out of his mouth, Andi spots us, smiles, and waves me over.

“Fucking kill me,” I mutter, unconsciously squeezing Jake’s hand. He squeezes back, and it isn’t until we reach Mase and Andi and her smile widens further at the sight of us that I realize how couple-y we look right now.

"Hey, guys," I say, pasting a warm smile on my face. "Fancy meeting you here."

"I was just talking about you," says Andi. "I feel like I've barely seen you since you guys played basketball on Sunday. I had to hear how your game was and whether you keep up."

She says it with a smile and I know she means zero harm by it, but the suggestion I might not be able to makes me bristle inside. "I think I did okay," I said.

"Law seemed to think so." The affection in her tone supercharges the bristling effect. "And you must be the basketball-playing boyfriend."

The word "boyfriend" catches me by surprise—I'm pretty sure I never called him that to Andi—but Jake takes it in stride. "Yes, ma'am. Jake Moss—nice to meet you."

"Andi," she says, returning his warm smile. God, she's so nice, and it makes my gut twist. This isn't a girl staking her claim on her man by pretending to be excited about mine; she has no idea that's something to consider. All she sees is her roommate being happily coupled, and this is her being supportive. The same way I should be for her and her boyfriend. "I can't believe this is the first I'm meeting you. You must sit with us."

"Oh," I say, "we haven't even gotten our food yet, and I don't want to keep you—"

"Don't be silly." Andi waves a hand dismissively. "I want to meet Jake! It'll be like a double date."

I guess that's supposed to be a good thing? It's hard to make excuses in the face of her enthusiasm, so Jake and I excuse ourselves to go get food. "She seems nice," he says when we're out of earshot.

"She is. Which kind of sucks."

Jake grins as we hold our trays for burgers, which are totally not on the lean-protein list I'm supposed to be adhering to during the season. Fuck it; I'll take my virtue in the form of a salad instead of fries. The burger stays. "She's too nice for him. Sunday morning was the only time I've ever seen him be a nice guy. He's been a total dick at practice since then, and he didn't do any more than grunt at us just now."

"He didn't used to be like that," I say as we both fill huge cups with water at the fountain soda machine. "He used to be like he was Sunday morning all the time—had fun, joked around, played well with others. It was nice to see again."

"I guess that makes it a *little* clearer why you like the guy," Jake says with a scowl. "Well, that and he looks like he could break you in half without using his hands."

I'd been sipping my water as he spoke, and at that, I splutter and choke on it. "Jake, you fucking pervert."

He shrugs unapologetically. "When he's not yelling or making us run an extra ten laps around the gym, I can appreciate that the guy is hot as hell."

Ugh, he really is. Those stupid long-lashed warm brown eyes; dark, smooth skin; and lush, full lips that used to part to reveal perfect white teeth all the damn time, back when he smiled. And I *know* that underneath the navy hooded sweatshirt he's wearing right now, he's still cut like a fucking Greek god.

I'm…not going to think any lower than that.

With no excuses left to linger by the food, we take our seats with Andi, who still looks thrilled to see us, and Mase, who looks like he'd rather die. "So, where are you guys coming from?" Andi asks cheerfully.

"Just the library. We're in Econ together." I take a huge bite of my burger, suddenly starving.

"That's how we hooked up," Jake adds, bumping his shoulder against mine. "Such a classic story—teaming up for a class project. This one's so smart, too."

I force my eyes not to roll out of my head as Jake lays it on thick as mud.

"So sweet," says Andi, looping an arm around Mase's and squeezing tight. "Did I ever tell you how we met?"

No. And please don't. "I don't think so!" *Please don't let me throw up this burger.*

"Oh, it's such a funny story. Law was still at Indiana, and he'd just sprained his knee, so he was hobbling around on these crutches, which of course had to be custom made because, well, look at him."

I'd rather not.

"We don't need to talk about me as an invalid," Mase says quietly, trying to sound like he's joking while most definitely not.

Andi rolls her eyes and pats his biceps as if he's a child. "Anyway, I was there visiting my cousin, who's a cheerleader, so she takes me to this party full of athletes. I of course have no idea how to talk to anyone there—I don't know a thing about sports—and I see this guy on crutches and think, 'Okay, there's someone else who doesn't play sports! I can talk to him!'"

I hate this story already—hate that *not* playing is what drew them together—but I just smile and nod, because Andi's eyes are sparkling at the memory and what else can I do?

"So we spend the entire night flirting, which is mostly me talking about Radleigh and my classes and stuff. Of course we can't dance, and he was still on painkillers, so no drinking. And the whole night I'm thinking he's gonna walk me back to my cousin's dorm after and maybe I'll actually get up the guts to ask him out, but duh, he can't walk. Well, I mean, he could walk, but not, like, across campus."

"I think they get it," Mase says with a strained smile.

Under the table, Jake flicks my thigh. I flick his back. No question about it—Andi and Mase have a strange dynamic, and just being in their presence is weirdly uncomfortable, history or not. But this is also the most animated I've ever seen her, so clearly there's some spark there I just do not get.

"So at this point, I've had a couple of drinks without even realizing it, just because I was totally nervous, you know? So I offer to *carry* him." She breaks into peals of laughter then, and I force a laugh too. I know if it'd been Lizzie or Frankie, the line would've been "I offered him a ride," infused with as much innuendo as possible; Andi's sincere silliness is totally new to me. "God, you looked at me like I was crazy," she says to Mase.

"Your tiny ass offering to drag mine around? You *were* a little crazy, babe," he replies, and I have to force myself not to wince at the genuine affection in his voice.

"But it was totally worth it." She turns back to me and Jake. "He *very* smoothly pointed out the easiest thing of all would be if I just stayed over. How could I argue with that, right?"

I don't even realize I'm clawing my nails into Jake's thigh until he gently disengages me with one hand and feeds me a fry with the other. I *never* eat fries, but I don't think twice before letting him do it in a nauseating display of faux-coupledom that keeps me blissfully distracted from the image of Mase and Andi going at it for a whole ten seconds.

"So cute," I finally manage when I've swallowed.

Andi beams, pulling her long dark curls up into a ponytail before returning to the salad she'd abandoned for her storytelling. "We didn't even stay in touch, really, but then one day he emailed me that he'd applied for a student coaching job here, and once he got it, well…how could we not reconnect?"

"What a coincidence," Jake mumbles around his bite of burger.

It does seem like a bizarre coincidence, unless he really was so taken with her from that one night that he followed her to Radleigh. That's a pretty intense move, and not one I'd ever imagine from Mase. But obviously I don't really know the guy sitting across from me anymore. Maybe their formerly one-night stand was just that good.

I try to catch Mase's eye but his are firmly fixed on the crusts of what I'm guessing were once pepperoni pizzas, if I recall his topping preferences correctly—and I'm sadly sure I do. I still can't process how a guy I used to know so damn well just keeps on becoming a bigger and bigger mystery to me. Finally, I go back to my burger and let the conversation change from their coupledom to our Econ project, then to Andi's major—Anthropology—and finally to some lackluster conversation about the basketball team. When both Jake's and my plates are clean, I jump up, grabbing him with me.

"It was so good to see you guys," I say apologetically as I pull my coat on, "but this project is pretty huge, and we have to get back to it before the library closes for the night. See you back at the room?" I ask Andi.

"Actually, I think I'll be staying at Law's tonight, but I'll see you tomorrow."

"Right, sure." I grab my tray with so much extra force I nearly send my cup flying. "Maybe I'll have Jake stay over then." I turn to Jake. "We should study in my room instead. Not that we'll get much studying done if we do that," I add with a wink that makes me hate myself so much I wish I could throw myself in the meat grinder that made the burger now churning in my stomach.

Andi laughs, and I wrap my arm around Jake's and yank him toward the tray depository. "This is getting a little pathetic, Johannssen," he warns me as we dump the garbage off our trays and return them.

"Like I don't know that," I mutter back. "Just shut up."

When he throws back his head and laughs and I yank him out of the room, I can only hope it looks like the romantic joking of a couple in love.

Pathetic.

• • •

I can't force myself to return to the dorm after that, so Jake and I walk off together for just long enough to suggest we're spending the night, and then I head off to Lizzie and Frankie's instead. Frankie answers the door with colorful smudges all over her face and arms, and ushers me inside, where I'm not sure what assaults me harder—the paint fumes or the absurd tableau in front of me. Lizzie's desk has been pulled out into the living room, and Connor's sitting behind it, looking like the paragon of college professor in an elbow-patched tweed jacket that's probably sending Lizzie into conniptions. Lizzie, meanwhile, is perched on the desk, vamping it up in a low-cut shirt and a skirt so tiny I think it might actually be one of my sweatbands. One hand is splayed out on the wood, showing off dramatic red-black polish. The other is curled around an apple she's extending in Connor's direction.

"Please tell me I did not just walk into some fetishist role play."

"This is *art*, thank you very much," Frankie sniffs, stepping in front of her easel and picking up a brush. I drop my stuff in the entryway and walk over, admiring the likeness on Frankie's canvas. Lizzie and Connor look spot on, right down to Lizzie's omnipresent black-framed glasses, but there are also jungle vines creeping around the edges, spotted with brightly colored fruit. As usual, I have no clue what I'm looking at, though I think Frankie's talented as hell.

"I give up—what's happening here?"

"It's my newest series," she says, peering around the canvas to assess the positioning of Lizzie's legs before dipping her brush into medium-brown paint. "Taking biblical characters and setting them in the modern world."

"Adam and Eve," I realize, looking at the apple in Lizzie's hand. "Frank, that is pretty fucking brilliant."

"Isn't it?" She squints at her handiwork, then dabs at a little spot with the tip of the brush. "These two sex fiends totally inspired me."

"Hey!"

"She means it as a compliment, Connor," Lizzie explains, brushing her foot up his leg. "Trust me."

"I do," Frankie murmurs as she paints, "but if you move again I will kill you both in your sleep."

"We've been sitting like this for hours, Frankie." Connor huffs out a sigh. "I'm about five seconds away from eating that apple."

"So impatient." Frankie clucks her tongue. "How do you teach children?"

"He doesn't teach *children*, you bitch," says Lizzie. "I can't believe you talked us into this."

"How *did* she talk you into it?" I ask, dropping onto the couch. "You're usually so good at evading Frankie's projects. And Connor, this seems pretty risqué for someone who's trying to stay out of trouble."

"She's oddly convincing when she wants to be," he grunts.

"You don't even know the half of how many people on this campus have already learned that lesson," Lizzie says with a grin. "But for what it's worth, her lasagna really is as good as she says it is."

Despite having just crammed a thousand calories into my face at dinner, the mention of Frankie's lasagna makes my stomach rumble. It's the only thing she knows how to cook, but she does it damn well. "Feel free to let me know what night that's happening," I say, pulling off my boots and putting my feet up on the couch. "I feel like I haven't had home-cooked food in months."

"Uh uh, Caity J. Lasagna's not free. You want my food, you'll have to pose."

"As what?"

Frankie frowns. "I'm not sure yet. Something that works with your height, maybe. Something warrior-like. Ooh, maybe Deborah! Or Yael! You would make such a good soldier."

"That'd be cool!" Lizzie agrees, and even Connor nods.

"Who are Deborah and Yael?" I ask sheepishly. Lizzie knows tons of random trivia, Connor's a major history nerd, and Frankie's dad is a former priest, so she has a weird amount of biblical knowledge, but this is totally not my area of expertise.

"Deborah was a general in the book of Judges," Frankie says as she stops to squeeze more paint onto her palette. "But I think I want you to be Yael. She was this badass woman who lured the opposing general into her home, soothed him into sleep, and then brained him with a tent peg."

"Hot damn. You may have convinced me," I say, curling my feet up underneath my butt. "Can I pick out who plays the general, by any chance?"

Lizzie laughs. "So that explains why you're here. Let me guess—you just had a run-in with the stargazing ex."

"More than a run-in," I grumble. "I got stuck with him and Andi for a whole damn dinner. I was clawing Jake so hard in the thigh I probably drew blood."

"And how exactly did you explain that to Jake?" Frankie asks.

"Who *is* Jake?" Connor asks.

Oh, crap. Right. Lying. "Jake's the guy I'm dating, and Mase is his coach. He's really unbearable, apparently." At least that part is true. "Neither of us wanted to be there. Hence the clawing."

Lizzie and Frankie exchange a glance. "I feel like we're missing something," says Frankie.

"Same." Lizzie shifts to work out a crick in her neck, and Frankie immediately clucks her annoyance. Lizzie rolls her eyes as she puts herself back in position. "You have twenty more minutes, Frank, and then I've got a Skype call with my brothers. Make good use." She looks to me without moving her head. "And you, we are clearly in need of some girl time. No offense, lover," she says to Connor.

"So, that whole conversation we had about not calling me that in public just kinda went in one ear and died there, huh?"

"Didn't even really make it in that ear, honestly. But Cait, girl date, yes? Next point at which we're all free, we need to go and do something. Maybe shopping? Shopping seems like a thing we should do."

The mention of shopping triggers the memory of Abigail's stupid email. "Well, I can tell you my dad and his fiancée would love that," I say wryly. "I'm supposed to be buying a bridesmaid dress for his stupid wedding."

"Perfect!" says Frankie, clapping her hands and immediately splattering paint on her face as a result, though she doesn't seem to care, any more than she acknowledges that my tone is meant to convey that I'd rather die. "Saturday?"

"I've got scrimmage on Saturday," I respond, already looking forward to my next game. Much as I loved lacrosse before, I appreciate it double now that I've got aggression to work out. The irony that my frustrations about potentially missing the championships are helping to drive my team there is not lost on me.

"Sunday, then," Lizzie says decisively. "I *know* we're all free Sunday."

She's got me there, and I reluctantly agree. I may have no interest in anything having to do with this wedding, but if anything has the potential to make it bearable, it's having my friends with me.

I think I've had more than enough testosterone in my life for a good, long while.

chapter ten

By the time we actually go, I've built up the dread in my head all over again, but of course, Lizzie and Frankie won't let up. "I can't even believe we're doing this. I don't even want to go to the stupid wedding," I grumble as Lizzie practically yanks me through the door of Sweethearts Bridal Shop. "The last thing I wanna do is try on a zillion stupid froufy dresses."

"You *are* going to the wedding, and you know it." Lizzie rolls her eyes, and I might be imagining it but I could swear her glasses magnify the attitude. "Be cranky and all that—I get it—but let's not pretend you're actually gonna miss your father's wedding for a fucking *lacrosse game.*"

I grab my arm back. "I know you think lacrosse is stupid—"

"Of course I don't think it's stupid, Cait. Just because I don't enjoy sports doesn't mean I don't understand that it's important to you and that you love it. But this is your *father*. This is his *wedding*. And however you feel about Abigail and the fact that your dad is marrying her, she's still gonna be your stepmother. You can't even imagine how much you'd hate yourself for missing this."

I bite the inside of my cheek to stop myself from letting out a heated response I'll regret. Six months ago, Lizzie would've been on Team Righteous Anger, no question. But now her parents are dead, and I know how much time she spends regretting every instant she fought with them, or displeased them. "We're not the same, Lizzie," I say quietly.

She snorts. "My parents weren't sick, remember? They were fine and then they weren't. They were *alive* and then they weren't. Sometimes, shit just happens. You don't think I imagined I'd have decades to make up lost moments with them?"

"So I have to do whatever my parents want because someday I may lose them in a random tragic accident and I'll regret that one time I disobeyed them?"

Frankie sucks in an audible breath, which is the ultimate in "You've gone too far," because Frankie doesn't generally believe there *is* a "too far." But I stand firm, setting my jaw as I watch Lizzie's eyes narrow. "I can't live my life as if I've been in your shoes," I say. "I haven't. What happened to your parents is *horrible*, but do you really think if I'd warned you there was the slightest possibility in the world that would happen, that would've been enough to get you to stop smoking or partying or whatever else your parents would've gotten pissed about?"

Lizzie exhales sharply and holds up her hands. "Okay, stop. Let's start this over." She fixes her stare on me. "Caitlin, you are going to try on dresses, because this is your father's wedding and it wouldn't take your father dying for you to regret not going. You're already upset that they're moving and you'll be missing out on their lives. How do you think you'll feel when you see family wedding pictures without you?"

"She's got a good point," says Frankie, and it's hard to disagree. I may not be sure either way, but if I don't get a bridesmaid dress, that *is* making a decision I'm not ready to make. I sigh and tell the saleswoman what I need, sure Frankie and Lizzie are exchanging triumphant glances behind me.

"I'm sorry," I mutter to Lizzie as the saleswoman walks off to look for some things in my size. "If I said—"

She holds up a hand. "You didn't. I get it. It's sort of impossible for me not to play the Dead Parents Card."

"Can't really blame you. I imagine it affects everything in your life."

"Yeah." Her lips twist into a wry smile. "Not a lot of people who can empathize, either. Which I guess is a good thing, but it gets rough."

We're all silent for a moment, because Lizzie's talking about her feelings and Lizzie *never* talks about her feelings, and for the first time, I'm actually glad to be out at this stupid dress shop. Then the saleswoman comes back with a rack of options that make me feel distinctly nauseated with their bright-and-shininess.

"Abigail said any color?" Lizzie asks, examining a hot-pink thing I wouldn't wear if it were my only protection against the fires of hell. "At least that's cool."

"Any color," I confirm, flipping through the dresses in the hopes there's something black. Or navy. Or dark brown. Anything that wouldn't be wrapped around an Easter egg. "As long as Cammie and I coordinate." I pull my phone from my back pocket and wiggle it.

"And what's Cammie wearing?" asks Frankie.

"Probably a repurposed trash bag," I mutter. If Cammie even comes to the wedding, there's no way she'd shell out any money to be part of it. "She said to pick something out first and then just let her know."

"No other bridesmaids?" Lizzie's moved on to fire engine-red.

"Nope. She wants this to be a small family thing, apparently. I'm guessing on account of the pregnancy."

"Okay, so this could be *way* worse." Frankie examines a wildly patterned thing critically, glances at me, and drops it. Good girl. "You're not *completely* dress-averse."

"No, just completely averse to this wedding," I mutter.

"We're ignoring you now," says Lizzie. "Here—how about this?" She holds up a floor-length dress in a stretchy fabric that's about the same shade of blue as the Patriots' away jerseys. At least that's something. When I hold it up against me, though, it's obvious it's inches too short.

"And now I remember why I stopped bothering with dresses." I sigh, handing the dress back. "Some articles of clothing are just not meant for girls over five-eight."

"There's gotta be something here…" Frankie mutters. As the two of them go through dresses, I pull out my phone and text Cammie. *I forgot how much I hate dress shopping. Can we re-discuss that wedding boycott?*

With pleasure, she writes back immediately.

I snort. I should be a better influence than this, but as Frankie and Lizzie hold dress after dress up next to me with frowns on their faces as they don't even brush my ankles, the disheartened feeling that always comes with shopping as a Tall Girl only increases.

There are only two dresses in my closet right now, and they're both dresses that are supposed to be knee-length but which I've embraced as minis instead, including the one I just wore to the Omega Nu party. Pretty sure that isn't gonna fly at the wedding, though.

I had a dress I loved, once. I'd bought it for Cammie's high school graduation, on my mother's insistence, and got so many compliments that I threw it into my trunk for camp on a whim. It was simple—strapless, white with a black lace overlay, fitted on top with a flared skirt that made it less obvious it was inches shorter on me than it should've been. I wore it with a cardigan to her graduation, but when I saw other girls at Stone Creek wearing dresses to the end-of-summer banquet after my sophomore year, I ditched my plan to wear my one nice pair of black pants and pulled out the dress instead.

After all, there was a certain basketball player's eye I'd recently caught, and I wanted to keep it.

Honestly, part of me had worried that Mase would find the sight of me in a dress silly, that he'd think I looked like a not-so-little girl playing dress-up. We'd already fooled around a few times, so I knew that despite the fact that he'd only really seen me in tank tops and shorts, he wasn't exactly clueless to my femininity. But still, I felt weirdly shy walking into the banquet all dolled up.

For about two seconds until Mase spotted me, froze in the middle of joking around with his friends, and smiled so slowly it felt like he was peeling the dress off me right then and there. It gave me the confidence to walk over to their group, and when I did, he wrapped an arm around my shoulders and pulled me to his side and I knew I didn't wanna be anywhere else that night.

I was glad I'd ditched the cardigan, because even as we talked to the other guys, his long fingers stroked the bare skin of my shoulder, sending trails of fire down my spine. Before long I was doing the same thing, tracing the muscles of his back through his shirt, both of us getting increasingly antsy before he finally leaned down and murmured in my ear, "We need to get out of here."

They were exactly the words I wanted to hear, though I didn't know it until he said them. "I have to go to the bathroom," I blurted to the guys, who all looked at me strangely, but I couldn't be bothered to care. There was only one single-room restroom in the gym and I ran toward it like my dress was on fire. Less than a minute later, Mase rushed in behind me and all but threw me on the sink, kissing me with a ferocity that matched exactly how I felt inside. My head slammed against the mirror but I didn't care. I was too busy wrapping my legs around his waist, my arms around his neck, inhaling the combination of his familiar deodorant and unfamiliar cologne.

I didn't even have to think twice when his hand slid up my dress and brushed against my damp cotton underwear; I just arched into his touch and made some sort of unintelligible noise against his lips that was meant to signify "Finger me *now*." I was so horny I came on his hand in about a minute, and it barely took him that to do the same in a bunch of rough paper towels from the dispenser on the wall. When we were both spent, we cracked up at our impatience and the speed with which we'd both come, but before we rejoined the rest of our friends at the banquet, knowing we'd take a ton of shit for disappearing at the same time, he kissed me.

It wasn't a desperate, hungry kiss like we'd exchanged a few minutes earlier when we were finally alone, nor was it one of the flirty, teasing ones we'd been exchanging in our late-night makeout sessions for the last couple of weeks. It was real, substantial, promising. It made me feel like what we'd done was more than just a spur-of-the-moment hookup. It made me feel…everything.

I promptly ruined the dress that night when the banquet spontaneously turned into a basketball game, as most things we did in the gym tended to do, but I still had it somewhere in the back of the closet at my mom's house.

I wanted a dress that would make me feel the way I felt that night. No, I wanted a *guy* who would make me feel the way I felt that night. But they only sold one of those things at Sweethearts Bridal, and it took two hours, but we finally found it.

Black lace over beige. Go figure.

• • •

In other things that shouldn't surprise me, I spot Mase through the doorway to the weight room on my way out of practice the next morning. I plan to just wave and keep walking, and have to hide my shock when he waves first. With no class until the afternoon, and my having locked myself in my room (sans Andi) to do my Communications and Greek Tragedy homework the night before, I have nothing better to do than walk in and say hi.

So I do.

"I thought I might see you at the community center yesterday morning," he says as he does another biceps curl. "The kids asked about you. Apparently you made quite an impression."

He doesn't say it to make me feel guilty, but somehow it does. Not that it would've occurred to me I was welcome; I certainly had no reason to think I could show up without Jake. "Maybe next week," I say, wondering if I'll feel more equipped to handle a morning alone with him and the kids then than I do now. "I had an errand to run yesterday."

"An errand, huh? How mysterious."

I snort. "Not exactly. I was getting a bridesmaid dress for my father's wedding."

He raises his eyebrows and puts down the dumbbell. "Your dad's getting married? I thought he and your mom split because he wanted to be a bachelor for life."

A little smile threatens to creep over my lips, and I bite one to stop it. He remembered. I don't know why that feels like a big deal to me right now, but for some reason, it does. And it makes me want to keep spilling my guts to him, knowing that he really listens. "Yeah, I'm guessing that would have been his life plan if he hadn't gotten his receptionist pregnant, but apparently that just wasn't in the cards."

"No shit." Mase whistles, then squirts water into his mouth from the bottle next to him with one hand while patting the bench with the other. I take the seat he offers. "So you're gonna be a big sister?"

"Oh, God, I hadn't even thought of the big sister part," I admit. "I mean, the fact that there'll be a kid, yeah, but not that I won't be the baby anymore. How weird."

"Do you like the receptionist, at least?"

"I've met her once. I was not particularly impressed."

"You gonna meet her again before the wedding?"

"I don't even want to go *to* the wedding," I tell him, twisting a strand of wet hair that's fallen out of my post-shower bun. "Get this—they scheduled it for the day of the lacrosse championships. Like, as if that was the *only* day they could possibly get hitched."

He sucks in a breath. "Man, that blows. I'm sorry. You think you guys are gonna go all the way?"

"We definitely have a shot," I say with confidence it's nice to actually feel. "I'm playing at my best, and so are a bunch of the other girls. We destroyed at our scrimmages the past two Saturdays." Instinctively, I push up the sleeve of my hoodie so he can see the welt there from a particularly impressive interception—we always used to proudly show each other our battle scars—but when he presses a finger to it and watches me wince, he's not grinning like he used to.

And then I remember he's got one very big, very final battle scar, invisible to the naked eye though it may be, and it's the last one he'll ever get on the court.

An apology rises to my lips and I force myself to swallow it down. It sucks what happened to Mase, but I can't say I'm sorry for the fact that I *didn't* injure myself.

I do, however, need to stop poking at the past. Unfortunately, as I search for a safer topic, I realize the past is all I know of the guy next to me. Well, other than the fact that he's dating my roommate, but I'd rather run another set of suicides than talk about that. "How's *your* mom?" I ask finally. It's kind of a reach as far as natural questions go—she never cared for me—but it's all I got.

He shrugs. "Same old." Silence settles between us until I start to feel silly for even trying, and then he coughs. "But, uh, Will's coming up for the weekend."

The mere mention of Mase's brother's name brings a smile to my face. Will didn't go to Stone Creek—sports aren't really his thing—but he used to come up for a weekend here and there and when he did, I always loved hanging out with him. He and Mase were such natural goofballs together, and whenever Mase had a game and I didn't, I'd sit in the sidelines with Will, checking out guys and rating their calves on a scale from one to ten. He was built like a beanpole—a few inches shorter than Mase and with half the muscle—but he could eat his own weight in burgers, and it was a sight to see every damn time.

Will was definitely a part of the past I'd be perfectly happy to see again.

"Sounds like fun! Does he, um…know I'm here?"

I watch his Adam's apple as he swallows, and even though he doesn't voice an answer, he doesn't have to. When will I learn to understand that I may or may not have meant something to Mase, but I definitely haven't elevated above Dirty Little Secret status with Law? "Of course not," I say, trying to keep my voice neutral but hearing the bite in my words. And I don't even know why it's there—I *don't* have anything to do with Law. Law is my roommate's boyfriend. He's a coach, not a player. This isn't summer camp; in a few months, I won't even be a teenager anymore. Whatever I'm clinging to, it isn't real. And it needs to stop, now.

"Well, have fun with him," I say. "I'll stay with friends on Friday night so you don't risk bumping into me with him in my room."

"You don't have to—"

"It's fine." I pull on my coat and hoist my gym bag onto my shoulder. "I'll see you around, Law."

He doesn't say anything to my back, and I don't turn around.

chapter eleven

I kill it at practice the next morning. Just absolutely crush it. By the time I score my fourth goal off Nora, I'm pretty sure she wants to kick me in the ovaries. I channel all my frustration and all my aggression into the game, and afterward, rather than joining everyone else in the locker room, I keep it up and run a mile around campus before returning to my room to shower.

When I come out of the bathroom, Samara's stretched out on the couch, and I realize I don't even know if she's been there the whole time; I pretty much walked into the suite with blinders on, hoping to evade Andi completely. Whoops. She looks up from her book when she sees me. "Hey, Cait."

"Hey. Reading anything good?"

She holds it up—a dark hardcover with a blurry picture of a girl hugging her knees on the cover. "Yeah, it's great. Enraging and powerful in the best way. You ever read any YA novels?"

"It's been forever since I read a book that wasn't for class," I admit. "It's hard to find the time between homework reading and practice. I actually have to read one of Sophocles' plays at some point before my class in the next three hours."

"Oh well. There's a contemporary romance series I think you'd love—they're almost all sports romances, but one of them's about a couple that reunites as camp counselors."

I don't miss the smile that plays on her lips before she glances back down into her book.

"Frankie told you."

"What else did you think we were gonna talk about at dinner without you?" She closes the book, leaving her finger between the pages to hold her place. "I haven't said a word to Andi, if that's what you're worried about, and no, she's not here. But are you ever planning on telling her the truth?"

"Pretty sure we missed the boat on that," I mutter, my stomach churning with guilt. "So, have you been secretly judging me this entire time?"

"Of course not. I understand that sometimes keeping a secret feels like the right thing." She looks like she wants to say more, but she chews on her lip instead. "Anyway, I'm sorry it kinda sucks."

"Thanks." I wrinkle my nose. "I still wanna kill Frankie for telling you. That girl does not make good decisions when she eyes prey."

Samara arches a perfect dark-golden eyebrow. "Prey?"

Oh, yeah, that was probably not the wisest word choice. "I just mean when she thinks a girl is cute."

The book slips in Samara's grip and nearly falls, but she catches it and badly plays like nothing happened. "Frankie…what?"

Uhhhh…shit. Was I wrong that she'd been flirting back with Frankie at the game? Had Frank not mentioned her sexuality at all the entire night? That definitely doesn't sound like her. But I can't tell what part of what I just said is throwing Samara, either. "She, um, thinks you're cute. You know, like…people think are people are cute."

"Oh. Uh, okay."

Wow, do I suck at this.

"Well then! I'm gonna go into my room and get started on Sophocles. I'll catch you later." I practically race into my room and close the door behind me, stopping just short of banging my head against the wall.

So much for taking charge of this day.

I sigh and settle back in my bed with the book, and only once I'm lying down do my aches from working extra hard that morning seem to settle consciously into my muscles and bones. My pillow and mattress feel like actual heaven, and it takes every effort to keep my eyes open and on my reading.

After a few pages, though, I'm definitely drifting, until the ping of an incoming text jolts me up. I grab my phone and am surprised and wary when I see Andi's name light up the screen. *Can I ask your help with something?*

This is a first, and even as I write back, *Sure*, I feel pretty certain I'm going to regret it.

K, lemme just get somewhere quieter so I can call. A minute later, my phone rings.

"Hey, what's up?"

"Hey! I'm with Law, and he was just talking to his brother, who's coming up for the weekend. Will's all excited about going out on Friday night, but I don't really party, and Law doesn't know the area yet… Help us out with a good spot?"

I cannot believe I'm somebody's party girl consultant. Given who my best friends are, both on lax and off, the idea that I'm the most connected person someone knows cracks me up. The truth is, most often when I go out, I'm just tagging along with my teammates or Lizzie and Frank to a frat party, but it doesn't exactly surprise me that Will doesn't want to hang out with a bunch of aggressively heterosexual jocks.

Suddenly, I remember that there's a gay bar not too far from here, one Frankie loves to go to with her friends from Rainbow House, the LGBTQ group on campus. Lizzie and I went with her once, and it was fun and campy and a total trip—I know without a doubt Will would love it. But how exactly can I recommend it without revealing that I know Will?

How did complicated secrets involving gay men end up becoming my life?

And just like that, inspiration hits for how I can accomplish everything at once.

"Well, you guys are welcome to join me and Jake and a couple of friends of ours at XO on Friday night, if you like. It should be fun."

"XO? I've never heard of that. Is it a bar?"

"It's a gay club, but it's really the only club around here with good music, if you guys are looking to dance. My friend Frankie loves it, and she's brought me a couple of times."

"Huh, that's so funny. Will's actually gay, so he might like that. But isn't it a little weird for the rest of us to go?"

Only if you think the rest of us are straight. "Nah, they're totally welcoming of whoever, as long as you buy their booze." I have no idea if this is true, but in addition to helping Andi out, it's a great way to get Jake and Troy on a date somewhere they can be comfortable and not run into anyone from their teams or frat. And if Frankie and I pretend we're going as their dates…

"Okay, well…I don't know. I guess we could do that." She doesn't sound terribly comfortable with the idea.

"There's also Delta," I offer feebly, knowing Will would hate it, "but it's a little…stiffer." *That's what she said*, Lizzie's voice sounds in my head. "More grad students, less…fun."

"Oh. That's probably not Will's thing. Okay, well, I guess I'll just offer both and see what they say. Thanks, Cait. I'll let you know."

As we hang up, I'm feeling pretty proud of my brilliant plan. There's only one flaw in it, besides the fact that no one's agreed to it yet: Will, Mase, Andi, and I are all gonna be together.

With a sigh, I put aside Sophocles and open up my text messages.

I've got work to do.

• • •

It takes some major convincing over my study session with Jake that he can bring Troy to XO in front of his own coach, but by the time the library kicks us out at closing, we have both a plan and our first finished presentation. Frankie's already on board, I'm sure Will was into it as soon as Andi suggested it, and Mase is happy whenever his brother is happy. Everybody wins.

Except, I realize far too late as I step out of Troy's car in front of the club, for me.

"Wow, this place is *super* gay," Will says with a grin as we walk inside—three gay guys, one pansexual girl, one hetero couple, and one straight ex who doesn't have a clue what the fuck she's doing here. At least I look good, in leather pants Frankie convinced me to buy last year and a sky-blue top cut so low I can only get away with it because I have no boobs to speak of. "Law, why didn't you tell me there was such a perfect spot nearby? I would've visited sooner."

"Shockingly, I had no idea," Mase deadpans, looking distinctly uncomfortable at all the neon lights flashing in his face. He shoves his hands into his pockets, like he's trying not to shield his eyes, and I have to bite my lip to keep from laughing. If possible, Andi looks even more uncomfortable, her eyes darting around as she averts them from bare chests and kissing couples.

Will winks at me, and I'm torn between laughing and punching him, and hating him because I can't do either one. He'd emailed me the night before to tell me Mase had filled him in, and that while he'd keep our dirty little secret, he thought it was ridiculous. I couldn't exactly argue with that, but he was getting entirely too much joy out of our predicament.

"I think we could all use a drink to start off with," Frankie suggests, looping one arm through Jake's and the other through Troy's, leading us in the direction of the glowing fountain overlooking the bar in the center of the room. "What are you guys having? Orgasm? Sex on the Beach?"

"I'm sure they have more clever names here," says Will. "I guarantee you there's a drink called a Jack & Cock."

Frankie slams a hand on the bar. "Well then! I think that's what we'll all be drinking tonight. Bartender!" A tall white guy with a clean-shaven head and a scraggly beard that looks like it sheds sidles on over. He gives our group a once-over and seems to settle his affections on Will, who takes the lead.

"A round of Jack & Cocks," he says with a grin.

The bartender nods his approval, and I wonder what the hell I'm about to put in my mouth, trying to ignore that I'm the only one in this group with no potential for action tonight. It turns out to be a mixture of Jack Daniels and Cream of Coconut, which is exactly as gross as it sounds in every way.

Immediately after I down it, I order a lemon drop to clear out the taste, and Frankie does the same.

"Do you want one too?" I ask Andi. She barely even sipped the last drink, for which I can't really blame her. "I promise, they're way better than that mess."

"I think I'm done for the night," she says with a tight smile.

I can't tell if she means with drinking or the club, but she doesn't offer any more than that, and Mase doesn't ask. He gets himself a beer, which earns a snort from the bartender, and Frankie, Jake, and Troy get themselves Rainbow Shots, whatever those are.

"So, you guys ready to dance?" I ask Jake and Troy as soon as they've downed their drinks.

"Yes!" says Frankie, tossing back the rest of her drink and gesturing for me to do the same to mine before she grabs my hand and yanks me onto the dance floor. I let her, pulling Jake and Troy along with us, and watching Mase and Andi follow while Will hangs back to flirt with the bartender. I'm not a huge fan of dancing, or the attention that usually comes with Frankie making me get down and dirty with her at a club, but here, no one's even looking at me; we're just another pair of girls in a club full of them, dancing with a couple of guys no one realizes are actually here as a couple.

Of course, it takes all of two seconds before Frankie pulls in another girl—gorgeous, with medium-brown skin, springy curls, and moves that make me look like a robot. With her attention totally gone, I allow myself to glance over at Mase, who's such an annoyingly good dancer that I realize I'm not the only one looking. They may be the only genuinely hetero couple dancing on the floor—and she's every bit as talented as he is, I note with not a little bit of envy—but it's not stopping people from staring with approval as they shimmy, dip, and curl their bodies in ways that should be scientifically impossible.

I liked it better when they hated this place.

Frankie and the other girl are about four centimeters from making out right now, and Mase and Andi are too preoccupied to notice Jake and Troy, so I imagine no one will mind when I excuse myself from the dance floor and reclaim a seat at the bar. The original bartender's gone, replaced by a girl with purple hair and a lip ring that glints under the neon, and Will seems to have disappeared, too.

At least I know how to pick a good spot.

You might've been right about this being a bad idea, I text to Lizzie after ordering a beer.

By the time Lizzie responds, my bottle is half empty. *Told you so. Why would you ever go somewhere with no promise of sex at the end of the night? Especially when you so desperately need to get laid?*

"Bitch," I mutter at the screen, even though she's right. I hate Mase for making me this person. I was *fine* with occasional flirting and the even more occasional makeout at a party (and, okay, once getting a little handsy in celebration of a particularly good win) that'd marked my romantic life the past couple of years. Then he comes in, and memories of how much I used to enjoy getting *way* more than handsy come flooding back, and now I'm as horny as…as…well, as Lizzie or Frankie on your average weekday, probably.

The thing about guys with me is they always assume I like to take charge because I'm aggressive in the gym, or on the field. They think I'm aggressive everywhere, and they love that. But when you have to be that fierce all the time—during practice, during games—sometimes it's nice to let your muscles relax, to stop being so conditioned and composed and just…react.

It's amazing how difficult it is to find a guy who gets that I love being a beast ninety-seven percent of the time, but every now and again, I just wanna feel small. Delicate. Feminine. It sounds stupid, I know, which is why it's impossible to say out loud, and yet also apparently impossible to ask anyone of the male gender to intuit.

Except Mase.

Mase, who'd seemingly internalized all of this after a week of screwing around in tents or shacks or in double sleeping bags under the stars. Mase, who totally dwarfs me. Mase, who knows how to use his teeth as well as any other body part. Mase, who—

"Hey."

Mase, who is right behind me.

I quickly shove my phone in the back pocket of my pants and look up to see him taking a seat on the next stool over. "Hey," I greet him back as he raises a hand to flag down the bartender. "Worked up a thirst dancing, huh?"

He gives me a funny look, then orders himself a Yuengling. He scowls when they don't have it—boy takes Philly pride seriously—and gets a Sam Adams instead.

"One Sam Adams," says the bartender, "unless the lady wants another one?"

"I'm good with this one, thanks."

She shrugs and goes to get Mase's. For some reason, it suddenly feels like a Thing that we got the same beer. It *isn't* a Thing, of course—it wasn't even his first choice—and yet, this is how my brain works now, all the time, every time.

"No dancing for you?" he asks.

"No one to dance with." I take a long drink from my glass.

"You can always ask someone."

I don't dignify that with a response, wishing instead that I'd gotten a second beer after all.

"But then, I guess you've always preferred to be asked."

My gaze flickers over to the hint of a smile playing on his mouth. Smug jerk.

"So, I don't know you anymore, but you think you know me?"

"I do know you," he says confidently, slipping a bill across the bar as the bartender brings him his beer.

"You don't change, Cait. You're at the college you always said you'd go to, playing the same sport you've always played, majoring in exactly what you knew you would. No hair dye, no piercings, no tattoos—"

"None that you can see, anyway."

He raises an eyebrow. "You're lying."

"Wouldn't you like to know?"

I see him give me a quick onceover, even as he huffs out a quick laugh to cover it. "There's no chance. I know you."

"You knew me."

"I *know* you." His dark eyes glitter in the flashing lights of the club, and the hint of possession in his voice does some unwelcome things to my insides. "You'd never get a piercing, because you're afraid it'd get tugged out during a game. *If* you have a tattoo, it's of the number twenty-one, which is your number and was also your dad's when he played basketball in high school and at UVM. But you don't have a tattoo, because there's no way you could commit to a body part for it; it takes you forever to make choices about anything that isn't food-related. I know that whatever you've got going on with Moss, you hate being here tonight and wish more than anything you were back in your room watching ESPN Classic."

I don't answer.

"Am I right?"

“What difference does it make?” Fuck the fact that I didn’t order a second beer; I grab Mase’s and chug it.

“None at all,” he says, amusement playing at his lips as he watches me.

I pull the bottle away and slam it back down in front of him, considerably emptier than when I’d picked it up. “If you say a word about me being unladylike—”

“I have never disliked your being unladylike.” The tone of his voice doesn’t change, but the volume of it lowers, reminding me that tonight is yet another night awash in secrets.

I’m not sure I’m up for any more of those.

But apparently, I have fewer than I thought, because Mase continues without missing a beat.

“I know you’re upset about your father’s wedding, and your friends think it’s about lacrosse, but more than anything it’s that you were his shining star and now someone else is coming in first. And that feels extra shitty because your dad is supposed to be someone you know as well as you know yourself.”

“Yeah, well, a lot of people have been disappointing me in that way lately,” I snap, refusing to let him have this.

“Cait—”

“You’re just…*here*,” I spit. “You’re here, and you didn’t even give me a heads-up you were coming. You show up in my fucking *room* and—”

I don't get to finish my words before he grabs my wrist and pulls me off the chair, toward the exit. My instinct is to childishly pull my arm back, but the fact is I *want* to have this conversation, and the noisy interior of a club is a stupid place to have it. We go around to the alley, but there are too many people standing there smoking, so we go out front. No one's around but the bouncer, who's not really a threat given he's shorter than I am in my heels and Mase could definitely kick his ass with an arm tied behind his back.

"I'd appreciate it if you *didn't* blow up in front of my girlfriend," Mase says when we're settled, keeping his voice low.

"And I'd appreciate some honesty, finally," I shoot back. "I want to know what you're doing here. I know you got a concussion, and that sucks, and I'm sorry. But there's no way they made you quit; you're clearly still eligible by NCAA guidelines. And even if you weren't, you didn't have to transfer."

"Says you and everyone else. Do you know that a couple of weeks before that concussion, I sprained my knee? It took weeks for me to get cleared after that hit, but the second I was, 'Mason, stop being such a pussy and get back on the court.' I knew I wasn't ready, but I sucked it up, because that's what a real man does, right? That's what you do when you're on a team. And if you're not completely stable, so you go down *hard* when some dick fouls you, and you bash your skull—who gives a shit? That's the game.

"But you know what? That's fucked up. It is *fucked up* that everyone who's supposed to have your back will ignore the possibility of permanent brain damage if it suits them. Fuck that. And it's not like I was making NBA money; I was making big fat NCAA zero. If I fucked myself up too bad to go pro? That's all I'd ever make. My mom needs more than zero from me. At least here I get paid, and I don't have to be around the guys who didn't have my back when I made my choice."

His mom. I knew it. If there's one woman who can actually affect Mase's choices, it's Sharon Mason. She wasn't a huge fan of mine—once she learned Will would never be bringing home a black girl, the idea of her other son with a white one got even less appealing—but she's a pretty objectively kickass parent. She raised both boys by herself—first while Mase's dad was away in the military, and then after he was killed in action. I'm not surprised she factored into his plans.

So that answers one question, but not the one I've been dying to ask; the one I know I shouldn't. Mase is with Andi. The fact that he and I have this history doesn't matter. But this is the first real, honest conversation we've had, and it might be our only one; I can't miss my chance to ask it. "You said before I'm at the college I always said I would be," I say quietly. "You remember Radleigh'd been at the top of my list for years. Did you remember that when you picked it to transfer to?"

He doesn't look back at me, doesn't move at all. If my eyes didn't stay trained on his face, I probably would've missed his eventual slow nod.

But I don't miss it. And he knows I don't.

"What the hell was your plan when you saw me?" I rasp, unexpected tears springing to my eyes. "You come to my school—following your girlfriend, no less—and knowing I'm here, and you were just…what? Never gonna say a word? Hope we'd go the entire time without bumping into each other? A warning might've been nice."

I expect him to fight back, but he doesn't. "I know." His voice is low and regretful and actually makes me feel bad for losing my temper. "I know I should've told you. But I didn't want you to think I came for you. I didn't want you to think you were the reason I came to Radleigh."

Ouch.

"But…I don't know that you weren't." He's not meeting my eyes as he says this, and my insides twist and turn unbearably at his words. "I mean, not that you were the reason, obviously, but…when I met Andi at that party and she said she went to Radleigh, something just clicked. I thought about how much we'd talked about your plans for this place, how much happiness I associated with it. I couldn't not look into it for a new start, ya know? Things were such shit, and I just…I needed that feeling."

Does Andi give you that feeling? I wonder, but I ask the more appropriate and generic version instead. "And? Are you happy here?"

"I should be. I got the job I was looking for. Andi's here. I didn't lose any credit transferring. I'm closer to home than I was in Indiana, which makes my mom happy."

"But you're miserable."

He doesn't answer. Instead, he looks up. "The thing about the stars, about everything that's bigger than us, is they never fucking change. The Big Dipper looks the same here as it did in Indiana as it did in Stone Creek as it did in Philly."

"Fools you into thinking everything's got that staying power," I say with a grim smile.

"But nothing does."

"Not nothing."

"Not for you, maybe."

"I'm not talking about sports, Mase," I snap, making his eyes flicker over to me for the first time since he got all confessional. "Friends have staying power, if you let them."

He inhales sharply, but doesn't say anything. Then his eyes drift back up to the sky, and so do mine.

Staring at the stars was a thing we used to do together all the time, him sharing his wealth of knowledge about constellations and how they got their names, and me listening to the fluid velvet of his voice and thinking how I could listen to it read the phone book. It seemed only natural when those long nights started including kissing, then more. During the day, we didn't talk about much other than sports, but it wasn't a secret. Everyone knew we were some sort of two-man team of our own. That we were always in each other's cheering sections. That you didn't fuck with one of us unless you were prepared to handle both.

I don't think either of us realizes our fingers are intertwining until he squeezes my hand in his, an instinctive gesture from the days of old. It's chilly outside but his skin is warm, a little less rough and callused than it used to be, but familiar nonetheless. For a moment, our gazes picking out the outlines of pictures in the sky, we are fourteen, fifteen, sixteen. We are smelling grass and summer sweetness, not cigarette smoke and fresh tar. We are bigger than us and so nothing changes.

But then the song inside switches and I think about how I want to dance with him and remember that I can't and why I can't and we are holding hands and this is not okay and I am not okay and we are not okay. We have changed and everything changes.

I let myself go limp in his grip and it jolts him. He looks down at our hands like he's never seen them before, doesn't know how they found each other in the night at all. He mutters something that's either "Shit" or "Sorry" and it doesn't really matter which so I don't ask him to repeat himself.

"I think—" I'm about to say that I should go when Frankie's long, streaked hair whips out the door and she sighs with relief.

"There you guys are! You need to get in here."

I don't even look to make sure Mase is following; I rush in after Frankie with my stomach sinking into my toes. There's a crowd of guys gathered around Jake, and Troy is nowhere to be found.

Mase and I inch closer until I can hear most of what they're saying. "I'm sure this is fucking hilarious to you, jock boy, but you can take your weak homophobic ass outta here. You wanna see girls fucking each other on the dance floor, go invite a couple of sad attention-seeking straight girls to one of your shitty frat parties."

One of the guys shoves Jake's shoulder, but Jake doesn't move. His jaw is set in stone as he seemingly contemplates his next move.

Before anyone can respond, another of the guys looks up, his eyes widening in fear. I realize he's spotted Mase. Jake may be built, but so are a lot of the guys here; he doesn't terrify them.

A six-foot-nine black man? Apparently scares the shit out of everybody.

"Dude, chill," the third guy in their group mutters at Mase, though he hasn't said a word.

"Touch my friend again and I don't think I *will* chill," Mase says calmly. "Thanks for the advice, though."

"What the fuck are all you guys even doing here?" the first guy spits out, though his bravado is wavering a little in Mase's presence. "Not enough queers to bully in your own clubs? Gotta come here to mess with the fa—"

"Don't you even fucking think about finishing that sentence." Mase's voice is still even but it's coated in a steel edge. "You don't put that word in my mouth. You don't say it in front of my fucking brother. No one's here to give you shit; everyone just wants to have a good time in peace. Stop running your damn mouth and let my friends be."

Despite the fact that he hasn't raised his voice once, the entire club has gone still. No one's dancing. The music level has lowered. All the fun and festivity seems to have been sucked out of the room.

The guy who shoved Jake juts his chin out like he's gonna respond, but he's not fooling anyone. No one in his right mind would go up against the quiet statue of fury that is Mase right now. No one ever has. I've seen him like this only a handful of times in my life, but I'll always remember the first. A couple of baseball players at camp had a little too much of their homemade moonshine and two of them tried getting me under the bleachers. I couldn't take on both, but one of the few sober guys on the team went to get Mase, and I was freed before he could even swing a punch.

I got to swing the punches instead.

Finally, the guys walk away, and the club resumes its normal activity, but none of us are really in the mood to dance. No one looks more pissed than Andi, though. "Can I talk to you?" I hear her say to him coldly, though she's obviously trying to keep her voice down. I can't imagine what she has to be pissed about, but judging by the way Mase sighs and hangs his head, he knows exactly what he's in for.

"I think we should probably go," I murmur to Frankie. "Or at least I should. You can stay and have fun or whatever. But I think the ship has sailed on my having a purpose here."

Frankie nods. "I'll come with you."

"Nothing doing with the chick from before?"

"Eh, I've seen her here before, and I'll see her here again." She glances at where Andi and Mase are quietly arguing in a corner, i.e. exactly where I'm trying *not* to look. "Let's get you home."

I silently bless Frankie for knowing exactly what I need right now, and I take Jake's hand and bring him outside while we call a cab. He's visibly shaking, and I hug him until he settles. "Where's Troy?" I ask quietly.

"Disappeared as soon as that guy got in my face," he mutters. "Recognized him from somewhere and panicked. Left me alone to deal with that fucker."

"That fucker" who accused Jake of being there to cause trouble. And because of my stupid idea to bring Mase and Andi, Jake didn't even feel like he could yell back that he belonged there. "This is all my fault. I'm so sorry."

The cab pulls up before he can respond, and we don't speak another word when we get in, or when I rest my head on Frankie's shoulder and take deep breaths through my nose to stem the feeling of my chest cracking from the inside. The entire ride back to campus is silent, and even bidding each other good night is practically a whisper.

Back in the room, I change into my comfiest pajamas and slip under the covers, sure that all my emotional exhaustion will catch up with me and put me to sleep in no time. Instead, I find myself waiting for the door to open again, for light to shine through the crack as Andi slips in, quiet and considerate as usual.

I fall asleep hours later, still waiting for her return.

chapter twelve

I wake up to my alarm at five in the morning with my entire head feeling like it's stuffed with cotton. My mouth is dry, my skull is throbbing, and I need a drink of water more than I need my next breath.

And then it hits me: I have a game today.

Not only do I have a game, but I have to haul ass to the bus right now; the game is a three-hour ride away.

I am so fucking stupid.

Dragging my ass quietly out of bed, I'm grateful to see when I check my bag Past Me was far more on top of her shit than Present Me and actually packed in advance. I'm about to start tiptoeing around to wash up when I realize I don't need to be quiet at all.

Andi never came home.

The realization that she stayed at Mase's—that they probably had sex within hours of him holding my hand outside XO—churns my stomach fiercely. I can't think about this today. I need to be on top of my game. It isn't fair to my team not to be, and anyway, I have no right to feel this way—it's my own fault I let myself sink back into these stupid feelings. I had him once, and I let him go. Maybe it wasn't my choice, but I didn't exactly put up a fight.

It was stupid, but it happened. And I need to move the fuck on and kick some ass today, the way a future captain would.

I force my brain on the game during my fifteen-minute warmup, recalling all the mental notes I've taken on Westfield's defensive strategies and their goalie's glaringly obvious blind spot. During my speedy shower, and pulling on my uniform afterward, my thoughts are on the plays we ran through this week. And when I dash out the door and to the gym where the bus is picking us up, I'm all about mentally pacing my run time and making sure I hydrate like I completely failed to do last night.

But once I'm seated on the bus with a smoothie in hand, it's just me and three hours of nothing. Usually I'm grateful for the silence of these early-morning bus rides during which everyone has their rituals, but right now all I want to do is shake Tessa awake or yank Tish's earbuds out so she can listen to me whine instead of Rihanna.

I'm only on a few hours of sleep myself, so eventually, I join Tessa in passing out with my face against the glass. By the time we arrive at Westfield, I'm a groggy mess with a sweating half-finished smoothie in my hands, meaning I'm also now under-nourished and under-hydrated. Fantastic.

"You all right there, Johannssen?" Coach Brady asks as I practically lurch off the bus. "You in game shape?"

"I'm good, Coach." I'm not sure whether this is a lie, but there's no other answer you can give if you expect to play on any given game day; we've all learned this quickly enough. I continue to work at my smoothie, keeping my sips as measured as possible so I don't make myself sick, and ignore the suspicious looks Tessa's shooting my way.

"You look like shit," she tells me when she gets close enough to without anyone else hearing.

"I feel like shit." Sip. Breathe. I've been doing this long enough to know exactly what I need in my system before a game, and I've still had too little, too late. Silently I curse Mase and Andi and Jake and my dad and every damn person who's gotten into my head this semester and disrupted the routines I had down to a science. I am so much better than this person I've become.

Tessa gives my shoulders a halfhearted squeeze. "You'll be fine. Just don't make yourself sick. Come on—let's go stretch."

I keep sipping as I let Tessa drag me out, and finally toss the cup as we start our warmups. It feels good to get the kinks out from sitting curled up on the bus for three hours, and once the team is in peppy, shouty mode, it finally pulls me out of my head. By the time I'm fully suited up with goggles on and mouth guard in, I've managed to channel most of my frustration and sadness into full-blown rage.

Mase followed *me.* Mase is at Radleigh because of *me*. He may not have known Andi was my roommate, but he knew I'd be around and he should've better prepared—should've prepared *me*.

Fuck that. *What he* really *should've done is returned my calls*, I think as I nearly mow down the Westfield cover point to nab a pass from Tessa and cut across the fan. *My texts. My emails. Anything.* I fire on goal with self-righteous heat pulsing through my veins, barely even noticing that I've scored until I hear my teammates whoop.

I should be elated, I know, but all I can feel are my muscles twitching to do it again and again.

The next time I get a pass, though, the Westfield cover point is on it, and she stick checks the shit out of me, landing the ball in the grass. I shove her out of the way to scoop it, but another defender gets there first, and in my mad dash to reclaim it I feel my elbow hit bone, and then there's the whistle.

Shit.

They hit me with a charging foul, which, whatever. Except that by halftime, I've got two more, and at least one has drawn blood.

"Johannssen, what's gotten into you?" Brady demands during a timeout. "You were half an inch from slashing their defensive wing."

I want to speak up in my defense, but I can't. Now that we've slowed down and my adrenaline is pumping to nowhere, I feel dizzy as hell. "I need water," I say instead.

"You need to sit out, is what you need," Coach snaps. "Coville! You're in for Johannssen."

"Coach—"

"Not another word, Cait. Go get a drink and sit on the bench."

I want to, more than anything, but my body won't cooperate. Instead, I run over to one of the huge garbage cans just in time to puke out my smoothie.

The sounds of spectators' repulsion carries over and on the breeze, but I don't give a shit; all I can do is lift my head enough to watch Christina Coville shove in her mouth guard and jog onto the field, her jersey and kilt spotless in contrast to my muddy, grass-stained uniform. Christina almost never sees playing time because I work my ass off to keep it that way, and I know she's not nearly practiced enough to take us to a win.

The team is gonna eviscerate me for this.

I wipe off my mouth, wishing I wore gloves, and accept the plastic cup of water someone behind me extends under my nose. Rinsing out my mouth feels good, but nothing will make up for the fact that I'm guaranteed benched for the rest of the game.

My dad's right—thinking we could make it to the championships is a fucking pipe dream. I can't even hold my shit together after one night of drinks and misery.

I sit my ass on the cold metal bench and watch Christina move a few seconds too slow for almost every pass, every easy retrieval. The Westfield defense blocks and stick checks her with ease, and my feet twitch to get back on the field and show her how a decent question mark dodge should be done.

The glares Tessa and Tish shoot my way every time Christina fucks up do not go over my head.

By the fourth quarter, even Brady's sick of watching her in my stead. He calls me back in, but not without as long a lecture as he can squeeze in as I go. He's in luck, because I'm finally hydrated and feeling humbled as shit by the time my cleats hit the field again, and I manage one more goal, bringing me to a hat trick and giving us the game.

Barely.

No one talks to me in the visitors' locker room—pretty sure the "fuck off" vibe I'm radiating doesn't help—or on the bus ride home, which I spend pretending to sleep. By the time we get back to the gym, I'm beyond exhausted, and the prospect of lying in bed with my laptop to do my dumb Communications assignment actually sounds welcoming. My stomach is still feeling queasy, even after grabbing a plain bagel at Westfield, and the sight of my suite door is such a relief, I actually manage to forget who's potentially behind it.

Until I swing it open and find myself looking right at Andi, sitting on the futon with Samara. Even in my totally messed-up state, it's obvious something's off. There's a bag of popcorn between them, and they both look glum as hell, staring at the TV without really watching. All I want to do is slip past them and collapse on my bed, but I'd have to be a huge asshole to ignore the vibe here. "What happened?" I ask, letting my bag slide to the floor and shrugging off my coat.

Samara glances at Andi, who sighs and digs her hand into the bag for another handful. "Andi, uh…"

"Andi's boyfriend dumped her," Andi says robotically, crunching on some kernels. "And so we are watching a chick flick, in time-honored tradition of girlhood, or something. You're welcome to join."

It takes a few seconds for everything to click into place.

Mase dumped Andi.

Mase is single.

Andi is my roommate, sitting in front of me with her heart cracked open, and I'm selfishly thinking of the fact that her boyfriend is now available.

Her boyfriend who is no longer interested in me, and even if he were, is now off limits anyway.

Or are the rules different if I had him first? It feels like they should be. I mean, technically, Andi dated *her* roommate's ex first…

Yeah, that's the same.

"Cait?"

I snap out of my selfish trance at the sound of Samara calling my name. "Sorry. I mean, I'm sorry about Ma—Law, Andi." God. "Are you okay?"

"Fine." She still hasn't made eye contact, and my stomach clenches as I wonder if I have anything to do with this. Which doesn't make any sense—nothing happened last night but a whole lot of fighting and a hand squeeze—but I still feel steeped in guilt. I'm dying to ask what happened, but it's so, so not my place, and anyway, I'm not really sure I want to know.

I wonder if Mase is feeling as calm as she sounds. I know I didn't, when he stopped returning my calls. But I tried to. And I sounded every bit as convincing as Andi does right now. But underneath it lay a world of hurt, and I can't help wondering if the same is true for her. No matter who her ex-boyfriend is, she's still my roommate, and she's probably in pain right now; I have to be a decent human being. "You guys seemed to be having a good time last night," I venture. They did, at least until that fight went down. "Are you sure it's nothing you can't fix?"

She laughs, and there's the audible pain I was waiting for. "We did, didn't we?" she says flatly.

"Then go after him," I argue, which is stupid for about eight billion reasons. But I feel so guilty, and trying to fix things between them is all I can do to even begin to alleviate it. "Why would you give up so easily?"

Andi's cheeks redden and Samara sucks in a sharp breath, and I know I've totally gone too far here. Andi's not Lizzie; just because she's my roommate doesn't mean I'm entitled to share my every thought on her relationships. But for some reason, I can't apologize like I know I should. I can't take it back. I need to know what happened, and why she's letting him go without a fight.

If I could take back giving up as easily as I had, I'd do it in a heartbeat.

"There are things about Lawrence you don't know," she says coldly, and all I can think is, *Try me. Fucking try me.* "Just because you're an athlete and he used to be one—"

"He's *still* an athlete," I snap, not caring how far I'm pushing, how many miles I'm overstepping.

"Cait," Samara says firmly, adopting the same warning tone I've used on Lizzie and Frankie a billion times. Because I am usually *that* girl, not this one. I don't fight battles that aren't mine and I don't demand information that isn't my business. I don't act like I have a right to know the inner workings of people who are basically strangers.

Who the fuck am I right now?

"I'm sorry, Andi," I mumble, feeling beyond shitty right now. "Bad day." I can't look either of them in the eye, so I don't; I just shuffle past them into my room and close the door behind me.

What the hell, Mase? I hop up on my bed and check my phone—nothing—then grab my laptop from where I keep it on my nightstand. I have a bunch of the usual emails—lax stuff, notes from professors and TAs, a couple of forwards from Matty, wedding crap from my dad and Abigail—but nothing from Mase. Nothing from Jake, either; I haven't heard a thing from him since last night.

Fuck, I have to get out of this room.

It's Saturday night, which means some frat somewhere on campus is definitely having a party; I just have to find out which one. I pull up Twitter on my phone and it takes two seconds to find the answer.

Unfortunately, the answer is the Sig Psi house.

Sig Psi isn't exactly on my list of favorites since Lizzie tangled with their president (both literally and figuratively), but tonight, I need a distraction more than I need to take a stand against a bunch of guys for being assholes. Unfortunately, there's no dragging Lizzie into that place, and Frankie's a little too much of a reminder of last night's partying right now. I take a deep breath and text a few of the lax girls instead.

If they're mad at me for losing my shit at the game earlier, it doesn't show. *I'm in!!* Latisha texts, and Tessa and Nora are quick to follow. *Meet in Shamblin lobby @ 9?* Nora asks.

Shamblin's the jock dorm all three of them live in. *Yup*, I write back, already glancing toward my closet, trying to figure out what to wear. But I already know I'm gonna have to ask Frankie for advice; no one can put together an instafuck outfit like my former suitemate.

One way or another, I'm going to clear my head tonight—of Mase, of Andi, of Jake—and when I wake up tomorrow, I'm going to be a new person.

Cait 2.0, here I come.

chapter thirteen

I'm two minutes early to meet the other girls in the Shamblin lobby, and they're already there. Not surprising—punctuality has been drilled into us by Brady and every other coach any of us has ever had in our illustrious lacrosse careers. Nora looks as sporty as she always does—her only alternative to the uniform is a plaid shirt and jeans, not that the rabid fangirl contingent who shows up to ogle her at every single one of our games seems to mind—but Latisha, Tessa, and I have all let down our hair (metaphorically, at least, considering Tish's pixie cut doesn't have far to go) and donned far more obvious fuck-me outfits.

"Looking good, ladies," Nora says with a whistle.

"Do I pass the 'would Nora fuck me' test?" I ask, spinning in a slow circle.

"If it weren't a Code Pink violation, definitely," she says, running a hand over the shaved side of her head.

Code Pink Violation: no intrateam banging. Learned the hard way at the 2011 finals, it is our single most important rule.

"Excellent. Let's go."

Talk shifts to this morning's game as we walk, and though the girls give me a little shit for it, everyone seems generally cool. We've got a game on Wednesday night, and we all know we're only as good as our next one. "Planning to be sober for it?" Tessa asks me as we hit the front lawn of the house, which is dotted with students talking, laughing, and making out.

"Scout's honor," I reply. "Those were my last drinks of the week. Brady will string me up, otherwise." We walk up to the front porch and buy our cups—white soda cups for me and Latisha, who never drinks, and red beer cups for Tessa and Nora. "I'm impressed he hasn't killed me already."

"Oh, please, you had a couple of nasty fouls," says Latisha, rubbing on some lip gloss before we enter the house. "You know Coach secretly loves watching you ride the shit out of the defense, and anyway, you're still his golden child."

There's a hint of bitterness in her voice, and I can't blame her. Last semester she was suspended for two games after failing a class, which only happened because she was trying to juggle a part-time job along with everything else. But my GPA is solid and my stats are among the best an attacker's had on the team in the last five years; my spot's not going down without a serious fight.

My chance at captainship is another story, but I'm not thinking about that tonight.

Inside the house, we quickly spot a couple of the lacrosse guys and head on over to talk to them. Tessa lets one get her a drink while Nora quickly gets swept up by one of her aforementioned fangirls, and Latisha and I laugh as we watch her try to extricate herself.

"Sporty Spice!" I look up to see Doug Leach heading my way, and I smile and accept a kiss on the cheek hello. Doug's one of the only guys I actually like in this house; he's one of Frankie's most frequent casual hookups, and a decent guy besides. "Haven't seen you here in a while. Are you, uh, with anyone?"

Okay, the poor guy might be a little more than *casually* into Frankie.

"Here with my lax girls tonight," I say apologetically. "I think you know Tessa; this is Latisha. Tish, Doug."

"A lot of sporty girls here tonight, then," he says with a smile that barely covers up his disappointment at Frankie's absence. No matter how often she tells him she has no interest in confining herself to a single person, he never stops hoping. It kind of sucks. "Anyone who'd like to dance?"

Latisha glances at me and I shrug and tell her to go

ahead; I'm obviously not gonna be hooking up with Doug tonight, and I want some time to nurse a Diet Coke and scout out the room. Andrew, one of the guys' midfielders and the guy who'd gone to get Tessa's drink, has returned, and I let the two of them flirt while I look around the crowd.

"Cait! Are you here with Moss? I haven't seen him."

I whirl around to see Daniel Gutierrez, one of the small forwards on the basketball team. "Hey, Dan," I say, accepting a peck on the check. "No, Jake's not here. I—" And then I realize my huge dilemma here—far too many people at this party think I'm Jake Moss's girlfriend. While I'm sure a whole bunch of them aren't decent enough to let it stop them from hooking up, I don't think it'll further endear Jake to me any if word gets around he's being cuckolded. Nor do I really need a rep as a cheater.

Dammit.

Alcohol is looking a whole lot more tempting right now, but I refuse to give in. The second I *need* alcohol to get through the evening, I know I've got a problem. I've got enough issues, so I just keep nursing my Diet Coke and ruefully think about just finding someone to distract me in other ways instead.

As if the very thought has somehow conjured him up, the door opens and in steps six feet and nine inches of My Issues.

Fuck me.

He's alone—either Will bailed after the breakup, or he's off hooking up with the bartender from last night—and I debate going over to just talk to him. It's not like I don't know I want to. But before I can even take a step, some guy calls "Law!" and I lose my chance. Not that he's tough to keep an eye on; now that we're not surrounded wholly by athletes, he stands out in the crowd that much more—literally head-and-shoulders above most of the other guys. His face is freshly shaven and his white T-shirt might be casual, but I know he knows how good he looks in it. If he's been crying over the breakup with Andi, not a drop of that shows in his current appearance.

Or maybe he's here to distract himself just as much as I am.

I don't know what I hate more—how badly I still want him, or how one-sided that is. I can't shake the feeling that there's still something between us, that I factor in to why he broke up with Andi. But if that were true, wouldn't he have told me when he did it? Wouldn't I have heard from him at all?

"Who is *that*?" Latisha asks, and I curse myself for not realizing she'd returned from dancing with Doug in time to tear my eyes off of Mase. "Basketball player? Brother looks seven feet tall, at least."

"Six-nine," I reply without thinking.

Latisha smirks. "Not that you're counting."

I can't do anything but blush at that. Tish isn't dumb. Unfortunately.

"I wouldn't have picked him for your type," she says.

"Because he's black?"

"Because you are *so* white. Like, Pumpkin Spice Latte white."

"Okay, I wasn't offended before, but I *am* at the suggestion I would drink that shit."

She laughs. "So, what's his deal? Because he's fine as hell and I'd remember if I'd seen him before."

What's his deal? That is an excellent question, Tish. "He's dating my roommate. Or at least he was until last night."

"Oh, well, that sounds like a fucking shitstorm. Who wants to be someone's sloppy seconds, anyway? Come on. Let's go find some single boys to chill with."

I let Tish lead me over to where a few guys I vaguely know are talking, but I can't stop turning her words over in my head. I have no interest in being sloppy seconds, but does that still apply when you came first?

"Johannssen! Heard you lost your shit this morning against Westfield!"

I roll my eyes as Scott Madden approaches, but accept the high-five he doles out. He's a harmless prick and a decent goalie on the guys' lax team, and one of the few who doesn't act like the girls' team is Less

Than just because we've got tits and aren't allowed to body-check the shit out of each other. "I may have lost my shit but at least we won the game."

"Heard there was a little puking incident too. Classy."

Okay, rehashing the crappy parts of the last twenty-four hours are *not* on my distraction agenda. "Fun seeing you, Scott." I start to walk away, but he dashes in front of me.

"Sorry, sorry, I'm just being a pain in the ass. I promise to stop talking if you dance with me."

I have no desire to dance, but when I turn to seek out Tish to use as my excuse, I see she's already in deep flirtation with James Nagawa.

Suddenly, I hate that I'm sober. "How about you stop talking and we get me a drink?" I suggest instead.

"Sure you wanna do that after this morning?" he asks, raising an eyebrow.

No. I'm not sure about a single fucking thing. "It's fine. I don't have another game until Wednesday."

He shrugs and steers me off to the kitchen, and I hate myself more with every step. Then we get inside and of course, there's the icing on the cake—Mase standing there, red plastic cup in hand, flirting with a gorgeous girl I don't recognize. Awesome. I freeze in place, trying to decide whether to go ahead and grab a drink like he isn't there or turn around and drag Scott back out to the floor, but don't have time to decide before he spots me.

I wait for him to say my name in that stupid deep, velvety voice of his, but it doesn't come. He just nods and then his gaze drifts over my outfit of skintight jeans and a tank top that reveals an inch of the abs I work my ass off for. Then he turns back to the other girl without a word, and I have never wished I could disappear so badly in my life.

"Forget the drink," I say to Scott, knowing that now a beer would *definitely* be a crutch, and exactly the kind I need to avoid. "Let's go dance."

"Yeah?"

"Yeah." I hate dancing, but I'm at a party and I don't want to drink, talk, or smoke, so I'm pretty low on options. At least the Omega house has a foosball table and a dartboard; Sig Psi's idea of recreation starts and ends with a beer luge. "Come on."

We go out to where a bunch of couples are grinding up on each other and push our way in. If I were more of a dancer, this would be where I'd let my brain drift off while the music carries me, but that isn't how my body operates; it runs on two settings—calculated, and reactive instinct—and dancing with Scott Madden doesn't trigger either of those things.

"Mind if I cut in?"

Dark. Velvety.

Speaking of triggers.

I'm pretty sure Scott wants to say no, but

something (everything?) about Mase has a way of getting guys to give him whatever he wants. Scott steps back without a word, and Mase wraps a hand around my waist from behind like we'd been partners all night and he'd just returned from getting a drink.

I don't say anything, and neither does he.

Whereas Scott's body feels like a stranger's, Mase has no problem triggering my reactive instinct. I know exactly how our bodies line up, know how to move with his. His long fingers splay on my waist, including the bare inch of skin, and my arm rises up to curl around his neck without a second thought. He may not be on the team anymore but every inch of his body from the biceps grazing mine to the chest pressing against my back is rock-solid muscle.

Fuck, he feels so good, and even though this is so wrong, I couldn't pry myself out of his grip if I wanted to. Instead, I melt back against him, rolling my hips to the music, shamelessly grinding against the fly of his jeans. He's every bit as shameless about tightening his grip, his fingers digging into my skin as he grinds back, and *fuck* he is getting so hard I can feel the entire outline of his sizable cock against my ass.

My clothing feels too tight on my body, tight and confining when all I want to do is burst out of it. I'm so horny I feel it *everywhere*—the nipples tightening in my tank top, the heat building just inches below where Mase's fingers currently lie—and if I don't get some relief soon, I'm gonna explode.

As if he can feel my desperation through my clothes, he inches his hand down until he's pressing my fly squarely over my clit with each roll. It feels so fucking good, I have to gnaw my lip to stop myself from crying out into the crowd. In my mind I'm begging for more, for the other hand to slide up my shirt and squeeze mercilessly, for his teeth to find my shoulder, for weeks, months, eons of frustrations to pour out of me.

Instead I hear, "Careful, you two!" The sound of a familiar smug voice snaps me out of my near-orgasm, and it's only Mase's firm grip that stops me from leaping away. Trevor fucking Matlin, vomit pile to the stars, president of this fraternal cesspool, and the guy who let Lizzie get fucked last semester in more ways than one. She said he apologized and she no longer wants to feed his nuts to a woodchipper, but I'm not quite as forgiving. "We take no responsibility for anyone getting knocked up on our dance floor."

From what I've heard, Trevor doesn't take responsibility for knocking girls up anywhere, but that's for him and his poisonous ex to deal with.

I expect Mase to tell him to fuck off, but instead, he just clasps my forearm and says, "Come on." Despite having no clue where he's taking me, I let him pull me through the house, up the stairs, and suddenly, I'm in a room I quickly realize my best friend must know all too well.

“What are we doing in Trevor Matlin’s room, Mase?”

“What we clearly need to do,” he replies.

I wait for him to say, “Talk.”

He says, “Fuck.”

“Mase—”

“We obviously need to get it out of our systems,” he says, sounding almost clinical. “I mean, if you don’t want to, that’s cool, but not really the impression I was getting downstairs.”

My cheeks burn as I think about how just a minute earlier, I was writhing against his hand, so close to coming I could practically feel the edge I’d been about to tip over.

Yes, I want to.

But this feels crazy, after barely talking since he got here. I don’t know what I’ve missed in the last two years. For all intents and purposes, I’m about to fuck a stranger.

His lips spread into a slow, smug smile. “And I brought you up here because there’s no sports shed around, and I assume you’re still a screamer.”

Just like that, all the weird feelings are gone, replaced with fiery, blazing want. I don’t give a shit about the last two years right now; all I see is the guy who snuck into the camp kitchen to make my favorite smoothie after we lost a big game to Camp Mitonka

Lake, poured two glasses, and watched me drink mine while he licked his off my body.

And this doesn't feel so random.

And I don't feel nervous at all.

"Strip," I order him.

He raises an eyebrow. "Excuse me?"

"You wanted to fuck," I remind him, locking Trevor's door. "That involves taking off clothing. And I'd like you to go first."

His lips twitch with a smile, but he doesn't argue. Instead, he pulls his shirt over the back of his head and tosses it to the floor. His ribbed white sleeveless undershirt glows against his skin, showing off his broad shoulders, rock-hard biceps, and the promise of an equally fuckhot body underneath. But I only have to speculate a few moments before he pulls that off too.

I hiss in a breath through my teeth, and immediately feel my cheeks warm up as a result. Mase's smug grin suggests he didn't miss my admiration of his toned, muscular body and lickably smooth skin. The boy has been working out, no question, and it is paying off like whoa.

"I think it's your turn now," he says, nodding at me.

"Nope," I say sweetly, because I already lost control for a second there and I won't do it again. "Still yours."

He raises an eyebrow and I'm sure he's gonna

come back with a snide comment, but instead, he toes off his sneakers and pulls off his socks. “Nothing?”

“Nothing.”

Long, strong fingers that can palm a basketball and lord only knows what else with ease move to his belt buckle and make quick work of it. He glances up and holds my gaze, watching me watch him as he unbuttons and then unzips his fly.

And then his jeans are on the floor, and he’s wearing nothing but a pair of black boxer briefs being strained to their limit.

Sweet Jesus.

“I think it’s your turn now.” His voice is deep, throaty, and I feel it tingling up and down my spine, out through my extremities. It *is* my turn, but I can’t make myself move.

He walks up to me, standing so close I can smell beer and mint gum faintly on his breath, and reaches for the hem of my shirt.

I don’t stop him.

Inch by inch, those long, thin fingers slide my top up my body with the patience of a surgeon, his jawbone set tight, his cheekbones in high relief, his long lashes dusting them when he blinks.

When he tosses it on the floor, he waits, as if I might stop him before he goes any further.

I have no intention of doing anything that crazy tonight.

Seemingly convinced I'm not putting the brakes on anything tonight, he moves his mouth to my neck, and I feel the touch of his tongue an instant before the nip of his teeth elicits a strangled moan from my throat.

He grins against my skin. "Fuck, I missed that sound."

Those large palms settle at my waist, slide up my rib cage. Thumbs stroke my breasts through the fabric of my bra with painful slowness. Anyone else might think he was being gentle, loving, caring with those soft touches. But I know he knows better than that.

He's torturing me. And he's enjoying every second of it.

"Are you going to take off those jeans yourself?" he asks, taking another little nip of my neck, followed by a cooling, soothing swipe of his tongue. "Or do you still need my assistance?"

I do like the way it feels to have his fingers working the buttons, but there's an edge of condescension in his voice, and it makes me not want to give him this. "I think I can handle it," I say with all the acid I can muster given the way he's firming his touches now, increasing pressure with both his hands and mouth.

I pull away and take care of my own boots, socks, and jeans, ignoring him all the while, just because I can.

But when I turn back around, he's staring at me, looking like a starving man as his dark eyes rake me up and down. I'm not even sure he realizes he's slowly slicking his lips. I only realize I'm doing the same when I bite down on mine.

He shakes his head, a little laugh emerging in that deep, throaty voice. "Christ, Jo. When the hell did you get that body?"

"Exactly what body do you think you were fucking before?" I shoot back.

"One that had a whole lot fewer curves," he says, stepping forward again. He takes a breast in his hand and stares at it as though it's a wondrous thing, even through the ice-blue cotton of my bra.

And then he leans down and takes it in his teeth, surprising me into crying out loud enough that they can probably hear me over the music blasting downstairs.

I immediately clap a hand over my mouth, but he straightens up and pulls it away. "We're not kids hiding in the woods anymore, Cait," he says, rubbing a thumb over my lower lip. "You can scream all you like."

I close my eyes and let my hands roam over his shoulders as he tastes every inch of my throat, my collarbone, and lower. His skin is so smooth, stretched over tight, rippling muscles. It's like groping a marble statue, except for the warmth of his body heat and the racing pulse beneath. He may not be on track to being a pro athlete anymore, but he sure as hell has the body of one.

"Make me."

Before I can even process what's happening, he lifts me by my waist and tosses me onto Trevor's bed like I'm some five-foot-nothing, hundred-pound cheerleader. I can't hold back a delighted little squeal as he does, and I know he doesn't miss it because he can no more stop the huge grin spreading across his face at the sound. Then he climbs over me and buries his face in my neck, turning my squeal into a moan with one hard suck on my skin that's definitely gonna leave a mark.

I've missed this roughness, the way his large hands grip and teeth sink in. He grunts his approval as his hands squeezing my breasts turn my nipples to diamonds, and takes his mouth off my chest just long enough to say, "This needs to come off, now," while one hand tugs at my bra strap.

"If you rip it, I'll kill you," I murmur. "Don't tell me you still haven't mastered one-handed removal."

He laughs lowly and the sound shudders straight through me. Fuck, I am horny. "Best you take it off."

I snort but roll away just long enough to do what he says and toss my bra on the floor. "Better?"

"Much." He takes my ribcage in hands that nearly span it and brushes his thumbs over my nipples until they're back in full force, murmuring in appreciation at his handiwork.

"Tits are still tiny," I say wryly when I've handled all the scrutiny of his stare that I can, especially given

Andi's impressive rack.

"Your tits are fucking perfect," he says without missing a beat, taking a nipple in his mouth and rocking his hips against mine so I can tell just how much he's enjoying them. If I thought I was turned-on before, that sends me over the limit. Much as I enjoy the foreplay, I'm about three seconds from exploding, and even that seems like too long to wait.

"Fuck me," I demand, pushing my hips back, letting him feel through two layers of cotton how wet and ready I am. It comes out less like an order and more like a plea but I don't even care. I'll happily cede some pride if it gets me off right the fuck now.

"Impatient, are we?"

"Get inside me right now or I will fucking kill you."

He laughs, loudly this time, and sits back on his haunches, then thankfully obliges by sliding my underwear down my legs. "Just as bossy as I remember."

"I make no apologies."

"I wouldn't want any." He tosses the panties to the floor, then glides his hands up my bent legs, parting them.

I reach out blindly for Trevor's nightstand drawer to grab a condom, but he's pulled me too far down the bed, and I can't reach. "Leave it," he says, his hands stroking up and down my legs, thumbs caressing the sensitive skin on the underside of my thighs.

For a moment, I actually let myself contemplate it—I *am* on the Pill—but I quickly shut it down. I may not have been with anyone else in the months since I was last tested, but he definitely has. "We need to use—"

"We will." He leans over and presses a kiss right below my bellybutton. Then another one a centimeter below that.

Oh. *Oh.* "But we don't—you don't…" He never did. He fully admitted he was totally freaked out by the idea of going down on a girl, just as we were about to try for the first time. His brother had convinced him he'd suffocate. (Probably should've been our first clue about Will.) "At least it means you don't have to try sucking me off," he'd joked, though I'd wanted to, so I did it anyway.

"I should have." He pulls me farther down the bed, sliding himself to his knees on the floor. His thumbs part me open and he takes a slow, hungry taste, then groans with approval. "I really fucking should have. God, you taste good."

Yes, he definitely should have. Holy shit. He might've had less scruff scraping the insides of my thighs back then, but that long, firm tongue—

"Fuuuuuck." Christ, I am loud. "Oh, God, Mase, holy shit." I didn't even know a tongue could work that far inside a person but if there's one thing Lawrence

Mason possesses, it's stellar control of the body's strongest muscles.

"Yeah," he mutters as he slides two of those basketball-palming fingers inside me. "I definitely should've done this sooner." He pulls out and pushes back in, repeating the motion while circling my clit with his tongue. "You don't even know how fucking hard hearing you makes me."

I want to know. I want to strip him all the way down and stroke his beautiful cock, feel how much I still turn him on these years later. But I can't say that, can't get out any words at all when he's fucking me with strong, purposeful hands, devouring me like he's starving and I'm his last meal. And then he adds a third finger, pushing in slowly, so tight it's a little painful, but fuck if I don't love that pain. I pant shamelessly as he works me, licking around his hand, sucking my clit between his teeth until I'm nearly in tears with the desperate need to come.

"Harder," I manage to grunt as I rock my hips against his hand, taking him as deeply as I can. "Mase, fuck me harder. Now."

Oh, how he complies, moving his wrist double-time until I'm muffling my screams as I come on his hand and tongue.

I'm still panting in the aftershock when he moves away, but instead of joining me on the bed, he storms over to the nightstand. He yanks open the drawer and withdraws a foil packet, then stalks back to the foot of the bed. I don't even have a second to get a word out before he flips me over onto my stomach.

We've never fucked like this; in the past, we were all about missionary, or me sitting in his lap. I'm used to seeing his eyes, touching his chest, feeling a sense of…reverence, I guess, even when we were going at it under the bleachers or whatever. But there's nothing like that here, just rough, raw hunger.

I barely hear the rip of the foil over the sound of my own panting, or the snap of the elastic of his boxer briefs as he yanks them off with a quickness. And then I feel his cock pressing hard and hot against my ass and I groan, already imagining how good it's gonna feel inside me. He pulls back to roll on the condom and then grips my hips to hold them steady before sliding inside me with a brutal slowness that has me biting ugly plaid blanket.

"Jesus fuck," he mutters as he pushes fully inside, then pulls out and slams home again. There's no gentleness to it, no grace, no sense that we've done this before, because frankly, we haven't, not like this, not just to get off and go our separate ways.

But fuck it. That's where we are now—*who* we are now. I push back on his cock with the same force he's giving me, and he grunts out in surprise, then clutches my hips tighter, tight enough to bruise. And maybe it's messed up that I like it, that I like the pain and even the anger, because it's *something*, it's feeling, it's proof that we're here, and fuck, fuck, *fuck* he's re-angled to hit the right spot and every snap of his hips makes me see stars until finally I explode into a million luminescent pieces.

Afterward, the room is full of our quiet panting, thunderous over the faint strains of music pouring in from downstairs. Slowly, the room comes into focus, and even more slowly, so does what we've just done.

"Shit."

I'm not even sure which of us mutters it. Especially since I'm sure we're both thinking it.

He doesn't say another word as he slips out of me, and I don't watch him remove and tie off the condom or slip on his boxers; I don't watch him at all. Instead, I pick up and throw on my clothes like I've just been rescued from the Himalayas in the dead of winter and given a pile of blankets.

I'm just clasping my bra with shaky hands when a knock pounds at the door, followed by "Who the fuck is in my room?"

Oh, perfect—Trevor has arrived.

"I know there were just people fucking in here! People heard you!" More banging. I officially want to die.

"Dude," another voice says through the door, "don't you have a key?"

"Why the fuck would I carry around a key to my

own room, you dumbass?"

I have to clap my hand over my mouth so I don't laugh out loud, and though I can't even look at him right now, I suspect Mase is restraining his laughter, too. I finally secure my bra then throw on my top, all the while eyeing the window.

"That's a bad idea." Mase's voice is low, bossy.

"And coming up here wasn't?" I shoot back, keeping my voice equally quiet. "Come on." I rush over to the window and swing it open, letting in a rush of cool night air. We're on the second floor, and there's no way I can see to get safely to the ground. Even just getting to the next window seems like a bigger stretch than we can pull off.

"We don't need to climb out a fucking window, Cait. I'm not afraid of some stupid frat bro fuckboy."

"Well you *should* be afraid of getting on the shit list of someone who probably has the power to get you fired. I assume your being here is contingent on keeping your job."

Mase tenses his jaw in lieu of a verbal response, which tells me everything I need to know. I make toward the window again, but he says, "*You* should probably be a little more afraid of sustaining an injury exiting a second-story window. I *know* you being here is contingent on keeping *your* job."

He makes an infuriatingly good point, which leaves me with only one thing to do. "You're being an asshole!" I yell.

"What the—"

I hold up my hand to shut him up as I dash to straighten out Trevor's sheets. I hate myself for where I have to take this now, but it's our only option. "You really hurt her. How dare—"

"I hear you in there!" Trevor calls through the door. "Don't make me—"

I swing his door open mid-yell. "What?" I demand, giving him my iciest glare.

His eyes bulge out of their sockets as he takes in me and Mase. Clearly not who he expected to contend with. "No fucking in my room," he snarls, but he sounds a little less sure of himself now.

Finally, Mase catches on to my plan. "Bro, no one's fucking anyone," he says in disgust. "Trust me, you're doing me a favor busting up this shit."

"People heard—"

"Me tearing him a new one for dickishly dumping my roommate?" I fill in, and Mase winces. It plays well, and I'm pretty sure he's not acting. "Yeah, well, he deserves it. She's a sweet girl, and she's been crying her eyes out all day."

"For the millionth time," says Mase, "this is none of your business. She doesn't need you to defend her, and—"

"Ooookay, everyone, take the bullshit out of my room." Trevor ushers us toward the door, and Mase and

I continue bickering until we've left Trevor behind. By the time we descend the staircase, we're stone silent.

And then I hear, "Cait?"

I jerk my head up, and see Jake giving me a quizzical look as he watches me and Mase descend the stairs. Of course, after not answering my texts all day, I'd run into him here and now. Mase and I may be able to hide what we've just done from everyone else, but Jake knows there's reason to be suspicious. And suspicious is exactly how he looks.

"Not now, Jake," I say with a sigh, because I have apologies to make to him, and questions to ask, but this isn't the time. All I want to do right now is go back to—

Fuck. Of course I can't go back to my dorm. Hell, Andi would probably smell Mase on me the second I walk through our door. Not to mention that the very idea just feels cruel. I can't see her right now. Fuck fuck fuck.

"Baby, don't be like that," he says, and now I look at him for real. However upset he might've been at me all day, right now he's asking for a favor, and it's in both our best interests that I grant it.

"You were late," I improvise, wondering when I became so good at public fauxmantic bullshit. "I had to walk here all by myself." I slap on a pout and walk over to Jake as if he's been the only guy in my life all night, as if Mase isn't towering behind me like an icy monolith. I assume he's drifting away too, both of us projecting that if you thought you saw something between us when we walked down the stairs together, it was all in your imagination. Two minutes from now, no one would think twice about seeing us together.

Thank you, Jake.

"I told you, I had shit to do." Jake opens his arms, and I allow him to wrap them around me and kiss my cheek. "But I'm here now. Come on. Dance with me."

I can't stay here and dance. I can't stay here at all. I don't wanna be around Mase or Trevor, and I don't want to stand here under the room in which I just got fucked within an inch of my sanity. "I'm tired," I say, realizing how true it is when I say the words. "Let's just go back to your room."

There are a couple of guys around us, and they all seem to hear that line and make those annoying congratulatory noises. But that's in our best interest too, and Jake gladly accepts the teasing while I make the necessary "Shut the fuck up" protests and then we sweep out of the party without a backward glance.

chapter fourteen

Neither of us says a word until we're safely inside his room—a single, same as all the other varsity basketball and football players in Shamblin. Then we both erupt at the same time.

"I'm sorry last night was such a shit show," I say, at the same time he says, "You fucked Mason, didn't you."

Clearly we're in different headspaces, but we both laugh. It feels good.

"I know last night wasn't your fault," he says. "You were doing me—us—a favor, and it got out of control. It was a stupid thing for me to attempt. There'll be a time for me to be in a normal relationship, someday, maybe, but this isn't it."

"That's so fucking bleak."

"Life is fucking bleak," he says shortly, hanging up his jacket and then holding a hand out for mine.

"I'm lucky to have whatever privilege I have. I've got a scholarship, I like my teammates, I've got a single and will for the next two years—if all I'm giving up for that is having a boyfriend for a couple of years, I'm way luckier than plenty of other guys."

I just nod. What can I say to that? We're lucky, as athletes. I know that. NCAA rules may bar us from getting paid, and our schedules may be absolute murder, but we get to play. We do what we love, and we get free rides to a good school to do so. I know what it's like now to feel like I'm constantly on the verge of having that taken away from me, and it's hell. So I can't exactly tell him giving it up for a guy would be no big deal.

Would I give it up for a guy? For Mase?

"You didn't answer my question." He drops onto his bed and grins up at me.

"I'm not dignifying it with a response," I say, slipping off my shoes.

"I'll take that as a yes."

"You can shove that yes up your ass," I grumble, and he laughs.

I settle into his desk chair, examining the few photos that fill the space. His family. The team. None of Troy, not that I'm surprised. He may have his own room, but Shamblin's basically one big open-door policy, unless you've got a sweatband hanging from the knob. "So what happened last night?"

"Exactly what you think," Jake says with a sigh. "Troy completely bailed to leave me with the crowd at XO, and has been ignoring every single one of my calls and texts since. I've spent the last twenty-four hours feeling like shit and eating so many chips it'd probably give Coach a heart attack. I haven't even left my room to go farther than the vending machine until I went out tonight. And that was just to find you."

"To find me?"

He holds up his phone. "A couple of guys on the team texted me that my girlfriend was running around by her lonesome."

"How nice of them to babysit me in your absence."

He laughs. "Hey, at least I know they're loyal, right?" Then his face grows serious and he pats the bed next to him, and I get up and walk over, sitting down next to him on his hunter-green sheets. "I need them to believe this," he says softly, "at least until I'm sure word about me and Troy being at XO last night won't get around. Just another week. And since I imagine you don't really want your roommate so much as suspecting you hooked up with her boyfriend—"

"Ex-boyfriend," I cut in.

"Is that so?"

"You're not the only one who had a breakup last night," I tell him, falling back on the bed. "I don't know details. I only know that it's over."

He lies back next to me. "That's good news, isn't

it?"

"It's no news. You don't fuck your roommate's ex-boyfriend of a day. What the hell is wrong with me?"

"What the hell is wrong with any of us?" he says, hooking a finger around mine. "Love and rules and all this shit is just so fucked up. Why can't *we* just actually like each other? Is it so much to ask for the easiest thing to be the truth?"

I turn to look at him, and see he's looking at me too. Without a word, we lean in and our lips brush, lightly at first, then not so lightly. A little clingy. Desperate. Not for each other, but for this—for something that makes sense—to work.

It doesn't.

He pulls away first, and laughs. "Shit. That was dumb. I'm sorry."

I shrug. "Worth a shot, right?"

"Honestly? You'd never be satisfied with my dick after his."

I burst out laughing and whack him on the chest. "Jesus, Jake."

"Hey, I've seen him in the locker room. I'm just being honest!"

"Be less honest," I say wryly, because now I can't stop picturing it, remembering its hot thickness pressed against my ass, pushing inside me, fucking me mercilessly. It's hard to imagine being satisfied by anyone else's cock after that, and considering that was my very last time with it, I really don't need or want that reminder.

He grins, and we both lie there for a minute, laughing quietly, before he says, "So I'm guessing you don't want to go back to your room tonight."

"Not so much. I'm gonna ask Frankie and Lizzie if I can stay with them." I slide my phone out of the butt pocket of my jeans, but Jake covers it with his hand before I can turn it on.

"You're welcome to stay here," he says. "You can borrow a pair of shorts and a T-shirt."

"And do a classy Walk of Shame tomorrow?"

"Hey, it's not shameful if you hold your head high."

I shake my head, but the idea of just crashing holds a whole lot of appeal right now. I don't feel like answering Lizzie and Frankie's inevitable questions, anyway. "Okay, fine, I'll stay. But don't you dare give me a Yankees T-shirt."

"Please, I would never do that to you." He reaches into his drawer and tosses me a navy-blue tee and a pair of gray shorts, then turns around to give me my privacy so I can change.

Only once I'm done do I see the tee is emblazoned with "New York Giants".

Asshole.

• • •

Jake's still passed out when I wake up in the morning and gingerly slide out of his bed. I creep over to the pile of my clothing on his desk chair, trying to figure out if it's only in my imagination that it reeks of sex and Mase's aftershave. Probably not, but it's between putting it back on and walking out of here in what are obviously Jake's clothes, so I suck it up and get dressed. Then I leave Jake a quick note and I'm gone.

It's still early on a Sunday morning, so the jeers and whistles are at a minimum, but they don't bother me; at least they think Jake is the guy I hooked up with last night. Considering Mase and I didn't exactly leave things on a hopeful, romantic note, and now I'm stuck having to return to the room I share with his ex-girlfriend, I almost wish everyone else was right.

The thought of seeing Andi makes me sick to my stomach, and I pull out my phone to see if I can delay the inevitable a little longer. But of course, because life is one hilarious conspiracy, my phone is showing four things:

One: an e-vite to a bridal-slash-baby shower for Abigail.

Two: a text from Frankie saying, *HI we're doing breakfast this morning.*

Three: a text from Lizzie, sent twenty minutes later, saying, *YOU ARE SO BUSTED, SHAMEWALKER.*

Four: a second text from Lizzie, explaining, *We're in the suite. Get your ass back here. And DON'T EVEN THINK YOU'RE NOT TELLING US WHERE YOU SPENT THE NIGHT.*

And then my phone dies. Fucking fantastic.

I have no choice now but to trudge back to my dorm, and the second I do, Lizzie and Frankie are on me like hyenas. "You *did* get laid!" Frankie declares.

"I slept at Jake's," I say, loading my words with as much emphasis as possible. The last thing I need is for Andi—who's sitting on the couch with Samara, staring glumly at the TV, exactly as I left her—to take note of any clues that I had sex last night, and with whom. "*Just* slept."

I expect the conversation to stop there, but Frankie shakes her head. "Then you hooked up with someone else. I can tell. I can *always* tell."

"You couldn't tell when I fucked Connor," Lizzie points out.

"That's different—you were in a perpetual state of having just been fucked for a year before that. Cait, on the other hand, wears her getting laid like the weed I smell on my mom once every six months."

"Did you just compare Cait's sexual activity to something having to do with your mother?" Andi asks, in her first sign she isn't catatonic since I walked in.

"Please stop talking about my sexual activity, period, both of you." I try to load my glare with extra meaning—usually at least Lizzie is more perceptive than this—but…nothing.

"Why must we constantly play these guessing games?" Frankie asks dramatically. "It's always pulling teeth with you two. You don't see me having any shame in telling you I made out with Doug last week at the pool hall."

"No, can't say we ever do see you having any shame," Lizzie concedes, stealing the words right out of my mouth. "But, good for you. Well, good for Doug. I like Doug."

I swear I see Samara stiffen on the couch.

We need a change of subject, stat. "We should get breakfast," I declare. "I'm starving." Actually, I've completely lost my appetite, but whatever—I'll choke down an entire buffet if it means ending this conversation right now. I don't wait for them to answer before I sail into my room, grab an armful of new clothing, and call, "Five minutes!" on my way into the shower.

By the time I emerge, Lizzie and Frankie have somehow talked Andi and Samara into getting their asses off the couch and joining us, proving once and for all that if we ever did have some sort of BFF ESP, it was severed when they moved out on me. But, I realize as we walk to the dining hall to chow down on waffles, Lizzie and Frankie are the only ones speaking in more than two-word sentences. Those of us who still reside in Barrow room 302 aren't quite as joyful. Certainly none of us are sneaking in dirty texts every few minutes, as I suspect Lizzie is under the table, or having to silence our phones because they keep ringing with different tones, the way Frankie's does.

No, the residents of 302 Barrow have become an unwitting Lonely Hearts Club, and it appears I'm the only one who knows why.

I stuff a huge bite of egg-white omelet into my mouth, just to faster clear my plate and get back to the dorm, where I plan on taking a nice, long, dreamless nap.

Ignorance is bliss.

• • •

The nap doesn't materialize; what *does* is a voicemail from my dad, imploring me to RSVP to Abigail's bridal shower. Which is quickly followed by a text from Cammie saying, *Plz tell me you are not going to that shit.* Part of me is envious of Cammie, knowing she doesn't give a damn if she's destroying her relationship with our father; it's not like she really has one anyway. But I have too many years of good memories with him for it to be this easy, and as angry as I am, I can't stop entertaining the possibility of going, knowing how happy it'll make him.

I don't know yet, I admit to Cammie, bracing myself for an angry response. But all she writes back is, *Whatever.*

I sigh heavily and toss my phone next to me on my bed, picking up my laptop instead. Andi's on her bed, too, but she's wearing headphones and listening to something loudly enough for the bass of the beat to travel all the way over to my side of the room. Part of me is so self-loathing that I actually wish she'd speak up, demand I confess—*something.* I feel so shitty sitting here, watching her stare at the wall while we both think about the same guy.

No. I am not thinking about Mase. That is stupid and pointless and will not lead to anything good. What I *should* be thinking about are my midterms, my game on Wednesday, my—

Andi's cell rings, making me jump up off the bed. When she doesn't pick up instantly, I glance over and see her staring at the screen, as if deciding whether or not to answer. I know immediately that it's Mase calling, and that I should give her privacy, but I can't seem to make myself move.

I'm sure she's about to let it go to voice mail when she takes a deep breath and picks it up, her "Hey" tinged with relief. My stomach tightens as she hops off her bed and leaves me alone in the room to go talk elsewhere. I try to refocus on my computer screen, but all the words on the assignment in front of me just look like a blur.

A gentle knock at the door is a welcome intrusion, and I look up to see Samara standing in the doorway, cradling a steaming mug. "Just wanted to check and see if you're okay," she says, quiet but knowing.

I don't know how to answer that. So I don't.

She closes the door gently behind her. "Look, I don't want to pry, but it's pretty obvious there's something going on between you and Law. Are you…do you have something to do with why they broke up?"

"No," I say immediately. "I don't really know what's going on between them." There's no point pretending she's wrong about the rest, though; she's been picking it up since day one. But that doesn't mean I have to burden her with carrying around the shitty secret I am. "And there's nothing between us…anymore. We were a thing, years ago. In camp. Before either of us knew Andi. And we just…thought it would be better not to mention that."

"Ah." She blows on her tea and takes a sip. "Is this, like, a 'we held hands around a campfire once' kind of thing, or…no, I'm thinking not."

I shake my head, impressed she got a little smile out of me. "Not quite."

"That…makes a lot more sense."

"What do you mean?"

"Just that it was obvious you guys are into each other, but I couldn't put together how and when that would've happened. I thought maybe in the gym, since you're both athletes, but—"

I hold up a hand. "You can stop right there. We're not 'into each other,'" I correct her.

She cups the mug in both hands and sits gently on my desk chair. "Yes, you are. I saw the way you were watching him at the game. And your reaction to their breakup wasn't exactly garden variety 'concerned suitemate.' I don't really know *what* it was, to be honest, but—"

"Okay, I think that's enough of that," I mutter. "Look, okay, yes, I've been a little thrown by him showing up again, but that's it. And he's made pretty clear he wants nothing to do with me."

Samara huffs out a laugh. "Yeah, okay. Maybe to your face, but the boy is not as good at hiding his feelings when you're not around."

"What are you talking about?"

She glances at the door. "He looks at your stuff when he's in here," she says, keeping her voice low. "Not, like, *through* it, but just…the pictures on your desk. The posters on your wall. One time I saw him pick up your Gatorade in the fridge and smile at it like it was a private joke."

At that, I smile too. "Well, we *did* have a thing with blue Gator—you know what? Never mind." I'm getting deep into oversharing territory, and what's worse is that I really, really want to. Mase looks at pictures of me? He remembers the thing with the Gatorade? If he really hated—or at least resented—me, why would he do that? Or were we actually okay until last night? The urge to spill everything to Samara is so strong, but then we both straighten up at the sound of footsteps on the other side of the door.

"Cait? You changing?"

I sigh. "Nope, just in here with Samara. Come on in."

She does, but it's impossible to tell from her expression what kind of call that was. I can't really ask—not after I flew off the handle a bit when learning they broke up—but thankfully, Samara does. "Everything okay?"

"Fine," Andi says lightly. "That was Law. He wants to talk over dinner, so, hopefully that's a good sign." Her smile barely shows any teeth, and it makes me think she doesn't have all that much confidence in what she's saying, but maybe I'm just seeing what I wanna see.

"That's great." Samara takes another sip of tea, probably as an excuse to avoid eye contact with me, and stands. "I'll leave you to get dressed for that. See you later, Cait."

I manage a weak goodbye as she walks out.

• • •

As I watch Andi leave for dinner twenty minutes later, I decide then and there to make my life a No-Mase Space. There are too many other important things happening in my life, and there's no room for pointless drama. Whatever feelings Samara's created in her head, they're obviously not real; Mase's attitude toward me has more than proven that. And I *don't* have feelings for him. Missing our friendship and finding him attractive isn't the same thing as wishing we were more than that. But clearly our friendship didn't really mean shit, which means there's nothing to miss.

So there.

I push him out of my brain, do the same with my father's wedding, and devote the next two days to nothing but class, studying, and practice. By the time Wednesday's game hits, I'm feeling peak.

Which of course is when Tish jogs over on the frost-crunchy field and says, "So, guess things worked out with Tall, Dark, and Handsome."

Adrenaline and warmups had been keeping me primed, even with the chill, but her words turn my hands cold around my crosse. "What?"

"Up there, in the stands. You didn't see him? He's kinda hard to miss."

Truth be told, I hadn't looked at the stands at all; only the most die-hard fans come to a mid-week game in February. But she's right—there he is, sitting in the back with a couple of guys I don't know, looking down at his phone.

He's here. Mase is sitting in the stands at one of my games. A rush of warmth fills me at the familiarity, the memory of the first time he did that at Stone Creek. It was close to the end of the summer, and I'd been pretty sure we were eye-flirting, but I had so little experience with guys, I couldn't be sure. And then one day he was there, sitting in the bleachers, a sly grin on his face as he gave me a little nod while looking me over in my lax uniform. I still don't know how the hell I got through that game, since I couldn't think about a damn thing other than that he was watching, but I got a pretty sweet goal toward the end of the first half. When he jumped up and roared a cheer, I knew I wanted to make him do that over and over again.

I did. Four more times in the second half. It was my highest-scoring game ever at Stone Creek, and I'm pretty sure they still talk about it.

Afterward, he'd walked over, shaking his head. "There was a rumor you were good, but damn, Johannssen. That was badass."

"Thanks." I hadn't even been able to keep the smile off my face. People kept walking by and smacking me on the back or tapping me on the shoulder with a crosse; honestly, I could not have looked more awesome in that moment, red-faced sweatiness and all. "So what brings you to our humble bleachers?"

He'd been so adorable right then, scratching the back of his neck as he looked back to the friends he'd been sitting with, who I realized only at that moment were watching us. They'd catcalled and laughed, and he'd laughed too. "My friends called me a sadass cliché for crushing on a white girl. I said if we came to your game and you scored, they had to shut the fuck up for the week."

Luckily, my cheeks were already burning from exertion, masking my hot blush at the "crushing" part. That answered that, even if I was a cliché white girl. "How long do they have to shut up for scoring five times?"

He'd laughed again, that low rumble, but then my coach had called my name, and Mase's friends called him back. We'd said goodbye and agreed to find each other later, which we had.

Somehow, tonight, I don't think there's a bonfire, marshmallows, and pickup game in our future.

What the fuck is he doing here, anyway? I've barely seen Andi since the night they went to dinner, but I assume that once he got his rocks off with me at the Sig Psi party, he went running back to her. So why the hell is he showing up here?

For the first time, I realize that I am *angry*. And I don't want him here—at all. But if he's gonna insist on watching, he's gonna get a hell of a show.

Throughout it all, I keep my eyes on the field and my teammates, refusing to acknowledge for even a second that Mase is in the crowd. This isn't about him; it's about me, and my team, and the sport I've loved for as long as I can remember. If he's going to hold his resentment over my head that I can still play, then he's right—we'll never be able to be friends, and we're certainly done being more. This is who I am, and I fell for the guy who understood that.

When the game ends, with me having posted two assists and scored three goals—my third hat trick of the season—I accept nonstop cheers, hugs, high-fives, and back slaps with what I know is the world's biggest goofy grin on my face. Only when I am one hundred percent sure that whatever Mase is expressing right now can't hurt me do I look up at the stands.

And see that he's gone.

chapter fifteen

I decline to spend the night celebrating, and I end up being beyond glad for it in the morning: the campus is a total madhouse. Even people who don't give a shit about sports are congratulating me all over the place, thanks to the fact that a seriously badass picture of me wielding my crosse is splashed across the top of page one of the campus paper. Congrats are flooding in for destroying Eastern Mass, and while I obviously can't take all the credit for that and always respond about it being a team effort, part of me is dying to say, "I know, right?"

Because, dammit, I was awesome.

Clearly, rage is every bit as good fuel as support was once upon a time, and now that I'm riding high on it, the sting is definitely soothed. Let Mase and Andi fuck all over the damn campus if they want to. I don't care. I've never been about romance, and I'm not gonna start to be now. For the first time in years, we have a real shot at the championships, and I'm sure that once my dad sees that—and sees what a huge role I've played in getting us there—he'll talk to Abigail about changing the date. There's no way he'd miss this, or let me. The first thing I did when I saw the paper this morning was send him a link to the site with a note that said, "Let's talk about that whole championships thing ;)" and I've been checking my phone non-stop waiting for his response.

Still nothing. But I'm not worried. I'm sure negotiating takes time. Matt, Cammie, and my mom, all of whom have always been considerably less interested in my lacrosse career, have been awesome about showing me their pride this morning, and I know that when my dad does too, it's gonna be good.

Spending a morning getting showered with adulation works up an appetite, and by the time I meet Jake in the cafeteria for our last meeting for our mid-term project, I am utterly starving, and, apparently, beaming like a fool. "Holy shit," he says when I slide into a seat across from him. "I have *never* seen you this cheerful. Guess you're enjoying your day of celebrity, huh?"

"Damn straight," I say, cutting into a huge piece of grilled chicken. "Eyes on the prize, Moss. Eyes on the prize. Those championships are going to be ours, and that captainship is going to be mine. *And*," I add, spearing the chicken with my fork and waving it in his face, "we are getting no less than an A on this project. Hear me?"

"I hear you, General Johannssen, sir!"

"Good. And one more thing."

"Yes'm?"

I put down the fork. "I figured out what favor I'm going to collect from you in exchange for…well, you know."

"Is that right?" He crosses his arms.

"Yep." I drop my voice. "In exchange for being your beard, you're gonna be mine, of sorts. How would you like an all-expenses-paid trip to San Diego?"

His eyebrows shoot up. "What's the catch?"

"Only that you need a tux. And you'll have to wear it to accompany me to my father's wedding. Date still to be determined. You in?"

"You sure? That seems like kind of a big deal. Don't you wanna bring a guy you—"

"In or out?"

"For you? Anything." We bump fists and go back to work, and to lunch.

One more problem down. *Life, you are back in my control.*

• • •

When I finally do hear back from my father later that night, the whole thing just says, "Congratulations, honey. We'll talk." It's not the flailing excitement and ready agreement I'd hoped it would be, but it's a start. And it's enough to push me to make my own effort, to show I'm worth making this change for. I take a deep breath and call up my sister.

"Sup, celebrity sis?" she greets me, and I grin for a brief moment before I delve right in.

"I need to ask you a huge favor you're going to hate me for."

She sighs. "No, Cait. Just…no."

"Just the bridal shower," I say quickly. "Please, Cam. I really think I can get Dad and Abigail to move the wedding off, and I would never ask you to go to that. But you know it's important for me to go to this. They'll never do it if I don't at least make the effort to show up to the bridal shower, though, and I can *not* do that alone."

"So bring one of your friends," she grumbles.

"Lizzie's going home to spend spring break with her brothers and meet her boyfriend's sister, and Frankie doesn't exactly make the best first impression with strangers."

"Hey, I thought she was very sweet."

"Yeah, because she hit on you."

"*And* she has great taste!"

"Cammie, come on. Please. Aren't you even the slightest bit curious? She's freaking carrying our future brother or sister. That kid's going to be related to you whether you like its parents or not. That has to matter."

She's silent for a moment, and that's when I know I've got her. "Fine," she says, "*but*, I reserve the right to leave as soon she proves to be utterly horrible."

"Deal."

"And ditto if you utter one word to me there trying to convince me to come to the wedding."

"Also deal."

"And I want that black-and-white top."

"Cam, we've been over this. That shirt is not going to fit over your new boobs. If you wanted to blackmail me with my clothing, you should've maxed out at a C when you got them done."

"Whatever, no regrets. And bring it anyway—I'm not taking your word for it, especially if I'm traveling all the way from Boston. Do we have a deal or not?"

"We have a deal."

• • •

As expected, my dad is thrilled to hear that I'll be going to the shower, while my mom is considerably less excited to hear I won't be going to her at all. In fairness, I'd never committed to going back to Burlington for any of the week, but the knowledge I'll be with my dad and his child bride does not seem to please her. Not that I can blame her, but I gotta do what I gotta do.

With my eye on the date-changing and championship-winning prizes, I actually do manage to keep Mase out of my head. Every day, I wake up to practice; take notes in class like a fiend; lunch with Lizzie and Frankie, girls from the team, or Jake; study my ass off; and get to sleep by ten. And yes, I completely destroy again at the final game before break on Saturday.

When I toss my stuff into the trunk of Lizzie's car the Friday night classes end, it's with the confidence of a girl on top of the world—a girl for whom failure is not an option. I'm going to this shower and I'm going to leave with the promise of both a bumped wedding date and my father's attendance at the championships we *will* be at. It's only two months until quarterfinals, and we've been at the top of our conference *and* the offensive scoreboard all season. I'm nationally ranked second overall in goals per game, but with only a .02 differential between me and the leader, I know I'm gonna take that top spot in our first game after break.

"That everything, Tiger?" Lizzie asks as I hop into the backseat of her car, thanks to her graciously offering to drop me off at my dad's on her way down to Pomona. She's taken to calling me "Tiger," declaring that I seem to be in a state of permanent ferocity now. I roll my eyes at the nickname, but secretly, I kinda love it.

"That's it. I didn't really put an end date on my visit, but I can't imagine it'll be more than three days, tops." Though no one would be happier than me if I'm wrong. Part of my newfound optimism includes hoping that I'll like Abigail once I spend a little more time with her, that despite the fact that they're moving across the country, we'll somehow be a happy long-distance family. That we'll video chat and I'll spend some time there this summer, or something. All I need is for this to go well, and I'll have everything I want.

Almost everything, my traitorous heart mentally amends as I watch Connor haul bag after bag of Lizzie's stuff to the trunk. Watch him subtly check out her legs when she pauses to send a text before getting in the car. Watch him remind her that he's happy to take over when she gets tired on the five-hour drive down to her house. Watch him produce a handful of grape lollipops for the drive, and see her laugh at the joke I clearly don't get.

Not that I'm a little lonely or anything.

"So what's it feel like to actually make Radleigh care about sports right now?" he asks as soon as we're on the road.

I laugh. "I wouldn't give me that much credit."

"I would. You know I've had two guys in my program ask me for your number already?"

"Bullshit."

"It *is* bullshit," he admits. "Only one's in my program; the other's in med school but lives in my hall. Historians don't generally have the balls to beg for athletes' numbers."

"God, that's sad. But I haven't gotten any mysterious phone calls from date-seekers lately," I point out, patting the phone in my pocket.

"Because you're taken, remember?" Lizzie says wryly, and for a split second, I think she means Mase, before I remember that of course, to the entire Radleigh campus, I am the girlfriend of Jake Moss. "Don't worry, Connor headed them off at the pass."

"Oh, good," I grumble.

"Always watching out for you, Tiger. So, did you ask Jake to come with you to your dad's wedding?"

"I did. And he is." *Assuming* I'm *going to my dad's wedding*, I mentally add, though I'm well aware that's not something I should be saying to Lizzie.

Lizzie beams with approval, but I ignore it. Just because she's got into her head now that love is wonderful and fairytales exist and blah blah blah doesn't mean happy endings are an option for all of us at present. At least I have Jake to keep me company.

"Enough about me," I say, because I really need it to be. "Excited to see your sister, Connor? Where's she been lately?"

Connor fills me in on his travel-blogger sister's adventures, which turns into Lizzie talking about what they're all gonna do in New York City for a day during break. That's interrupted by Frankie calling to ask us for wardrobe advice for a party, which turns into her telling us a hilarious story about how she met this girl at a rest stop when she was stretching her legs after pushing it too hard on her Vespa. Before I know it, there we are, in front of my dad's little white house. There's no sign of Cammie's Prius, which means I'm on my own for now.

I wonder if I could beg Lizzie and Connor to go for a drive in scenic Middle-of-Nowhere for a bit.

But before I can say a word, the front door opens, and my dad comes out with flannel-covered arms open. His blond beard is frosted with white and he looks about five years older than the last time I saw him, but joyful all the same. "Caity," he says warmly, enveloping me in a hug. "I'm so, so happy you could make it." The words are muffled in my hair—at six-five, he's clearly the source of my height genes—but they make me really happy I chose to come, too. Now I just hope his and Cammie's reunion is equally nice.

Yeah, right.

I say goodbye to Lizzie and Connor and tell them to drive the remaining four hours safely, have a good week, and report back on all interesting things. Then I follow my dad inside his messy, newspaper-filled house. I love the familiarity of it, even though he's only lived there a few years—anywhere he lives smells like mustiness and newsprint. For all that he's adjusted to email and text messaging, he just cannot read full coverage of sports on a website.

Judging by the mess, Abigail hasn't moved in; it's hard to imagine another human living in this nest of paper piles, beer bottles, and cigar smoke. My dad is the consummate bachelor, which just makes me wonder for the millionth time how the hell he's going to be a new groom and papa all over again.

"I'm guessing Abigail doesn't spend a lot of time here," I say, sniffing as I round up the bottles and toss them into his recycling bin. "She must get hives every time she steps over that threshold."

He just grunts and clears a stack of papers off the couch, and I take a seat, dropping my bag on the floor and sending up a cloud of dust.

"How were midterms?"

Midterms? Seriously? That's what he wants to ask me about, when I'm having the best lacrosse season of my life? When I just gave him the opportunity to talk about The Child Bride? Ooookay. "They were good. My partner project for Econ went really well, my Stats exam was a piece of cake, Communications was totally open book, and Greek Tragedy was just a paper—I wrote half of it on the bus to Albany."

"Atta girl. Have you figured out what you're taking next year?"

I shrug. "Another Econ class, probably another Communications class…not sure yet what else. I haven't really started thinking about junior year yet." *Except the part where I want to be captain.*

He drops into the battered Eames chair he's had my entire life, but there's a tension in his body as he searches for his next words, and I realize what's coming before he even opens his mouth. "You know, sweetheart, those are classes you could really take anywhere, and UCSD—"

"Is not Radleigh." He sucks in a sharp breath at how quickly I cut him off, and I realize I'm not gaining myself any points here. I try again a little more patiently. "I'm really happy at school, Dad. I'm doing well, I've made really good friends, and I'm seriously killing it on lax. I mean, you saw that article—at this point, Coach Brady would probably break out into tears if I left."

Dad chuckles in this most annoying way that suggests he's not taking a word I say seriously. "He's a grown man, Cait, and he's used to losing his best players to graduation. He'll live, and *you* can stop playing lacrosse on a layer of frost."

"In case you somehow forgot, I'm from Vermont; I could care less about the frost. And this isn't about Brady; it's about me and where I want to be."

"You haven't even given San Diego a shot."

"Why would I?" I ask, jumping up from the couch, already getting sorry I came. "You—" The ringing of my phone cuts me off, then, and I think it's probably for the best. I pull it from my pocket, and see that it's Cammie. I flicker an annoyed glance at my father and then pick it up. "Hey, Cam."

"Hey, you here yet? I just got to my motel."

Shit, I should've known Cammie would stay at a motel. Without a backward glance at my dad, I let myself out of his house and take a seat on his cold stone stoop. "I'm at Dad's house. Any chance of you coming over here?"

"Hell no. How's it going?"

I glance back at the door I've closed behind me and sigh. "Not great."

"Want me to come pick you up?"

I know I should say no, that I should stick around and talk things out with my father. But…man, I really don't want to. And anyway, it's not like I've seen my sister at all this semester either. I'll see him later tonight. "Yes, please," I say, wincing at how small my voice sounds.

She sighs, and in it I hear the world's loudest "I told you this was a bad idea." "I'll see you in five."

"Thanks, Cam." I hang up and turn back to my dad. "Cammie's coming to pick me up."

I know the comment will bruise, and it does; I see it in the way his jaw tightens when I make no mention of her coming inside to say hi. Or maybe that's a response to the fact that I'm leaving this conversation in the middle, the same way I have been for months. Either way, I don't care; he chose this.

He wanted distance between him and his daughters, and he got it.

chapter sixteen

Cammie'd never actually been to Harborville, the tiny town my dad had moved to after the divorce to take over their paper's sports section. I'd gone for weekends a bunch during the off season, though, so I was able to direct us to the lone coffee shop with ease. To her credit, Cammie quietly sipped at her latte while I filled her in on my ongoing issues with Dad and Abigail, and then provided the welcome distraction of telling me about her work life in Brookline and the weird sexual tension between her and her boss.

After a couple of hours of talking about nothing at all, my dad called and asked to take us out to dinner—just the three of us—and we reluctantly agreed. Sitting with him and Cammie was painful, and I kept sneaking texts to Lizzie and Frankie under the table. Cammie went back to her motel after that, and I went back to my dad's, grateful there was always sports on to keep our own awkwardness at bay.

Unfortunately, tonight is basketball, and watching the Knicks in stark silence just lets my mind drift to a certain center I haven't allowed myself to think about in days. This could've been his life in a couple of years, if things had gone differently, if he hadn't gotten hurt. This is where we'd always thought he'd be, where he seemed to belong.

March Madness starts next week, and instead of getting on the court with Indiana, he'll be watching on the sidelines from Radleigh. Despite all my anger *and* my supposed apathy, at this moment my heart is breaking for him. I want to reach out, want to tell him that I get how sad and frustrated he must be. I want to make sure he's okay, bring him Cheetos and Mountain Dew—his favorites—and curl up on the couch with him to watch the games and rant at every bad play, the way we used to do on the phone, before he stopped taking my calls.

I never stopped missing the sound of his voice in my ear during games. He's not wrong that I'd rather be in my room watching ESPN Classic than doing most things, but the missing piece is how badly I miss—how badly I've missed for years—his enthusiastic whoops and gravelly laughs in my ear. The way he used to practice his announcer voice, cracking me up. The promises he used to make that we'd go to games together someday and give everyone something to see on kiss cams.

Thoughts and memories and half a beer lull me to sleep on the couch, and when I wake up, my dad is gone and I'm stretched out, covered in a blanket, the room around me silent and dark.

I slide my phone out of my pocket to check the time, and smile at the sight of a picture message from Lizzie of Connor and her two little brothers all passed out on the floor in front of the fireplace. It was sent a couple of hours ago, along with a text that says, *How's it going over there?*

She's probably asleep, but I type back, *Not great. Fingers crossed tomorrow's better.* I hit Send, then add, *Make that today.*

Unsurprisingly, there's no response—it's after three and after driving five hours that day, I'm sure Lizzie's zonked. I peel myself off the couch and head into the second bedroom with its two twin beds, covered in plaid sheets—my dad's entire aesthetic—and drop onto one. I'm wide awake now, and I don't know what to do with myself, which of course brings my thoughts back to the last place I want them to go.

I knew when Mase got his concussion; even though we'd been drifting before that, it was big news on the college sports grapevine. But I'd never wanted to know details, maybe because I'd always needed to believe it wasn't that bad, that he'd go back when he was healed. Not to mention that I was hurt—I called him so many times after it happened, and never received a single response. Eventually I let it go. The futures we'd discussed so many times under the stars were only coming true for one of us, and I was so wrapped up in myself and so determined to forget him, it never occurred to me he wouldn't eventually get back on his feet.

And I guess he did. Just not the way I would've thought.

I wonder if he likes coaching. We'd talked about it, in the past, if there was anything we could see ourselves doing on the field or court other than playing. Neither of us had been able to imagine a time past slamming the ball into the net, though. Not really. But here he is, at twenty, doing the thing we never wanted to believe we'd do before we were twice this age.

God, I want to talk to him. The urge to call him right now makes my fingers physically ache, and I'm relieved it's an absurd enough hour of the night to talk me out of it. For all I know, he's in my dorm room right now, curled up with Andi in post-coital slumber. And I'm here with Brandon, the stuffed poodle I've kept here since I was fourteen, just to have something to hug.

I fall asleep with Brandon squeezed tightly in my arms.

• • •

I feel like crap when I wake up in the morning, and my greasy hair and the circles under my eyes show it. Fortunately, Abigail's bridal shower isn't until noon, and my internal clock wakes me up at six, but it's so fucking cold in my dad's house that it takes half an hour before I can even squirm out from under the covers.

He's still asleep when I get up, so I leave him a note before going for a run—only a fraction of the spring break training regimen Brady handed out, but it's a start—and let the not-yet-spring chill wake me up. He's awake when I get back, the smell of freshly brewed coffee just bordering on burning permeating the entire house. "Hey, Caity," he greets me, overly sunny, as if it'll put me in exactly the right frame of mind he wants me to be for the bridal shower. "I was just gonna run out and get some bagels. Still sesame with cream cheese?"

Bagels aren't exactly on the Future Captain Diet, but he's trying, and I appreciate it, so I say sure. Then he hesitates before asking, "What would your sister like?"

Not me, if I drag her here for breakfast. But I can't say that, nor do I want to tell him that I'm pretty sure Cammie hasn't touched a carb since the Bush administration, so I just tell him she'll have the same. As soon as he leaves, I play the guilting game, promising her the moon and more just to get her to sit down to coffee. Then I jump into the shower and finish just in time for them to pull up to the house nearly simultaneously.

"Camille!" The already frigid air drops ten degrees as Cammie lets my dad kiss her on her tightening jaw. She doesn't even hate her full name, but I know it bothers her that he uses it; she thinks it's proprietary, like, "I gave you this name and don't you forget it." I wish I could've given him a primer—just some basic tips for not pissing off the daughter you haven't spoken to in years—but our conversations have been otherwise occupied with enough bad feelings already.

"Hi," she says stiffly, trying to paste a smile on her face, unquestionably for my benefit. The actual breakfast isn't any more comfortable than dinner last night, with basic small talk about Cammie's job and what we all hear from Matt. When Dad asks how Mom's doing, I actually think Cammie's gonna hiss, but she just says that Mom's great and really happy with her boyfriend—a boyfriend Cammie has absolutely made up on the spot.

By the time my dad says, "I'm so glad you girls are here," everyone at the table knows it's a lie. Cammie just grunts in response, picking at the edges of her barely touched bagel, and I force a smile I hope gets across that I'm sorry for putting them both in this position. I've never felt this distant from my dad, but there's only one reason I'm here, and if he has any interest in the conversation about bumping the wedding date, I'm not seeing even the slightest hint of it. In fact, he's gone out of his way to avoid talking about lacrosse at all, despite the fact that it usually dominates at least the first hour of all of our conversations.

Or at least it did before Abigail.

"We are too, Dad," I lie, because the part of me that wants to make him happy is still there.

The little fib seems to satisfy him, enough that he feels confident jumping into talk of San Diego, and the weather, and how much we'll love the beach and the zoo and their little house. Cammie and I mostly nod, and I'm grateful she's polite enough not to point out that considering this is her first time here, the odds of her ever seeing his San Diego abode aren't likely.

On my fiftieth glance at my watch, I see it's finally ten, and I announce it's time for us to get ready for the shower.

"Since when do you girls need two hours to get ready for something?" Dad asks. "What happened to 'Dad, we only need five minutes'?"

I claw Cammie's thigh before she can provide the snarky response I already see forming on the tip of her tongue. "Important occasion," I say weakly. "I'm wearing a dress."

He nods as if that makes sense—maybe it does? I really don't wear dresses often—and lets us go, and even though I'd fully planned to get ready at his house, it's so easy and natural to escape by bringing my stuff with me to Cammie's rental car and motel. So I do.

"This whole thing is ridiculous," Cammie says as soon as we're safely on the road and out of earshot. "You haven't even said a word to him about moving the wedding since we got here, have you?"

"I thought I'd have a chance when lacrosse came up," I admit, "but so far he's avoided talking about it like the plague, even after I sent him those emails."

"Yeah, because he's a self-centered dick and always has been," Cammie snaps, apparently at her end with patience for him. "Seriously, Cait, if you're not gonna talk to him, then what the fuck am I even doing here?"

"I don't think he's going to listen to me as long as she's set on it," I say. "She's the one I have to convince, which isn't gonna happen unless we play *super* nice at this shower. That's it. It's the last thing, Cam. Can I count on you?"

She grumbles in response, but I know it's as good as a yes.

We don't talk about it anymore after that, instead taking turns doing each other's hair while we laugh remembering what it was like when Mom tried to dress us in matching outfits and hairstyles. (It never worked, because I was always running around and making everything a mess, and Cammie was such a space cadet, she'd twirl her hair into knots and pull at threads without even realizing it.) Even with all our primping, we still have half an hour until we have to leave, so we sit back on the bed and watch an episode of *House Hunters*, miming taking shots every time someone says “open concept” or “I really wanted stainless steel.” And then there’s no more avoiding The Event, and off we go.

chapter seventeen

The shower is at a friend of Abigail's cute bungalow. (Open concept, no less.) Said friend—Jillian, according to the invitation—swings the door open wide to greet us with a big smile, revealing an explosion of pink décor, helium balloons shaped like bottles and diapers, and, in the center of it all, our future stepmother.

"I'm…guessing it's a girl?" Cammie murmurs to me as Jillian ushers us inside. I can only shrug, because I'd had no idea they knew the sex of the baby either. But I guess I shouldn't be surprised at surprises anymore.

"So, you're the daughters!" A blonde who must be Abigail's mom squeezes our arms, just enough distress in her eyes for me to know she's still processing the fact that her daughter's about to become a stepmother to women her own age. "Abigail didn't mention how tall you are!"

I've never been good at clever responses to people marveling at my height, which I prove by saying, "Yup! Tall." Next to me, Cammie chokes on a laugh, and I elbow her. Hard.

"Indeed. Well! Welcome. I'm Judy, and it's so nice to meet you both…"

It's clear then that if she ever knew our names, she doesn't anymore. "Cait," I fill in. "And this is Cammie," I add, just in case my sister won't.

"Ooh, both C names!" another woman chirps, this one Abigail's age. "Is that gonna be a problem for Esme?"

"Who's Esme?" I ask, at the same time Cammie says, "Our dad's name is Steve."

Abigail smiles serenely and rests her hands on her basketball belly. "Your future sister is Esme. We just decided on her name last week."

Esme. My beer-swilling, cigar-smoking, sports-obsessed, flannel-wearing father is going to have a child named Esme. We've all heard from my mother numerous times what a struggle it was to get my father to agree to Camille because it was "too fancy." And now he's gonna have an Esme, which I suspect wasn't a battle at all.

"Is she named after someone?" I ask, because that seems like the polite thing to do.

Judging by the way Abigail's smile flickers, it was not. "Nope, we just love the name."

We. Okay.

"It's a beautiful name," says Jillian, sweeping in as if to protect Abigail from an hour's worth of nasty insults hurled in her direction. She fixes me with a Look, and next to me I can feel Cammie stifling a laugh.

I nod, even though whether I like the name or not is beside the point, and then, mercifully, Judy interrupts. "Have you girls seen the beautiful food Jillian put together? She's such a wonderful hostess."

"No, we haven't!" Cammie says cheerfully. I follow her gaze to see she's spotted an arrangement of mimosas on the end of the long, pink-covered table. "Wouldn't want to let that go to waste. Come on, Cait."

I let her drag me over to the table of food, which does in fact look pretty damn good. After already choking down a bagel for Dad, Cammie skips right to the mimosas, but I pile my plate with crudités, two kinds of salad, a piece of salmon, and, with only a moment's hesitation, a slice of quiche; it's not like Coach Brady's watching. Besides, the busier my mouth is with chewing, the less I have to talk.

It's a strategy that does me well when everyone takes their seats in a circle around Abigail and starts gushing about how much they'll miss her when she moves to San Diego, and she replies by extending an open invitation, then jumping into everything she knows she "and Steve" will love about it. As if my dad can't wait to be surrounded by Padres fans. Please. But it isn't until she says, "And Matt's so excited to start at UCSD," that I almost choke on roasted golden beet.

"You okay, dear?" Judy asks me, her voice dripping with what's probably genuine concern but fills me with annoyance anyway. The idea that Matt's "so excited" to be coerced away from his friends for his senior year of college is such bullshit. Maybe he'd be excited to move after he graduated, but there's no way he's happy about this.

Of course, while I'm seething with the truth in my head, Cammie takes it upon herself to state it out loud. "Who wouldn't be excited about having their tuition covered for a year after working like a dog and drowning in debt for the last three? I mean, sure, all he has to do is leave the school he loves and move across the country from his friends, frat house, and the rest of his family, but yeah, that's definitely genuine excitement about moving for his senior year. No doubt."

"Cammie!" I force a laugh and squeeze her tight around the shoulders as everyone else gasps in horror. "What have we said about your bad jokes?"

She just shrugs and tosses back the rest of her mimosa.

"Well," Abigail says weakly, but she doesn't follow it up with anything. I don't know whether to feel sad for her or keep being mad. I guess I feel both.

Maybe it's my turn for a mimosa.

Another woman speaks up, then, suggesting Abigail open a present. "That's a great idea, Jessica!" Jillian says. "Mom, could you grab the bingo cards?"

Bingo cards? Before I can ask anyone to interpret, Judy places a card in front of me. It says "Baby Bingo" in pink and blue up top, and in the squares are different baby-related items I guess could conceivably be presents. Judging by the way people attack their cards when Abigail opens up the first gift, I'm guessing I can put one of the little pink discs Judy distributed over "bathtub" in the top right corner.

Cammie promptly gets up and gets us both drinks, returning just in time to see Abigail pull the last scrap of baby block-printed wrapping paper off something apparently called a Diaper Genie. Everyone else oohs and ahhs as if it actually grants wishes fueled by baby poop, and Cammie and I toss back our mimosas.

As Abigail continues to open gifts, I stuff another forkful of food in my mouth every time I feel the urge to say something like "What the hell is that?" or "Don't you worry about the kid suffocating from that many ruffles?" or "How much was I supposed to spend on this??" and before I know it, my plate is empty. As I hop up to get more, I can see Cammie's lips moving, and I'm sure she's asking me to get her another drink. But she's drowned out by a woman frantically asking, "Does that count as layette?" and I pretend I didn't hear.

The longer I stand at the table, the less time I have to spend in the seventh circle of hell, so I take my sweet time plucking individual baby carrots and spinach leaves. I only turn when I hear a loud groan, followed by Abigail saying, "Oh, God, Steve, give it up."

The other women in the circle laugh. "I thought you told him sports weren't happening this time," one says.

"It's sort of cute, how desperately he holds on, like a little boy," says another.

"He does realize you're having a girl, right?" another jokes.

While they all joke around about my dad's sad attachment to the Red Sox and the Patriots, Cammie turns around and gives me a questioning look. I nod as much as the lump in my throat will allow. The pair of sports-themed onesies aren't from my dad—they're from me (and, technically, Cammie, who had no interest in helping select the present). I happen *not* to have known it was a girl, thank you very much, but what the fuck does it matter? Do these people seriously think girls can't like or play sports? I swear, I have half a mind to challenge them all to a scrimmage right the fuck now.

But of course, I can't do that—can't do anything to rock the boat before I've had my conversation with Abigail about the wedding date. Then again, I can't really *not* say anything here, either—if I let her think they're from my dad, it'll look like I didn't bring a gift at all. Plus they'll both probably figure out what happened as soon as she mentions it to him, anyway.

"Uh, those aren't from Dad," I say, extra awkward, since I'm still standing at the food table. "Those are, um—I sent those. Me and Cammie. I guess the card is buried in there."

Aaaaand silence.

"Oh, Cait!" Abigail flushes as pink as the ribbons around her throne of honor, and I wish it made me feel better. But so far everything about being here feels like dirt. It's all proof that my father wants a very different life with a very different child than the ones he's got—that both of them do. And I don't know if that'd be any different if I'd agreed to move out to San Diego or not, but I do know that's never felt less like a possibility than it does right at this moment. "That's so sweet, thank you. I know your dad will love them."

Probably, but you don't, so Esme will never wear them. She'll probably never watch football with him on Sunday afternoons, and we'll never have matching jerseys and watch games together via video chat when she's a little older…I hadn't even realized the ways I'd been imagining bonding with my baby sis-to-be until it became clear they'd never be happening.

I smile weakly in response, wishing I could think of some way—any way—to turn this afternoon around.

And then, like magic, Abigail gives it to me.

"Actually, Cait, I'd love to hear more about the plus-one you're bringing to the wedding," Abigail chirps as she plucks a baby carrot between her pink talons. "Your dad didn't know you'd been dating anyone! So, now that it's just us girls, dish!"

Cammie gives me a "seriously?" look. I feel like shooting the very same look at Abigail for bringing up my dating life in this group of strangers.

But fuck it. If she wants to hear about my plus-one, I will talk alllll about my plus-one.

"His name is Jake," I gush as I take another mimosa from the table and sit back down next to Cammie. "He's on the basketball team at Radleigh—point guard—and he's also in my Econ class."

"A jock with brains!" Jillian lifts her champagne flute in the air.

"Mmhmm. Brains and a whole lot more," I add, because why the fuck not. "He's sooooo hot. And such a great boyfriend." I touch one of the pearl studs I borrowed from Lizzie—inherited from her mother. "Look what he got me for one month together."

Cammie's eyebrows shoot up, but I pretend not to notice. "I'm so excited for everyone to see how good he looks in his tux. He has a serious basketball player's body, if you know what I mean. Six-five, killer biceps..."

"Suddenly I am *very* excited for this wedding!" one of the three Jessicas present declares with a giggle, and the rest of the circle cracks up.

"Do you have any pictures of this Golden God?" Abigail asks.

I pull out my phone, find a cute selfie we took for show after a game, and pass it around. I may have lied about my relationship with Jake, but I wasn't lying about the fact that he's hot, and it's gratifying to hear everyone's exclamations of admiration and envy. Even Cammie takes a peek and whistles.

Which, unfortunately, draws Abigail's attention right to her. "What about you, Cammie? Haven't gotten your response card yet."

Apparently, Abigail also hasn't gotten the memo that Cammie has zero intention of going to her wedding, and wouldn't have a date even if she did—something we discussed at great length the day before. The last thing anyone needs is Cammie's three-mimosa response, so I do the only thing I can think of and tip mine over on to her skirt.

"Oh, shit!" she yelps, jumping up.

I gasp, covering my mouth so no one can see me laughing behind it at Cammie's very real dramatics. "I'm so sorry, Cam! Jillian, can you point us to the bathroom? I'll help Cammie clean up."

She's a little fuzzy on her alcohol-filled stomach, but even Cammie finally realizes I was saving her from Abigail's line of questioning. We let Jillian shuffle us along to a little powder room, into which we both squeeze as I close the door behind us.

"Jake, huh?" she says as soon as we can no longer hear Jillian's footsteps. "That's funny—I don't seem to recall any mention of a Jake during our conversation yesterday."

Actually, I'd avoided talking about my love life with Cammie altogether, because it was so nice to have a conversation that wasn't obsessing about it. But now that it's on the table, I feel the urge to spill.

Everything.

"He's just a friend," I tell her, keeping my voice just loud enough to be heard over the sound of the water she's running onto a washcloth. "A gay friend. With whom I have an arrangement of sorts."

She throws back her head and laughs, flicking water everywhere. I squeeze the spigot shut, and she dabs at her skirt, her teeth still bared in a smile. "Cait Johannssen, in an arrangement of convenience. I thought you were the queen of drama-free living."

"I know, I know," I groan. "Shut up. Trust me, it wasn't my first choice. But he needed a cover when he was hooking up with this guy, and with Mase at school, it was just really convenient for both of us."

"I thought you said Mase is dating your roommate." She examines the stain, then looks up at me. "Am I remembering wrong? I know it was a while ago."

"You're remembering right, but they're not dating anymore," I say. "Or maybe they are. I'm actually not a hundred percent sure. There was definitely a breakup in there somewhere, but I'm still fuzzy on whether there was a reconciliation."

"Okay, so where do you fit in to that? I thought you guys were sweeping your entire history under the rug. Wasn't that the plan? I mean, not that I thought it was a particularly realistic one, especially since I remember when you guys were head-over-ass about each other, but—" She purses her lips, clearly trying to stem another round of laughter. "You still are, aren't you?"

"You don't have to sound so damn smug about it," I mutter, wishing I'd poured my drink on her hair instead of her skirt, which already looks clean. "And I'm not saying we like each other, just that...attraction is still there. But that's it."

"Oh really. That's it? The attraction is still there between you and a super-hot ex—the same super-hot ex, who, if I recall correctly, held your hand through a *ton* of Mom and Dad's divorce shit? The one you talked to on the phone through an entire Thanksgiving dinner the time Mom shipped us to Grandma's? The one who used to handcraft you birthday cards every year?"

Little by little, blurry memories from the past come back in hi-def, reminding me of all the ways Mase had been there for me through the worst of the worst. It's no wonder I miss him now more than ever; he'd been instrumental for me surviving my family's issues in the past, and now that new ones are surfacing—the worst I'd had since we were together—it's only natural to miss his reassuring hand on my back, his patented distraction tactics of having me name the starting lineup of the '86 Celtics or the stats of every midfielder on every girls' lacrosse team that played Stone Creek.

Even the stars…the stars were a distraction too, once upon a time.

"How do you remember all that?" I ask Cammie.

"Because I remember thanking him," she replies quietly. "Your last visiting day. I thanked him for helping you in all the ways none of the rest of us could. There were times I thought you were seriously gonna lose it, Cait. You'd call home so angry at Mom, I was afraid she was gonna send you to live at Dad's. Then I'd text you later that night and you'd be okay, filled with some story of how Mase had done this or that to cheer you up.

"I couldn't believe it when you guys stopped talking. You actually seemed to have something special between you. And you never told me what happened."

"I never knew." I sigh heavily, sliding down to the floor with my back against the wall. "I still don't."

Cammie cocks her head. "It wasn't mutual? I always assumed…"

"I kind of let you assume," I admit. "Because it was embarrassing and confusing and it hurt like hell. I wanted to think it was for the best, because we were gonna be so far apart anyway. But it sucked. And yeah, it sucked less over time, but now that he's at Radleigh…it sucks over and over again every damn time I see him."

To my horror, I realize there's a tear rolling down my cheek. I can't even remember the last time I cried; the mimosas must be making me extra emotional. Thankfully, Cammie doesn't give me shit; she just slides down next to me on the floor and wraps her arms around my shoulders. Neither of us realizes her heels kick the door open until a shadow casts over us both, and we look up.

"You girls okay in here?" Judy asks.

Cammie and I look at each other, splayed out on the bathroom floor, tears and undoubtedly mascara running down my cheeks, a washcloth draped over her lap, and what else can we possibly do?

We laugh.

• • •

By the time we clean up and return to The Circle, all the presents are open and someone's collected all the bingo cards and pieces. Jillian, Judy, and a couple of other women are carrying platters into the kitchen, dusting off the tablecloth, and setting down doilies. Cammie and I try to help, but they shoo us out, and Abigail calls us over to come sit in the seats vacated by her nearest and dearest.

"I feel like we've barely gotten to talk today," she says as I slide into Jillian's chair. "I'm just so happy you both came."

"Me too," I lie, wondering whether she's going to address any of the many pink elephants in the room, only one of which is literal. But she doesn't do anything other than smile and rest her hand on mine, and I realize it's probably now or never. "Actually, there was something I wanted to talk to you about."

"Is this about the bridesmaid manicure color? I know it's hard to find, but I booked appointments for all of us at a salon I made sure has plenty in stock. Don't worry about that!"

"I...what? No, not that." *I didn't even know there was a bridesmaid manicure color.* "No, I was wondering about the date. I'm sure my dad's told you about my lacrosse championships being the same day as the wedding."

Her jaw tightens and she swallows, and I realize all at once that this was a very, very stupid idea. The woman's already booked manicure appointments for the days before the wedding, and I think she's gonna have any flexibility about the date? Especially after showing me and the rest of the room exactly what her attitude is toward sports, and particularly girls playing them.

"He has told me," she says slowly, "and frankly, I'm a little sick of hearing about it. I thought you were here because you'd finally let it go. Your father and I would both appreciate if you'd stop harassing him—"

"Harrassing?" Cammie snaps, and I blink; I'd actually forgotten she was there.

"Yes, harassing," Abigail hisses. "How many times does the man have to tell you the wedding date is not negotiable for a *game*? You think telling him every single time you score a goal is going to make him suddenly drop the biggest day of his life?"

I'm struck completely dumb, but Cammie is decidedly not. "You think the biggest day of our father's life is his *second* wedding, forced by the impending birth of his *fourth* child? I realize you're basically a child yourself, Abigail, but even you have to realize—"

"Cammie, stop," I say quietly, my throat raw with tears I absolutely refuse to shed again today. I turn to Abigail. "Are you really speaking for both yourself and my father? Or are you just putting his name on your words? And before you answer that, remember how shitty it would be to lie about this."

"Your father and I are a team," she says firmly, jutting her chin out. "I realize you haven't grown up with a good example of that, but you're seeing it now. Your father and I are getting married on May 26th in San Diego whether the two of you are there are not, and frankly, I don't care which you choose at this point."

Somehow, I get myself to standing on two shaky legs, and Cammie immediately rushes to my side. "Not," she spits at Abigail. "You and your friends will just have to eye-fuck someone else's date who's actually your age while you marry a man who's twice it." And then she escorts me out, both of us unwilling and unable to thank Jillian for hosting us so graciously.

Just as we reach her car, though, she says, "I'll be right back," and dashes into the house. When she emerges a minute later, she's dangling a onesie in each hand, and I crack up laughing when I see she's rescued my gift. "Fuck Esme," she says as we get into the car. "You and Mase will make much better use of these someday. Now come on—let's go see a crappy movie until I sober up and then I'll drive you back to school."

chapter eighteen

It's only an hour drive back to Radleigh, and Cammie driving me is a whole lot more convenient than taking the bus, but I still feel completely wiped by the time I drag my ass back into Barrow. All I want to do is drop my bag and pass out for a million years.

Unfortunately, life seems to have other, terrible plans.

"Andi?" I drop my bag on the floor and look at my roommate, who's perched on the couch in the common room, her laptop balanced on her knees. "I thought you were going home for the week."

"Tonight," she says, her tone flat, no sign of surprise that I've returned unannounced. She hasn't even lifted her eyes from the screen since I walked in. At least when Mase dumped her, she pretended to watch TV with Samara. Now she just looks like a zombie.

"Oh." I slip off my coat and hang it up, unzip my boots, wait for her to say something, anything else, but nothing comes. I'm afraid to ask what's wrong, to throw myself in a whirlwind of Mase drama after the day I've had and the thoughts that are still consuming me. I decide to leave her alone and take my nap after all.

I only get as far as our bedroom door when she says, "You knew each other."

Fuck.

There's no point in denying it. She isn't asking a question; she's stating a fact. A rush of anger surges through me at the fact that Mase didn't warn me he told her, not even a two-second text message saying, *Heads-up, we're busted.* But this isn't about my anger right now. "Yeah."

"You lied to me. Both of you."

Again, not exactly ripe for denial. I turn around so that I'm actually facing her. "I'm sorry, An—"

"Don't tell me you're sorry." I've never heard Andi snap before, and the harshness of her voice is unsettling, all the more so because I deserve it. Because I'm a dirty liar and she's a good person and I don't really have a good excuse at all. "Tell me why."

"It's not what you think," I say quickly, which is dumb. I don't know what she thinks, and I don't know what Mase thinks either. "We were just surprised to see each other, that first time. We hadn't spoken in years,

Andi. We were close and then we weren't. I was just meeting you, and it wasn't exactly a decent time to reconnect. It was just reaction."

"Okay," she says slowly. "So that was the first meeting, but what about after that? You could've told me. I mean, God, we all hung out. You met his—" Her mouth twists into a frown. "You didn't 'meet' Will, did you? You already knew him. That's why you picked XO. God, I'm such an idiot."

"You're *not* an idiot," I say firmly. "*We* were idiots, okay? We should've just told you. Lying was stupid. But…" But what? But there's absolutely nothing between us? If that's true, then why did we hook up at that party? Why did he show up at my game? Why did I ache with missing him today? Why did every time I saw them together feel like a stab to the heart? "I don't know what he told you—"

"Nothing," she spits. "He told me absolutely nothing."

And then she turns her laptop around, and I feel a twinge in my chest as I recognize the picture on her screen. It's a shot of Mase, holding up a trophy, looking exactly how I remember him at sixteen—massive smile, glowing with joy, teammates all around him in various states of yelling and cheering…and me, in his other arm, laughing into his chest. His other golden trophy.

"I missed him. He barely takes pictures anymore, but I remembered seeing the pictures on his camp website once, how happy he looked in them. And I missed his smile. So I looked. And there you were. Everywhere. God, I'm surprised I didn't recognize you, you're in so many of these."

I don't respond. What can I? I've given whatever defense I have, and she's right to be angry. I would be too.

I'm just not sure what I would've done differently.

"I'm sorry," I say hoarsely. "We thought we were doing the right thing."

"No, you didn't. When he called me and said he wanted to see me again, after we broke up, I thought 'He's gonna realize he made a mistake.' And then when it turned out he just wanted to apologize for hurting me and talk it out, I thought, 'Okay, at least I'm getting more of the truth.' But that was bull, too. And here I've been beating myself up over what I've done wrong, but the truth is I'm just not *you*, and that's clearly who he's wanted all along."

"It's *not*," I insist. "Andi, *nothing* happened between us while you were dating. I swear."

"And after?" she asks, raising her meticulously arched brows.

Shit. Bad word choice on my part. "Once," I admit. "Just once, and never again."

She looks like she's gonna throw up, and the very least I can do is spare her the sight of my face. "I'm just dropping this off, and then I'm heading back out," I promise, walking past her into our room. Her clothing is spread out all over her bed, waiting to be stuffed into a suitcase—an uncharacteristic mess in the half of the room that's usually clean. I drop my bag on my own bed and slip my phone out of my pocket, opening up my ever-running group text with Lizzie and Frankie.

Cait: *Hey, can I stay at your apt tonight?*

Neither one answers right away, but the question's basically a formality; I have a spare key, and with Lizzie and Connor in Pomona and Frankie home in Longmeadow, no one else will be using it. I pack another, smaller bag—pajamas, my toothbrush, deodorant, and something to go running in in the morning, after which I can return safely to my room. The idea of walking over there now instead of passing out in my own bed right now exhausts me even more than I thought possible, but I've had enough interpersonal misery for one day, and I'll happily trade my own mattress for some blissful solitude.

My phone beeps.

Lizzie: *Uh oh. What happened?*

Lizzie: *And yes, of course you can, duh.*

Cait: *I'll fill you in when I get there.*

I hoist the bag onto my shoulder and take a deep breath before walking back out. Andi's still sitting on the couch, staring stonily at her computer screen, though whether the pictures of us are still on it, I have no idea.

When I say, "Have a good break," it's over my shoulder, and I don't look back.

• • •

It takes a minute to remember where I am when I wake up the next morning, squinting into the March sunlight streaming through Lizzie's window. By now, Andi should be in her own bed in…God, I can't even remember where in Jersey she's from. I really am a shitty roommate.

I drag my ass out of bed, wash up, and get dressed for my run. In a flash, I remember that it's Sunday; if I jog over now, I'll make it in time for youth basketball at the community center. It's highly unlikely Mase will be there—presumably he's in Philly for break—and I know Jake's in Miami with a bunch of guys from his frat, but I could use some company, even if it's just of the kids. Hopefully they'll vouch for me and let me stick around even without the boys. And if not, well, I need the run one way or another.

It turns out being vouched for isn't necessary; the first person I see when I step inside is Mase, smiling smugly around the whistle in his teeth as he holds the ball on his fingertips over his head, out of reach of the kids jumping for it. It's been a few weeks, but I recognize the kids as Peter, Carlos, and Xavier, and I love that they love working with Mase enough to keep coming back. It's easy to see he connects to them really well, and if he really doesn't have a career in playing professionally anymore, he'd make a pretty kickass coach or even gym teacher.

For the millionth time since I first saw him again, I feel a pang of sadness that I have no idea what the guy I used to discuss everything with has planned for his future.

It isn't Mase who notices me standing in the doorway of the gym; it's Peter. "Hey, Miss J!" he calls. "You playing with us?"

I glance at Mase, but his expression's impossible to read. I should probably say I was just running by, but my blood is pumping with the desire to move, and the fact that I haven't even started on the spring break training schedule Brady gave us isn't helping. So, fuck it. "That all right?" I ask, directing the question at him and the other guys rather than the statue between them.

"As long as you're on our team!" Xavier replies, just as Carlos jumps and knocks the ball off Mase's fingertips. "We need someone tall."

"Hey!" another kid, DeShaun, says as if he's insulted, but there's no way he tops five-nine.

"You wish, Winslow," Carlos says with a snort, which sets off a mini-battle that Mase promptly breaks apart with his whistle and obnoxiously sexy arms. He divvies the teams up, and for the next hour, I let myself sweat everything out—the awkwardness with my father, the fight with Abigail, the "I told you so" radiating from Cammie the entire ride back to Radleigh, the horribly uncomfortable conversation with Andi... The only thing I can't ignore is the fact that once again, I've come to Mase—consciously or not—to take me back out of my head, to bring me to a happy place when everything else is miserable. And he's delivered, is still delivering, is making me smile over and over again as he teasingly dribbles just out of my reach or groans when I hit a particularly nice three or dunks with such awe-inspiring form, the kids' mouths actually drop open.

The time passes too fast, and then it's time to go, and reality comes rushing back. Mase and I fall into step together on the walk back to Radleigh, and as we chat casually about the kids and the game and the fact that he's still on campus because he's working as a personal trainer on the side, the urge to bring up my conversation with Cammie bubbles just below the surface until there's finally a lull, and I can't resist.

"Do you remember that visiting day when both my parents came to camp and they got into that huge, embarrassing fight?"

He grins. "Hard to forget. I spent half an hour helping your dad wash marinara sauce out of his hair."

"Oh, yes, that was particularly epic." It's relief to be able to laugh about it now; at the time, I thought it'd traumatize me forever. "I had no idea how I was going to make it through the summer after that. How I was gonna make it through the day. And then you…"

I can't finish. It's too much. And anyway, I don't need to; it's clear from the little smile on his lips that he remembers. He was at my side for the rest of the day, making sure no one would dare say a word. And as soon as they were gone, he took me down to the lake and let me cry in his lap for an hour, no teasing, just stroking my hair until I was all cried out. And then, when I was feeling like a gross, snotty mess, it was his idea for us to strip down to our underwear and jump in.

Under normal circumstances, I might've hesitated, but teary and disgusting and miserable, faced with the option of seeing the object of my massive crush in his boxer briefs…I got down to my sports bra and patterned cotton boy shorts in three seconds flat.

That was the night he told me about Will, all the shit he got in West Philly, how painfully closeted he had to be to everyone—even Mase—for a while, and how shitty Mase felt for it.

That was the night we talked about our hopes for college—not just pipe dreams but the plans that burned in our blood at night, keeping us awake, dreaming of collegiate uniforms and March Madness. The little things, like hoping we'd be able to keep our numbers—

21 for me, because it'd been my dad's; 47 for Mase, for his dad's birthday.

That was the night he told me what it was like growing up without a father—how hard it was to watch his mom struggle after her husband died, to see his whole family hurting every day, to be able to do nothing except this, and dream of being good enough at it to bring them all better lives someday.

That was the night I fell for him.

"That was the night I fell for you."

I'm shocked at myself for saying it aloud, and then I realize I didn't; he did. I freeze in my tracks and look up at him. "Really? I was a teary mess, practically using your mesh shorts as a tissue."

He laughs, and there's just a little embarrassment to it, a shyness I've never seen from him before. It's incredibly fucking cute. I have thought of Mase in many complimentary terms before, but "cute" isn't really one of them. It's surprisingly unsettling.

"I liked that you were comfortable crying in front of me. It's cool to have someone get that vulnerable with you."

"Oh really? So if Brockhurst had cried into your lap, that would've been cool?"

He grins. "Sure."

"Liar."

His smile turns into full-blown laughter. "Fine. It's cool when a hot girl gets that vulnerable with you, especially when she's such a stone-cold badass most of the time. Better?"

"Much," I say, jealous that his cheeks hide a blush much better than mine do. But talking like this, joking like this…it's like all the blood rising to the surface of my skin is bringing all my feelings with it. One prick and I'll bleed everywhere.

"It's cool when a hot girl blushes, too."

And there it is. His voice is teasing, but it doesn't matter whether it's just a joke; it's never been that to me. "So then what's been up with you since you got here? With us? If you liked me so much then, why do you hate me so much now?"

His dark eyes flash as the smile drops from his face. "I don't hate you, Cait."

"Oh, really? Because you haven't exactly seemed happy to see me, and honestly, at times, you've been pretty downright shitty. And don't pretend you're like this to everyone. I've seen you with Andi. I've seen you with the team. You're a different person around them, or you're different around me, but don't pretend we're okay.

"It isn't just because I still play, either," I continue. "You wouldn't be coaching, or doing this at the community center, if you really hated being around active athletes that much. So what is it about me, Mase? Because before you stopped returning my calls, we were pretty damn good friends."

He snorts. “Friends?”

“Yes, friends,” I snap. “Stop pretending we were just fuckbuddies, Mason. I won’t let you rewrite that. We *were* friends—”

“Of course we were friends!” he explodes. “You were my *best* friend. Being with you, sleeping with you—it meant *everything* to me. *You* meant everything to me. And like a fucking idiot, I thought I needed my freedom more than I needed to be with you, and I spent months regretting that decision, months trying to work up the nerve to ask if you felt the same way. If you’d wanna try long distance.”

I did, I scream in my brain, but I’m frozen in place by his words; I can’t push out any of my own. I’m too scared to see where this is going, because we’re standing here as living proof this story doesn’t have a happy ending.

“I got up the nerve, finally,” he says, his voice brimming with bitterness. “I was having the game of my fucking career, and I thought, ‘This feels incomplete without Cait. She should be here. This should be *our* victory.’”

The quiet that follows is thunderous. Finally, I ask the question I’m pretty sure he’s just hinted at the answer to. “How long after this epiphany did you get that concussion?”

He closes his eyes, and I wonder what he sees behind his lids. “Sixteen-point-four seconds.”

The telltale choking of imminent tears climbs up my throat. "I wish you'd called me." It comes out as a whisper, but I mean it, so strongly. "I *should've* been there."

"To watch my career end? My life end? Is that what you want?"

"It would've been our victory had you won, Mase," I say, more forcefully now, "and it would've been our tragedy, too, if you'd just fucking called. Love isn't only being there for the trophy shit. I would've been there in a second if you wanted me to, and I would've *stayed*."

"Out of pity, maybe. Don't kid yourself, Cait. Being the Dream Team couple was half the draw. I couldn't pick up a ball again for months. I stopped being an athlete. You think you would've wanted to be with that?"

"Don't tell me what I wanted."

"Then be honest, with both of us. Stop romanticizing the past based on who I was when you knew me. I stopped being that person long before I walked into your dorm room with another girl."

My instinct is to argue again, but for once, I shut it down, and I think about what he's saying, and whether there's any truth to it. And if I'm honest with myself, the answer is that I don't know. I don't know if who Mase was is too intrinsically tied to the guy I loved, or if the man standing in front of me now could still be it.

I don't know.

We keep walking in stubborn silence, and it's only when we reach campus and turn to go our separate ways that I ask my last question. "Why were you at my last lacrosse game?"

He turns, dark eyes cold and glittering, jaw stiff. "Old habits die hard."

And then he takes off and so do I.

chapter nineteen

For the rest of break, I do nothing but follow my training schedule, do some advance reading, and watch old lax games online to study up on our competition. Knowing Mase is the closest thing I have to a friend on campus makes me feel even more isolated, and I don't dare go anywhere I might run into him, other than the gym, where I practically have on blinders. I eat my meals in my suite like a creepy shut-in, and by the time the weekend hits, I feel like I'm going out of my mind.

And it doesn't help that Andi's imminent return is hanging over my head.

Friday night, as I'm curled up in bed with my laptop and halfheartedly watching old episodes of *Parks and Rec*, my gaze won't stop drifting over to Andi's side of the room. How the hell are we going to share this space now? We haven't spoken once all week, not so much as a text. Do we just pretend nothing happened when she gets back? Do we live in awkward silence?

I sigh and pick up my phone, opening the group text with Lizzie and Frankie. It's grown monumental in length this week, mostly with my whining. *Please tell me they've changed the school calendar and the semester is officially over. I can't deal with Andi coming back this week.*

Bless Frankie's heart, I see she's responding immediately. *Sorry, Caity J ☹ But you know you're always welcome at our place!*

I start to type a response, but Lizzie gets there first. *Srsly, C, we can work something out if you need.*

I know they mean it, and I love them for it, but I can't exactly just move all my stuff into their apartment. Besides, between Frankie's frequent hookups and Connor, they really don't need an extra body living on the couch and cramping their style, especially since I'm…not the neatest. *<3 you both, but you'd prob both kill me after three days of my stuff all over your floor.* I send the text, then sigh and send another. *Plus, there's prob some mature way I'm supposed to deal w/this.*

Fuck mature, they both respond immediately, and I crack up. God, I miss them. Life was so much more fun when it was the three of us living here, our trio against the world. I know why Lizzie had to move, and I know it made sense for Frankie to go with her, but sometimes, my loneliness with them gone feels like a physical ache even hours of Icy Hot can't cure.

Maybe Samara can help? Frankie suggests.

If this is you "helpfully" suggesting she sleep at your place so I can take her bed...

Hahahahaha. Lizzie's being equally helpful.

That too, says Frankie, *but I meant maybe she has an idea, seeing as she lives w/u.*

Fair point. I've chatted online with Sam a little this week—she checked in to see how the shower was (I said it was Fine) and I asked her about some fancy dinner she had to go to with her family, including her small-town mayor dad (she said it was Fine)—but I've steered clear of the topic of Andi. Which is silly, because A) she's not completely clueless about me and Mase, and B) Frankie's right—I need her help.

I check to find that Samara's indeed online right now. I open a chat window and type, *Hey, how's it going over there?*

Samara: *Is it terrible that I cannot wait to come back to school?*

I'm tempted to say I'd switch places with her in a heartbeat, but then I remember how much I enjoyed my recent vacation time spent with family and think better of it. *Trust me, I'll be very happy to have you back.*

Samara: *Are you just being sweet, or is that loaded?*

I wonder if she's that smart, or I'm that transparent. Probably both. *Does it have to be one or the other?*

Samara: *Uh oh. Fill me in.*

So I do, cringing through every second of my clash with Andi as I imagine Samara's judgment on the other end, and how badly she wants to say, "You should've told her the truth from the start." Frankly, it's exactly what I would've said to someone in my situation, and I have no idea how the hell I became someone who makes such idiotic decisions.

I blame sexual deprivation.

Any ideas for how we can get through the rest of the semester without her killing me in my sleep? I finish.

Samara: *Yiiiiikes. At least she's an early sleeper (though so are you), and you're an early riser, so maybe you can just avoid each other?*

Cait: *Hmm, that's true. Maybe I just have to be a* less *early sleeper.* The idea physically pains me—I'm usually drop-dead exhausted by the time I fall asleep, and the two-a-days awaiting us for the next two months are only gonna make it worse—but it's less awful than the nauseated feeling I get when I imagine Andi daggering me in my bed, if only with her sad eyes.

Samara: *If you can keep yourself away at night for long enough to let her pass out around ten like she* *usually does, I can stay on watch and report in when it's safe for you to return.*

The idea of a lookout spying for me is hilarious…and oddly comforting. *I can't believe I'm saying this, but would you? I know this is completely ridiculous, but drama is not my specialty.*

Samara: *Not a problem! Kinda fun to have a "mission."*

I love that she's not making me feel like an idiot about it. As much as I miss living with my best friends, I'm glad to have met her. *Thank you*, I reply, adding a little heart at the end.

Samara: *Anytime. You're like a real life YA novel. Or NA novel, I guess.*

Cait: *What's NA?*

She starts to type a response, then deletes it, then types again, *Dammit, I gotta run. Another Dad thing. I'll text you some recs when I get some downtime later.*

Cait: *Wait, one more thing before you go?*

Samara: *Yeah?*

I take a deep breath and type my question, nervously, having thought about this a lot over the past week. *Despite all my drama, any chance you might wanna consider living together next year? Just the two of us?*

My cursor just blinks on the screen as I wait for her to reply, and I quickly wish I could take it back. I haven't exactly proven my capabilities as a drama-free roomie, and if I were her, I wouldn't wanna live with me either. What I *should* do is suck it up and move to Shamblin with everyone else, but I've always liked living separate from the other jocks—gives me a little headspace from the game to focus on my homework.

I'm about to tell her not to worry about answering right now when she writes back, *Sure! Would love that. Talk more later!*

Samara Kazarian has signed off.

I sigh with relief and put the laptop aside, then pick up my phone again. *I'll officially have a lookout for the rest of the semester*, I write to Lizzie and Frankie.

Awesome, says Frankie. *And hey, if you need anyone to look at *her* for the rest of the semester...*

FRANCESCA.

At Lizzie's sympathetic *hahahahahaha*, I decide to call it a night. But I'm feeling the tiniest bit better, knowing they've all got my back.

• • •

Sam is every bit as good a lookout as promised, but after two weeks of showering at the gym and doing work at the library or at Jake's instead of in my room, and going to sleep later than usual even though two-a-days have my eyelids dropping hours earlier, I pretty much want to die. The bright side is that I haven't seen Andi, and she hasn't done anything like leave me passive-aggressive notes or text me asking to talk. I haven't seen Mase, either, though somehow that feels less like a good thing. I know I could show up at the community center, or play the dutiful girlfriend at one of Jake's games, but what's the point? I don't have any more to say to him than I did on the walk home a few Sundays earlier. Maybe I don't know him well enough now to know how we'd fit.

Maybe I don't know me without lacrosse well enough to, either.

The thought ribbons in and out of my head throughout the day, every day, but for practice, and for games, I push it aside—if I'm gonna be at odds with my family and the guy I…maybe sort of still have feelings for…over lacrosse, then I'm damn well gonna make the most of lacrosse.

It's been three games and plenty of traveling, but I've used the bus rides for strategizing or catching up on reading instead of wallowing. (Mostly.) I'm clearly one of the few who actually followed the practice schedule over break, and while everyone else gets back into form eventually, I smugly accept Nora and Tessa's muttered resentment at my general kickass-ness on the field. The irony is that I've never been on a shittier sleep schedule, but exhaustion somehow gives way to adrenaline at game time, and I'm not questioning that magic.

We're just getting ready to file out of the locker room for practice on Friday, fresh off another blowout win, when Brady halts us all with our gear still in hand. "Girls, huddle up."

We do, gathering around obediently in a mass, the excitement in the room palpable. Yesterday's game proved us to be a well-oiled machine, and we're all ready to kill it again tomorrow. Even our current circle around our coach is as perfectly formed as possible, given the locker room's structure, though it's obvious from everyone's jittery feet and white knuckles around their crosses that we all just wanna get on the field already. This is the first time Brady's stopped us like this.

Which can only mean one thing.

"I was gonna wait until after tomorrow's game to make this announcement, but I want us to go into it with a strong sense of leadership," he says, confirming my suspicions. "As you all know, Mariana will be graduating in a couple of months. Although obviously no one can replace her"—pause while everyone cheers and shakes our crosses in our fearless leader's direction—"we will need a new captain. I've thought long and hard about this choice, along with Larissa and Kathy, and I think you'll all agree your new captain is a talented and hardworking leader, who helps hold this team together, and has been instrumental in taking our team to new heights this season. We know she'll continue to help bring us home that championship trophy."

My face is on fire, and I don't dare return any of the stares I feel picking me apart, or acknowledge the hand—Tessa's, most likely—on my back. I want this more than anything, and everyone knows I've worked and sacrificed like hell for it, but I don't want attention; I just wanna lead. Which I've practically been doing for the last couple weeks anyway, since Mariana spent her spring break in Cabo with a couple of the other girls, celebrating our victorious season with a few dozen margaritas too many.

"Congratulations…Tessa!"

Blood freezes in my veins. Tessa? Not that I don't love her and she isn't a great player, but…captain? If she's ever even wanted that, it's news to me.

"Um, what?"

Apparently, it's news to her, too.

Her fingers are still on my back, and all I wanna do is shake them off and run. But this isn't her fault, and if there's anyone I should be able to be happy for, it's Tess. The silence in the room as everyone looks from Coach to us and back is awful, and shitty as this feels, the thought of Tessa getting hurt is worse. I force myself out of my stupor to say, "Congrats, Tess," with as much warmth as I can muster, squeezing her shoulders. "You're gonna kick ass."

"Damn straight," Latisha says quickly, and Nora agrees, and Tessa's hand finally falls from my back as she accepts congratulations from the whole team. I watch, feeling like I'm underwater, everything around me vaguely blurry and muffled. I hate how embarrassed I feel. I have the best scoring record on the team right now, and I'm the *only* one nationally ranked for goals per game. I'm at every practice on time—even earlier, now, to make sure I've escaped my suite before Andi stirs—and I'm usually the one people ask to stay late to help them practice passing. How could I have screwed up badly enough that they'd take this away from me?

"Okay, enough chatter, ladies," Brady admonishes. "Goggles on. Take the field."

Everyone obeys. Including me. Just as I always do.

• • •

Practice is full of the worst kind of crackling tension, people staring at me as if waiting to see whether I'll blow up in some way. As if I'd put my pride before the team, or before my friend. But the worst is when Tessa comes up to me after practice and tries to *apologize*.

"Tess." I put a hand on her arm, hoping to end this conversation once and for all. "First of all, you have nothing to be sorry for; you're a great player, everyone gets along with you, and obviously Brady, Larissa, and Kathy think you deserve it."

"You're better," she argues, as if it's fact. Which, I guess, statistically it is. "And yeah, it's been a little rockier for you this season with the team, but everyone loves you. Everyone wanted this captainship for you. This is fucked up. I don't even want it."

I know she means to be kind, but that last bit hurts the worst of all, even though I already knew it. "Tessa—"

"Seriously, I'll tell Brady that. This isn't my life the way it is yours, Cait. I love lax, but it isn't my whole heart and soul. You deserve this. You put lacrosse before *everything*, and they should recognize that."

Welp, turns out there's even further to twist the dagger.

They're not that different from the thoughts I've already had, but…my life? My whole heart and soul? I think of myself as passionate and devoted to a sport that's meant a lot to me, that's given me sanity during hard times, that's paid my way through a college I could never have afforded otherwise. It's a way to physically express myself, and a healthy distraction from life's drama. But between Mase and Tessa, I'm suddenly seeing the love of my life in an entirely different way: pathetic.

And it feels like shit.

Worse, it feels like Mase was so, so right.

"Thanks, Tess," I manage weakly, my crosse suddenly feeling like it weighs a thousand pounds. "But really, please don't. You deserve this. I can always try again next year." I can't handle any more of the conversation than that, so I forge on ahead, past the locker room, past the gym entirely, leaving her and the rest of the team behind.

• • •

With my mind full of that conversation, I don't even think to pull out my phone and text Samara; I just head back to the dorm. And of course, because luck is never on my side, the first person I see when I walk in is Andi, standing over the stove, stirring a pot of what smells like tomato soup.

"Oh," I say, then instantly feel like an idiot for the obvious surprise in my tone. "Hey."

"Hey." She glances over just long enough to take in that I'm still in my lax uniform, then turns back to the stove. "How was practice?"

I'm so surprised at her attempt at civil conversation after all this that I couldn't recall the honest answer to the question if I wanted to; it takes me longer than it should just to stammer out "Good."

"Good." She shakes something into the pot, which already smells so delicious, my stomach lets out a little rumble.

"Welp, guess that's my sign I should hurry up and shower so I can get lunch," I say, glad I have a good excuse to extricate myself from this awkward little encounter. I get as far as putting my hand on the doorknob to our room when I realize that doing so isn't fair. She's been stewing in this for weeks, is dealing with a shitty breakup, and had her roommate lying to her on top of everything else. And I've let myself not care because—how did Tessa put it?—oh yes, because I put lacrosse before *everything.* Well, not today.

I turn back.

"Why did you break up?"

She answers so tersely, I wonder if she's been waiting for this question for weeks. "Ask him."

"I'm asking you. He and I have had enough conversations about this…triangle that don't include your voice. You're clearly upset about that. So tell me."

She sets her jaw, and I realize my biggest fear is that she'll say it was my fault, that I'm the kind of homewrecker I've never wanted to be. Yes, I wanted them broken up, and I was happy it happened. Yes, I wanted him to want me again. But I didn't want her to get hurt.

If only relationships—and life—were ever that neat.

To my surprise, she sighs into a slump. "I liked him for who I thought he wasn't. When I met him, it was right after that knee injury, and I guess it was just the pain meds talking, but he really made it sound like he was gonna quit. Put sports behind him for good. I'd recently been dumped by one of those cocky jock types—dropped me as soon as he realized being able to hit a ball with a stick meant he could get way hotter girls. And Law was…well, you don't need me to tell you he's hot. It felt like such a jackpot to get a guy who looked like that and *wasn't* a jock."

But he was. He would always be, in some way. And if Andi had really known him, she would've gotten that.

It doesn't need to be said aloud. So it isn't.

"What about you?" she asks. "Why'd you break up?"

For so long, I thought the answer to that was just physical distance, real life, whatever. I thought he got bored, or it was too hard, and I should feel the same way, so I pushed myself to. But it wasn't any of that. Not really. And Tessa may be right that I put things before lacrosse, but she isn't right that lacrosse has my whole heart. I hate that I've given that impression—both to her and to Mase—but the question of who he and I could be now doesn't detract from who I know we were then, how I know I *felt* then.

"I guess I loved him for being someone he isn't anymore." My voice is a whisper, and only when I see her flinch do I realize she used the word "liked"; I used the word "loved." But I really did. He got me through some of my very worst moments; he was the reason for some of my best.

And those moments that were all me? He celebrated those with me too, as proud as Cammie, as Matt, as my dad used to be, once upon a time.

He didn't need to be on the court for any of that.

He still doesn't.

Fuck.

"You sure that 'loved' is past tense?" asks Andi, her tone dry but her voice thick with hurt.

I hate that she's hurting.

I hate that she's right.

I shake my head, and she smiles, just slightly. Resignedly. I feel like crap. But…honest crap. Finally.

"I'm sorry," I say. No qualifiers, no explanations—just an apology, for all of it.

She nods, but even without words I think we're gonna be okay. Not BFFs okay. Not living together next year okay. But I don't think I need a lookout anymore, and I'll take that.

chapter twenty

It feels good to sleep in my room again, to lie in my own bed reading Greek plays and typing up Communications presentations while Andi sits at her desk, poring over her anthropology textbooks and Spanish flashcards. But it's also way more restless sleep. Whereas before I'd been able to focus my five or six hours, now my solid seven are full of tossing and turning, things I wish I'd said back to Mase when I had the chance, and questions for Brady about why he gave the captainship to Tessa. I dread having to tell my father that he was right to be apathetic about my lacrosse career. He's been continuing to send me wedding things without any hint of acknowledgment that my plans might have changed. And maybe they shouldn't.

I'm obviously not valued on the team. My own teammates don't seem to care nearly as much as I do.

And the guy who used to make me love all this stuff no matter how hard it all got wants nothing to do with me.

What's the fucking point?

"Caitlin Johannssen, if you sigh one more time—and then say 'nothing' when one of us asks you what's wrong—I am making you an appointment with Doc Locke," Lizzie says firmly from the couch, where she's currently lying in pose beneath me as the Sisera to my Yael, for another of Frankie's paintings. I'd tried to beg off when Frankie requested my presence, but she promised it'd only be for an hour or two while she sketched, and it'd seemed like a good distraction at the time.

Apparently, it wasn't good enough.

"Lizzie, you've been in therapy for like three seconds," I remind her. "It's a little early to be pushing it on me like you've been bellowing the gospel for years."

"I can't decide if giving your therapist a rhyme-y nickname helps or hurts your evangelism," Frankie adds around the pencil in her mouth.

"I'm guessing helps with you, hurts with Cait," says Lizzie.

"Accurate," Frankie and I say simultaneously.

"Is this still about Tessa?" Lizzie asks. "Or are we past that and onto how you should obviously be telling Mase that you're still into him?"

I growl at Lizzie, my knuckles tightening around the hammer I'm holding over her head. "For the millionth time, words aren't enough. I have no right to ask for another shot with him if I can't prove we have a future without the thing that bound us."

"Didn't you say he was a fantastic fuck?" asks Frankie. "Let that be the thing that binds you."

"Jesus Christ, Frank," I mutter, though it probably gets lost in Lizzie's cackling from the couch.

"You guys are ruining the pose!"

"Maybe don't talk about my sex life, then!"

"Well one of us needs to," Frankie says. "Now get back into position."

"Hee hee."

"Oh, shut up, Lizzie." I sigh. "It's complicated, you guys."

"So uncomplicate it," Frankie suggests. "Tell him you wanna be fuckbuddies. Then you don't need to worry about the rest of this shit."

"I *don't* want to be fuckbuddies," I snap. "I *want* a relationship. I miss the fuck out of him, and I miss how good he makes me feel, in *and* out of bed. I was in love with him, and I think I still am. Okay?"

You could hear a pin drop in the silence that follows. Or, more accurately, a pencil drop. "Shit."

"Caity!" Lizzie flings her arms around me, completely fucking up our pose, but the yelling I'm waiting for from Frankie doesn't come. Instead, a second pair of arms circles me—us—and squeezes tight. "I didn't know you were in love."

"*Was*," I clarify. "Now, I don't know what I am."

"But you want a real shot to find out," says Lizzie.

I nod.

They both squeeze me again. "Okay," says Frankie. "We need a plan."

"A plan?"

"You said the problem is convincing him that you're in it for real, right?" I nod again. "So we do that."

"But—"

"Yes, I have an idea of how." She holds up a hand. "You're not gonna like it. I'm telling you that now."

"Also, you're probably gonna need to break up with Jake," Lizzie adds wryly.

Oh, fuck. I'd completely forgotten about that. I'd never even told them that relationship was a farce, but I'm guessing from her apathetic tone they've both already figured that out a while ago.

"You knew."

"I told you, Caity J.," says Frankie. "My gaydar is stellar."

I should've known. "I'm sorry for lying, but—"

"We get it," Lizzie assures me. "Forget that. But you do need to tell him the jig is up, or whatever the kids are saying these days."

"And then what?"

Frankie grins, her dark eyes glittering. "And then you ask him to help."

• • •

I text Jake to ask him to meet me that night at his favorite diner; if I'm pulling his beard—and his free trip to San Diego—I figure there should at least be a great burger in it for him. My stomach drops when I see him walk through the door with a smile on his face, certain he has no idea what's coming, but the instant he sits down across from me, he says, "You're dumping me, aren't you."

"How the hell did you know that?"

He laughs. "This is the first time we've hung out outside of the library and class in weeks. Either you're trying to seduce me or you're trying to dump me, and you more than anyone know that the first one isn't happening. Though I'd be flattered. Really."

The busboy comes over then and fills our water glasses, saving me from the necessity of an awkward response. "Do you hate me?" I ask once the busboy is gone.

"How could I hate you for wanting to live your life? Honestly, this has gone on longer than I even hoped, especially considering I thought Mason was gonna chop off my nuts when your name started coming up in the locker room."

I snort, trying to squash any warmth I feel at Mase's jealousy. "So, I've been locker room talk, huh?"

"Sorry, babe—goes with the territory of being a jock's girl." He rolls his eyes and takes a sip of water. "For what it's worth, the entire team is impressed that you give stellar head."

"My life's ambition achieved two whole months before my twentieth birthday." I pick up the menu and pretend to study it for about ten seconds before the question bursts out of me. "So, Mase didn't like it, huh?"

Jake throws back his head and laughs. "He's what this is about, isn't he?"

I narrow my eyes. "You answer, then I'll answer."

"Well, since you've asked so nicely, no, he did not like it. I believe his exact words were 'Moss, shut your fool mouth before I shut it for you.' Charmer you've got there."

I don't have him, my brain automatically corrects. *Yet.*

"The dude really is a raging hardass, and I mean that in more ways than one. What is it about him, anyway?"

"He's sweeter than you think, when he wants to be." The waiter comes and we place our orders—cheeseburger and fries for Jake, turkey sandwich for me. "You've seen him at the community center, with those kids—when he's fun and kind and makes you wanna be around him all the time? The guy I used to know was like that all the time. And he was a great listener, and he…I don't know. He always made me feel good about myself, you know? Guys like that are in short supply. And I think he's still in there somewhere; it's just been a while since he's had someone bring it out."

I expect Jake to laugh, to tell me I'm being naïve, but he just smiles softly and starts shredding the paper napkin in his hands. "I believe that. He seemed cool, that night at the club. And I like him on Sundays at the center. I'm sure the rest of the team would be happy to have him be that guy all the time." He levels me with a stare. "That *is* the idea, I assume?"

"God, I hope so," I mutter.

"Not convinced of your powers of seduction?"

"Well, my last boyfriend turned out to be into dudes, so."

Jake grins. "His loss."

"Speaking of." I cover his hand with mine. "I'm really sorry about Troy. I know I said that already, but…I really am. You deserve a good guy, Jake. Whenever you're ready."

His cheeks turn pink, and there is just something too adorable about a hulking basketball player blushing at the idea of an actual romance.

"You know," I say quickly as I spot our waiter coming back with our food, "if you really wanted, I bet

Frankie would be perfectly happy to play your girlfriend for a while. Though, fair warning, she doesn't really understand the idea of 'acting.'"

"Nah, I'm good," he says with a smile. "If you can be brave enough to go for the guy you want, maybe you'll inspire me to do the same."

Now I'm the one blushing, but the waiter's arrived and we both clam up. I wait until he's out of earshot before saying, "There's just one more thing I need to ask you, but it should be a piece of cake. Probably. Maybe."

"Well, that's promising."

I ignore the twinge in my gut. Frankie was right—I *do* hate her plan—but the more I think about it, the more I think it's the right one on every level. However, Jake would hate it even more than I do. Thankfully, he doesn't need details. "I need you to get Mase to my playoff game on Sunday."

He raises an eyebrow. "That's it? Wait, is it—"

"It's at home," I assure him. "Just a matter of getting him to show up in the Radleigh stands. This is not a request to drive him to Maryland or something."

"Fair enough. Not sure he'll be up to doing any favors for your 'ex,' but I'll do what I can."

I grin and nab one of his fries. "That's all I ask."

chapter twenty-one

Come game day, my worries over whether or not Mase will actually be in the stands take a backseat to my heart pounding and palms sweating over whether I can actually pull this off at all. Seeing the rest of the team pumped and ready to kick some ass gives me a billion butterflies in my stomach, and Tessa's awkward attempts to sound captain-ly when she's been more of a quiet, background force all season make my heart ache in my chest.

What will it do to them—to her—if I go through with this?

Nothing, the little devil on my shoulder tells me. *This isn't Tessa's life the way it is yours, remember? She made damn sure to tell you that.*

I set my jaw, snap my goggles on around my ponytail, and line up on the field.

We form as if we're a solid unit, as if nothing's changed. It probably hasn't, for anyone else. I run out at the call of my name and number, waving my crosse in the air under the canopy created by everyone else's. I accept the applause and stand quietly with my hand over my heart during the national anthem, searching the stands until I see a little group of guys, a head taller than everyone around them. Jake is in the middle, and on his right, his expression unreadable from this distance, is Mase.

I tear my eyes away from him, look around at my team as I get into position at the draw, and think, *I am about to screw you all.*

Nobody gives a shit what good I do here. Not Brady, who gave the captainship to someone else. Not the actual captain. Not anyone in my family. How much easier would it be with my dad if there were no championships in contention to start with?

And Mase…there's only one way I know to prove that lacrosse is not my everything, and that's to give it up, right here, right now, while he watches.

Of course, the ball lands in my crosse almost instantly, fed by Mariana, and I instinctively run, plowing through a line of defense, their uniforms nothing but a yellow blur. They're so poorly spread out, it'd be the most glaring fuck-up in the world if I didn't run it down the clear alley they've made to the right of the goal and hammer it in.

Goal one, fifteen seconds in.

I pray St. Mary's will pick it up, fast, because the more they suck, the harder this game's gonna be to throw. Thankfully, their midfielder pulls it from Mariana on the next draw and runs it down the field, out of my realm. They pass it around the 12-meter for what feels like an hour before Cassie Duvall finally takes a shot to the top right of the goal, which Nora saves easily.

That, finally, kicks St. Mary's into high gear, and both Duvall and Freya Clayton try riding our defense, to no avail. Nora passes it to Olivia Bonner, who promptly clears it to—of course. Me.

It's a smooth overhead pass, in perfect position for me to take a quick-stick shot right into the St. Mary's goal. All I'd have to do is take a single step forward.

There's a twinge in my stomach as I let it bounce off the top of my crosse onto the grass.

"Oh, shit," I hear Tessa yell as she runs in to recover it, but the defender on her is built like a fridge. The one on me scoops it up and passes it upfield until it's back with Duvall. I see Nora make the mistake of leaving the goal circle an instant before she realizes it herself, and bam, we're tied at 1-1.

And it feels like hell.

"It's all right," Tessa assures me, patting me on the back as we get back into position for the draw. "It's just one play."

Then Mariana heads into the middle of the circle, her eyes flashing. When she pulls the next draw control, I'm in position for a pass, and I see her notice it for a second before she opts for Tish instead. But Tish barely pulls it in, and she ends up passing right to me. I run it down, keeping my pace slow enough to let the St. Mary's defense get in my face. Tish manages to make herself available for a pass, but I pretend I don't see her, and take a wild shot on goal instead. It hits the edge, then gets salvaged by St. Mary's, who runs it back down and scores on Nora.

I know I made it happen, but my stomach turns at the sound of their cheers anyway.

"Girl, I was open," says Tish as we retake our positions for the draw. "Why'd you take that shot?"

"Sorry, I didn't see you," I mutter, but lying to Tish feels worst of all. Especially when I see her put on her supportive teammate face.

"It's okay," she says, even though it isn't. "Just nerves, probably. But don't worry. You got this, C."

Do I? What *am* I doing right now? Did I really convince myself this game doesn't matter to them just because they don't live and breathe this sport like I do?

And is it worth doing this to help get a guy to like me if it makes me not like myself?

I'm sorry, I think, to both Mase and to my dad, for ever thinking this was something I could pull off, something I'd want to. I want to show them I care, somehow, but this isn't the right way. I love lacrosse, and if it's an unhealthy amount, well, that's just who I am. But it's who I was when my dad was proud of me and who I was when Mase was with me, and even without them, I don't want to be anyone else.

I'm sorry to my team, too, but not for much longer; my shitty day ends now.

• • •

We win the game by only a goal, but it's enough. I was flustered enough to make a few more (genuine) fumbles, but I also had two assists and two goals, one of which was so damn lucky I must've actually earned karma points with some higher power. Afterward, I avoid the team, too embarrassed to face them, but Jake finds me before I can disappear for good. "Congrats on the win," he says, giving me a peck on the cheek. "Now do I get to hear the great mystery behind why I basically got down on my knees begging my student-coach to come?" He nods over at where Mase is talking to Ryan Pfeffer, the only other basketball player present, who comes to almost all our games to watch Jamie.

"I thought I was going to prove something I didn't," I grumble. "Just…can we not talk about it?"

"You don't have to talk about it with me, but you do need to talk about it with him, whatever it is," he says.

"Did you tell him? About you and me?"

Jake snorts. "He's known since the night we went to XO, Cait. Did you really think you were fooling him with that plan?"

I smile sheepishly. "I don't know, I thought it was smart. Why'd you go along with it if you thought it was so obvious?"

"Guess I wanted to go on a date with Troy more than I cared if Mason found out," he says with a sad shrug. "Solid prioritizing on my front, clearly, since Troy turned out to be such a winner."

I squeeze his shoulder. "Someone will be, Jake. I promise. We're gonna find him."

"Yeah, maybe. Someday." He cocks his head. "You think Law's little brother's coming up to visit again anytime soon?"

"Oh, God, Jake—"

"Kidding," he says with a smile. "But your boy's heading over here, so I think it's time I see myself out. I've really gotta get packing, anyway. Going home in a couple days."

"You're not coming to the victory party tonight?"

"Nah. It's too weird with everyone thinking we just broke up; it makes all the guys into even bigger pussyhounds than usual, trying to find me a rebound girl or three. Pass."

"I'm s—"

"Stop apologizing, Cait." He leans down to peck me on the cheek. "You're fine. *We're* fine. I'll give you a call tomorrow so I can say goodbye and good luck before I head out."

I don't have time to say anything in response before a shadow falls over us. "Hey man," says Jake, before I can even take in that Mase is standing behind me. "I was just heading out. I'll see you later."

Mase grunts a goodbye, just as I turn around. "Hey," I say meekly. "You came."

"I was informed my presence was requested, by your ex-boyfriend," he says, with only a trace of sarcasm to his words.

I choose to sidestep that last bit. "It was, but I was being stupid. I shouldn't have dragged you out here."

"Then why did you? Because if you're trying to prove to me that you're still a great player, I kind of already knew that."

"That wasn't it."

"Then what was?" he presses.

I take a deep breath, knowing I can tell some stupid lie right now, maybe even drive him away if I really am too scared to pursue getting him back. But I don't want to lie, and I don't want to give up again; I've spent too long hating myself for how easily I gave up the first time. "I thought I was going to prove it to you—that you matter more than this," I tell him. "That I don't need to be an athlete. That I can walk away anytime. But I was wrong. This is it. This is me. I'm sorry I dragged you out here."

"Wait. You *what*?" He pulls us even further from the crowd. "You were gonna throw the game? For me?"

"Among other reasons," I mumble, feeling immeasurably stupid about it now. "I thought I could, but—"

"Cait. Fuck." He wraps a hand around my wrist. "I never—I would never want that. I love that this is who you are. I love what you can do. I'm sorry if I made you think otherwise."

The praise and apology suffuse me with warmth, and I don't know what to say. I retrieve my arm from his grip, nod jerkily, and manage a "thanks" before turning away, cheeks burning with too many emotions to name.

But then, again, my name. His velvet voice. I turn to look up into his long-lashed eyes, despite my better judgment. "You wanted me here."

"I did," I acknowledge. "I'm sorry."

"Why are you sorry?"

"I just told you—"

"Cait." He takes a step closer. He smells like mint gum and Right Guard; I shudder to think of my scent after an entire game of running around like an animal. Not that he seems to notice. "You wanted me here."

The truth. "I always want you here."

"Even when I've been an asshole."

"Apparently."

"Even though I don't play anymore."

Now I look him squarely in the eye. "You play. You don't have to be on ESPN or make the front page of the school paper to be an athlete, Mase. You're doing something real with those kids, with our basketball team. I'm not letting you rewrite your present any more than I'll let you rewrite our past."

His lips curve, just on one side, just an inch, but it feels like the ice around us has finally cracked. Like I can finally breathe. "Mase."

"Yes?"

"Why'd you come?"

"Because you wanted me here. Because—" He sighs. "I always wanna be here, Cait. I always wanna be on your damn team."

"Even when you're being an asshole."

"Especially then," he says, velvet vanishing into smoke as he dips his head and brushes his lips against mine. It's the slightest of kisses and yet the sparks it sends through my blood could set this field on fire.

I wrap my aching, sweaty, filthy arms around his neck and nip his lip, forcing him to look at me, to listen. "Our victories, from here on out. Our victories, our losses. All of them."

He's quiet for a moment, though his hands find my waist. "As long as it's *my* blue Gatorade."

"You selfish bas—" My words are lost in his kiss, fierce and hungry and victorious.

For once, I let him win.

• • •

That night, I go the victory party. And for the first time in two years, I actually bring someone.

"So, this is our first 'date,' huh?" Mase had asked when I told him that not only did I want to go—together—but I wanted him to pick me up. (Then I realized how tremendously awkward that was and amended it to have him pick me up at Double Trouble's apartment instead.)

"Yes," I'd said firmly, "and we are doing it right, like a normal couple. Well, starting after the part where you can't pick me up at my own dorm room because my roommate's your ex. But *then.*"

He'd laughed, and so had I, and it felt really damn good to laugh, even though I still feel really shitty about Andi. When Mase shows up at Lizzie and Frankie's door, looking so fucking good in jeans and a button-down I could weep, I vow to put the bad stuff behind me, at least for a night.

And then he whips out a bouquet of lilies from behind his back, and forgetting everything else gets really, really easy. "Impressive, Mr. Mason." I mean it to come out light, teasing, but it comes out a little choked. It makes my heart ache that he's really trying, that he wants this as much as I do. He might've thought the idea of emphatically making this A Date was silly, but that's the thing about Lawrence Mason—he always takes me seriously when I need it.

"You, too," he says with a shameless onceover, sounding a little choked himself. Dresses may be hard to find for my height, but I've always loved this one—it's cobalt-blue and makes my eyes look like sapphires and my legs look a billion miles long.

It would appear Mase is a similarly big fan.

"You *guys*," Lizzie coos, clapping her hands together like a proud parent at prom. "Don't make me cry."

"Aren't they adorable?" says Frankie. "So fucking adorable I could just bang them both."

"This is why I asked you to stay in your rooms," I say with a sigh.

Mase just laughs and squeezes my hand. I know then that he likes my friends, and that's probably the best thing about this night so far.

"So is this just the lacrosse team getting drunk together in a dorm room?" Lizzie asks.

Frankie perks up. "Wait, is there room for one more?"

"It's in the basement of Shamblin, and my friend Tish said a whole bunch of athletes are crashing. You're welcome to come if you don't mind non-stop jock talk *and* if you promise not to lay a finger on a single one of my teammates," I add with a glare in Frankie's direction.

"Hard pass," she replies, and Lizzie nods.

"Well then, we're gonna head out."

"Here, gimme those—I'll put them in water." Lizzie takes the lilies from me and whisks them off to the kitchen. I never thought I was a flower person, but I miss them immediately. At least until Mase fills the empty spot in my hand with his. "Hopefully they'll drop very subtle hints to Connor that some girls occasionally like flowers, and not just DVDs of old documentaries from the History Channel."

"Girls like what now?"

I shake my head at Mase. "We do not attempt to understand Lizzie's history nerd boyfriend. We just go with it."

"Noted. Good to meet you, officially," he says to Lizzie, "and to see you again," he says to Frankie.

They both chirp back "You too!" and Frankie adds a "Don't do anything I wouldn't do tonight!"

"Don't worry," I tell Mase. "There is literally nothing on that list." Then I yank him out the door before any of them can get out another word.

chapter twenty-two

The first thing I realize when we step through the door is that I wildly underestimated how awkward it would be to walk into an athlete party with a date who *isn't* the guy everyone thinks I've been with for months. It's impossible not to notice how many heads turn to stare at me and Mase as we walk through the door, fingers interlaced. While I accounted for the fact that it might be a surprise to see me dating a guy almost no one's seen me speak to, there are a bunch of pissed-off looking basketball players I realize think their coach stole me from one of their players.

Huh. I guess that would be pretty fucked up, if it were actually what happened.

"Cait! Hey!"

I'm relieved when I see Latisha hop off her chair and make her way over. She's the only one on the team for whom this probably isn't much of a surprise, and it makes seeing her oddly validating. "Hey, Tish." I let go of Mase to exchange a squeeze hug with my teammate, just long enough for her to whisper, "Nice job, and I expect *many* details."

"Smoothies after practice tomorrow," I promise, and she releases me. "Tish, this is…" My inclination is, of course, to call him Mase, but that isn't how anyone here knows him. Hell, I don't even know if he hates the nickname now, if it reminds him of glory days past or something.

"Mase," he fills in with a little chuckle in my direction as he shakes Tish's hand. "Or Law. Or 'that fucking asshole,' when the guys on the basketball team don't realize their student-coach is in the locker room with them. I'm not picky."

There is no better sound than one of your friends laughing at your boyfriend's jokes, I swear. God bless Tish, because some of my anxiety about this party melts right then and there. "This is Latisha," I say to Mase. "She's on lax with me, as you presumably saw earlier."

"Definitely noticed," he says with a warm smile. "Always happy to see a sister representing in this white-ass sport."

"Someday, maybe there'll be two of us," she replies in a mock-fantasizing voice.

"Dare to dream." He raises a fist in the air.

A couple of drinks and an hour later, the party has blown up. We've got an undefeated season behind us, a week until our next game, and most of our finals done with; tonight, we're here to have a good time like nothing else matters. Of course, with Mase's arm around my waist, his fingers stroking dangerously close to my ass, the definition of "good time" keeps getting more and more singularly focused in my mind. His touch is a drug to my already beer-soaked brain.

"So, Johannssen," Scott Madden says, "you think you'll be the one to pull the Fabe from Lewis this year?"

His tone is friendly, but I'm ninety-nine percent sure he's actively trying to be a dick. "The Fabe" is the Donald and Emily Fabian Award for Scholar Athletes, and Keisha Lewis, girls' basketball captain, has locked it down for the past two years. Even if there was a chance of them not giving it to her in her senior year, I killed that chance by losing out on captain, and Scott knows it. Everyone knows it. Not that anyone's talked about it to my face since Tessa's painful attempt.

"No one's prying the Fabe from Lewis's cold, dead hands," I say evenly, and everyone around me laughs, oblivious to my sourness.

Well, almost everyone. The tension I'm carrying in my back slowly melts as Mase draws his hand across my waist and creeps it under the hem of my dress. "I'd give it to you," he murmurs in my ear as he traces a pattern on my skin. The conversation's moved on, but he's still here, with me.

I cover his hand with mine, just loosely enough to convey I have no intention of moving it off. His hand slides up my thigh so slowly under my grip, it's like a moving Ouija piece—I have no idea who's actually steering.

"You guys are all going to the award ceremony, right?" some dude asks.

Mase's fingers inch higher.

"Of course."

There's chatter about outfits and finals schedules and who will win what awards and I can't hear any of it through the roaring rush in my ears. One finger, two, brushes against the little scrap of silk I'm wearing under my dress. It's my only nice pair of underwear, and it's not faring very well right now. Bits and pieces of the surrounding conversation filter in, just enough to remind me we're not alone, but not enough to make me care.

"Are we supposed to, like, bring dates?"

Another brush. Beneath the table, the dress, the silk, I am liquid fire.

"You looking, freshie?"

"Ugh, back off, Layton."

Touch me.

All I get in response to my mental begging are lazy trails of heat—torturous but responsible, given we're in a room packed with friends. Only I don't care about responsible; I am going out of my fucking mind.

"We should go," I murmur, but when I turn to look at him I see he's deep in conversation with a guy on the basketball team. I don't wanna interrupt—my impression from Jake is that Mase could use all the fans on the team he can get—so I re-focus on the conversation.

Which is exactly when one of his fingers dips inside, finding me wet and wanting.

I glance up at him, and see him trying to keep a sly smile from spreading across his face.

Fucker.

Two can play at that game. I glance down to make sure his lap is as hidden by the table as mine is, then skate my fingers over his denim-covered thigh. He tenses immediately, knowing what's coming, but it doesn't make me inclined to show an ounce of mercy.

"So, where's Moss tonight?" The question from Dan Guttierez—the one he seems to love asking me—drips with blood, and stops both Mase's and my teasing hands in place.

"Maybe you should get a tracker, and then you can stop asking me that," I reply as lightly as I can manage.

"Nice move, snaking the girl of one of your own guys," he spits at Mase. Then he turns to me. "Don't you think it's a little slutty to start fucking his coach five seconds after you guys break up? If you even waited that long."

Conversation in the room grinds to a halt, and everyone turns to look at us—particularly at me, since I jumped out of my seat the second I heard the word slutty.

"Don't you think it's a little fucking presumptuous to think you know *anything* about our relationship? In case you missed it—which you might have, since you don't seem to realize this is a party to celebrate *my* team's achievement today, not yours—Jake was in the stands at our game. We're just fine. You're the one with the problem, and you can feel free to take it elsewhere."

Dan looks like he wants to spit nails, but his gaze flicks over to Mase standing behind me—hand on my back, a tight expression on his face that I know is masking a whole lot of rage, ready to let loose if he determines I need it—and he keeps his mouth shut. As player and coach, there are infinite reasons they cannot have a throw down here and now, and as gratifying as it would be to see Mase deliver the pop to Dan's jaw he so desperately deserves, it's probably a good thing for all of us I can take care of myself.

Instead, Dan stalks off, a few of the other guys behind him. I'm glad to see them go, but I feel so queasy at how shitty this is for Mase. At least their season is over and done with; their record picked up after Mase's hiring, but not enough to dig them out of the hole.

"You okay?" Tessa asks as soon as the door slams behind the basketball players.

"Fine," I mutter. "But I think we'll probably head out too. I've had enough celebrating for the night."

"Cait—"

"I'll see you guys at practice tomorrow." I blow a kiss and a bunch of the girls blow them back. Then Mase and I get the fuck out of there, all thoughts of fun and fooling around forgotten.

I storm toward Shamblin's exit, barely conscious of whether Mase is even behind me, but his arm curls around my waist and pulls me back toward the elevators instead.

"Where are we going?" I demand.

"Up to my room, so you can take a breath before you go back to the room you share with my ex in a ball of rage. Especially since I can't exactly walk you inside."

Fair point. I hadn't even known he lived in Shamblin—I would've steered clear far more often if I had—but of course he does; the entire eighth floor is full of singles for student coaches. I don't say anything, but I watch in silence as he presses the button, keeping his arm around me, and then brings me up to his room.

The familiarity of the Sixers poster on his wall sloughs only the roughest edge off my anger; I'm too tense to notice anything else. "I am so sick of all this shit," I say as soon as he closes the door behind us. "All I've wanted this entire semester is the captainship I've worked my ass off for, to go to the championships my team has earned without getting in a family feud over it, to help a friend, and to get the guy back who was mine in the fucking first place. None of this is unfuckingreasonable."

A little smile plays on Mase's lips. "The guy who was yours, huh?"

That stops my rage in its tracks with flames lighting up my skin. "You know what I mean."

He cups my chin in his hand, stroking a thumb over my lower lip. "Fuck it; I was. I am. I always have been. I'm man enough to admit it."

Christ, that might be the hottest thing any guy has ever said to me, and he's close enough for me to feel his body heat, to kiss with nothing but a tilt of my head. But I need to clear the air, first. "I'm so sorry for all the shit you've had to go through for us to find our way back here," I say, my voice barely above a whisper. "I hate that I fucked things up with you and Andi, and with you and the team. I know at least one of those was necessary, but it doesn't make me feel any better."

"I can handle it."

My man of few words, I think, but however spare he is with his conversation, I know he always means what he says. He can handle anything. *I* just can't. "Fuck, I wanna hit something."

He steps back. "Go for it."

"Not *you*."

He grins. "I know, but do it anyway. It'll make you feel better."

"I feel like you're mocking my strength here."

"Never," he says seriously.

Fuck it. I step toward him, aim a hand at each of his broad shoulders, and shove. And he's so surprised I did it that he actually stumbles back. I do it again, and again, until he falls back onto his extra-long bed.

And then I climb over him, straddling his hips on my knees. "I feel mildly better now."

"Me too," he says, skating his hands up under my dress. "Me too."

The heat of my anger is slowly but surely morphing into something else, and even though this is gonna be our first time since officially getting back together, I can't slow this down into the sweet, loving thing it should be. I bend forward to cover his mouth with mine while my fingers rip his shirt apart, the clinking sound of flying buttons hitting their marks like firecrackers in the quiet room.

As if in revenge for destroying his shirt, there's a quick burn on my thighs from the tear of fabric, and I see a flash of black out of the corner of my eye as my collection of good underwear dwindles to zero. "I liked those," I say as I work open his belt.

He flips me over in one smooth motion and shoves my dress up to my waist. "My guess from the fact you soaked through them is that you'll like this better." He pushes a finger inside me easily, then adds a second and grazes my clit with his thumb. I couldn't feign indignation over my breathless moan even if I wanted to.

"Feeling any better about those panties yet?"

I rock into his hand harder. "Shut up."

"How about those assholes downstairs? They still bothering you?" He brushes against my clit again as he withdraws his hand and slides it back in.

"Shut up," I just barely manage on another moan.

"And—"

"Lawrence Mason, so help me God, you better put that mouth to better use right now."

There's a low chuckle and then the only sound in the room is my howl as he shifts back on the bed and licks around his fingers. Somewhere in the back of my mind, I'm aware that I'm chanting "fuck" like a sailor while I writhe against his firm hand and maddeningly playful tongue. Still I'm missing something, craving a little more of an edge, a little pain. I push back harder, and am rewarded with the addition of a third finger.

"Good," I gasp out. I'm not particularly articulate when I'm this horny, apparently, but it's enough for

Mase. He closes his teeth around my clit and flicks his tongue mercilessly until my brain explodes in white light and I come so hard I couldn't recall my own name if you asked.

I shudder against his mouth for what must be a century. Then he slides up the bed next to me. "Am I forgiven for the panties?"

"What panties?" I ask sleepily.

He laughs. "Have I lost you for the night?"

"Please. I think you know I have way better endurance than that." I roll over on my side and tug him to me by his open shirt, pressing my mouth to his. The taste of me is sharp on his tongue, and I feel particularly grateful he's upped his game in the past couple of years. "I mean, unless you're too worn out…"

He shrugs out of his shirt and shuts me up by fusing our mouths together, sliding his hand in my hair and tugging. I shove his jeans down his hips and he pushes them the rest of the way off, then helps me out of my dress. When he sees I'm not wearing a bra underneath—small boob perks—he sucks in a breath through his teeth, and looking down at the enormous tent in his boxer briefs, I know exactly how he feels.

He's sitting up and I straddle his lap, fully aware I'm soaking through the cotton of his boxers. Boosted by his thighs, we're almost the same height, and as I rub gently against his cock—just enough to keep us both on the edge but not enough to make either of us go off—I let myself appreciate how fucking beautiful the man is who's holding me right now. Those gorgeous, warm brown eyes with their mile-long lashes; high cheekbones I could trace with my tongue; the full mouth that brings me comfort in so many different ways…

If I open my mouth, I'm going to tell him I love him, and it's far too soon for that. Instead I lift myself higher, arching for him to easily take a nipple into his mouth. He does, sucking so hard it feels like a lightning bolt straight to my clit, making me forget to keep my rocking gentle.

"Oh *fuck*," he groans, gently pushing me back. "You do that one more time I'm gonna come in my shorts. Gimme a sec to get a condom."

I drag myself off him, forcing myself still because I know if my clit brushes anything now I *will* come whether that gorgeous cock is inside of me or not. By the time he suits up and rejoins me on the bed, I feel like I can probably last at least thirty whole seconds. I climb back into his lap, hyperconscious of how different this is from the last time we fucked—when he took me from behind in a space that wasn't ours, no kissing, no affection at all. I came, sure, but it wasn't like this.

Nothing in my life has ever been like this.

Our lips melt together as I fit him inside me, sliding down slowly to adjust to his size. It feels so fucking good to be pressed against him, chest to chest, arms wrapped around each other, nails digging into each other's skin as we pick up the pace, careful gentleness giving way to raw, primal need until we can barely catch our breath in each other's. It's impossible to tell who comes first, impossible to be aware of anything at all except that the world suddenly seems full of stars.

chapter twenty-three

I drift off to sleep in Mase's arms sometime afterward, and am woken even before my internal clock by his impressive morning wood. I'm too sore from last night to fully go again—plus, admittedly, I've never been one of those people who can ignore morning breath—but I gladly take my own advice from the night before and put my mouth to good use. Much as I'm not looking forward to this day, his filthy praise definitely feels like the right start to it.

Afterward, I realize I've got nothing to put back on except for my dress. You'd think I'd have learned from spending the night at Jake's, but I'm still highly unpracticed at sleepovers. While I could generally give less than half a fuck about doing a walk of shame, I really don't want to bump into Andi looking so glaringly post-coital.

"You okay?" A gentle kiss lands on my shoulder, then another, and I swear if I could spend this entire day in Mase's bed, I'd do it in a heartbeat.

"Yeah, I just gotta get back, sadly. I've got practice, a study group for my Comm final, and I promised I'd meet up with Tish today so I can fill her in on…well, you. I'm just trying to figure out what to wear back to my room."

"Don't you have friends in this dorm? Just borrow something."

Oh, duh. "I knew I liked you for more than your body," I say, reaching back to cup his cheek. Then I climb out of bed and search for my phone to text Nora, the closest to my size, crossing my fingers that she's awake.

The first thing I see is a Missed Call from my mom.

"Okay, now I *really* have to go," I mutter, tapping out a quick text to Nora, Trish, and Tessa, who share a suite on the fourth floor. Luckily, Tessa's awake, and she tells me to come by. I beg some toothpaste from Mase, change in the girls' suite, and call my mom on the way out.

"Hi, honey. Busy night last night? I called you twice."

It's a patented Molly Holt-Johannssen opener. Whoever thinks Catholic and Jewish moms hold the monopolies on guilt has never met my Lutheran mother. "We were celebrating our first playoff win," I explain. "There's no cell service in the basement of the dorm I was in."

"Don't you have finals now?"

"I'm doing fine, Mom. Promise. Everything's done but Communications, and I have a study group for it this afternoon."

"How'd your Econ project go?"

"We got an A." Jake and I may not have done everything perfectly that semester, but we sure as hell did just fine in class.

I recognize her sigh for what she'd never admit it is—wishing I were more of a shitshow so she'd have a reason to keep stronger tabs on me. One of the reasons she and I have never really clicked is because she needs too much be needed; unlike Cammie, who was a party girl extraordinaire in high school, I haven't come up with much for her to do. "All right, then. And you have another game tomorrow?"

"Yup—got practice in an hour. I'm heading home now."

"Heading home?" She perks up, and I clap my hand to my forehead as I realize my mistake. "From where?"

"I stayed over at the dorm the party was in last night. It's the jock dorm—most of the lax team lives there." All true things.

"All right," she says again after a few moments of silence. "Well, I'm calling because your father wants to know what you've decided about going to his wedding."

Ouch. My parents do not talk when they can help it. For my father to be reaching out to my mother…that's pretty bad.

"I guess his child bride still hasn't filled him in about our conversation at her bridal shower."

"Do I even want to know?"

"Probably not." The spring sunshine is delightfully warm through the cool morning breeze, and I take a seat at one of the benches on the quad and watch the usual runners go by.

I haven't officially said this to anyone yet, but after yesterday's game, the one thing I'm sure about is that for better or for worse, lacrosse is coming first in my life. It doesn't matter if anyone else understands that, or if people think it's crazy, or if it's unhealthy that it's all-consuming. The fact is that right now, in my life, it's who I am—more than I'm my mother's daughter and apparently more than I'm my father's daughter. I chose it when I thought it was mutually exclusive with being Mase's girlfriend too. "I'm not going, Mom. Don't be mad. My team's in the quarterfinals next week, and then it's just the semis—right before the rehearsal dinner—and then the championships the day of the actual wedding. I can't—"

"Honey, you know I don't get all this sports stuff. That's always been between you and your father. As long as your choice is right with you, I'm not going to interfere. I don't agree with your decision not to go, but I don't agree with his decision to make it that day either. So, you do what's right for you."

"I really do think I am," I say quietly, my heart swelling with how grateful I am for her trusting me. "I really do."

"Okay, then. I hope it's worth it."

Ouch. But I guess I deserve that. Hell, I hope it is too. But I have the faith it will be, and I have to, if no one else will.

Even though I've said it to my mom, there's one more person whose blessing I feel like I need to make my decision official. "Mom, I gotta go. I'll call you after I talk to Dad, okay?"

"Okay. Good luck, honey."

She's right that I'll need it, but right now, it's not my father I care about speaking to. I say goodbye, tuck my phone back into my purse, take a deep breath with my eyes on my dorm up ahead, and then I turn west.

• • •

I take a deep breath and ring Lizzie's doorbell, praying I haven't caught her and Connor mid-bang. Not that it's a typical banging hour, but with Lizzie there isn't really any such thing; a few times freshman year, I came back to a knee-high tied around our door knob during lunch. Thankfully, she comes to the door in sweats and a T-shirt after a few seconds, and with no sign of company.

"Cait! Hey! Did you text, or just in the neighborhood?"

"Neither. Sorry," I add, because even though Lizzie and I shared a room for a year and a half and it's hard to think of a space being hers and not mine, that's exactly what her apartment is. Plus, she's got that whole "serious boyfriend" thing happening now; presumably that makes drop-ins a little less welcome.

She waves her hand and steps aside to let me in. "Please. Mi casa es su casa—you know that. Walk in whenever. Just, you know, be prepared to see the occasional bare ass if you do."

"I've been prepared for that since the very first day I made the acquaintance of Francesca Bellisario, thank you very much."

She grins. "Touché. Want a drink?"

"Thanks, I'm good." My mouth actually does feel a little dry, but I don't want to draw out the pleasantry stuff; I'm afraid if I don't say what I have to say, I'll lose my nerve. "I wanted to talk to you about something."

"That sounds serious."

"Kind of." I take a deep breath. "Listen, I just got off the phone with my mom, and I've thought a *lot* about this…and I'm not going to my dad's wedding. I just can't. I've worked too hard for the championships, not just this year but ever since I first picked up a crosse. I know it's just a sport to you, and to Frankie, and to pretty much everyone on the planet, but it's what got me through my entire adolescence. It's what got me through the shitty years of my parents' fighting, and then the shittiness of their divorce. It's what got me into college after years of being afraid I wouldn't be able to afford it. And in a couple of years I'm gonna have to say goodbye to it for good, but I'm not ready to throw it away just yet. I can't let down my team, and I can't kill their faith in me, captain or not. I just can't. I'm sorry."

She shoots me a startled look. "Why are you apologizing to *me*?"

"Because I know it feels to you like I'm taking my dad for granted, when you lost yours. And I get that—I do. Maybe I am taking him for granted. But he's taking me for granted too, and he's disappearing, and he's starting a new family that very clearly doesn't have any room for me in it. So—"

"Hold up. Cait." Lizzie puts a hand on my arm. "I am on your side. I'm always on your side, okay? I just don't want you to make any decisions you're gonna regret later."

"I know, and I love you for it, but I feel firm about this one."

"Then I support you a thousand percent, and say fuck that stupid wedding." She throws her arms around me, and I squeeze her back so tight I think I might bruise a few ribs. "I'm sorry if I made this about me when you really needed it not to be. I'm still…adjusting. Badly."

I relinquish my lobster-claw grip, but keep my hold on her at arms' length. "Elizabeth Brandt, hush your mouth. You are doing as well as any human possibly could in your situation. Right now I'd rather streak across the lacrosse field during the championships than see my father, but I don't know how I'd handle it if I *couldn't*."

She just nods and hugs me again, and this time she's the one squeezing so tight I can barely breathe. But I can, so I do—just a little exhale full of all the relief into the world.

chapter twenty-four

The blankets are scratchy, there are moths mating in the fluorescent lighting, and Tessa's been snoring for hours, but I wouldn't trade being in this hotel room just outside Philly with my three closest teammates for anything in the world.

Tomorrow, we'll be playing for the championship trophy.

I should be following Tessa's lead and sleeping, or Tish and Nora's—they've been going through the starting lineup of our opponents, Carolina U, for hours, talking about weak spots and favored scoring sides and angles. But I can't sit still; my mind is racing with thoughts about the game, the wedding, and how badly I wish I'd asked Mase to come. I didn't, out of a combination of fear that him seeing me have this opportunity just might be too much, and consideration, since I know sitting in a car that long with an old knee injury is murder, but God, I could use the support. Once upon a time I would've been certain I'd see my dad in the stands, but that's obviously impossible this year, and I know I'll be on my own tomorrow.

At least the other girls will have parents and siblings there, and Tish's mom always brings cookies.

My phone beeps with a text, and I grab it, eager to talk to Mase. But the message isn't from him after all: *Dude, you need to call Dad. He seriously still thinks you're gonna show up.*

Matt, texting from San Diego, i.e. Wedding Central.

Wha?? I told him I'm playing tomorrow. I'm IN PA.

Yeah, I know. I think Abigail got it into his head that you'd change your mind at the last minute or something.

Of course she did.

Lol

I freaking hate the idea of calling my dad, but Matt wouldn't tell me to if he didn't think it were absolutely necessary; he's even less interested in inserting himself in drama than I usually am.

Can't you just tell him?

Soooo not getting in the middle.

Probably should've seen that coming. *Fine.* I take a deep breath, find my dad's number in my cell, and hit Send.

"Hello?"

Abigail. Of course.

"Hi, Abigail. It's Cait. Is my father there?"

"Cait!" She sounds almost…happy to hear from me. Is that possible? "Are you at the airport?"

Oh, well, that makes more sense now. "No, I'm in Philly. My championship game is tomorrow, remember?"

I keep my voice gentle, as if there's a chance she actually forgot, but it doesn't help her reaction. "You really did it," she says venomously.

"Got to the championships? I told you both we would."

"Skipped your own father's wedding for a game," she says in disbelief. "He said you meant it, that sports were your heart, but I couldn't believe it. I couldn't believe a twenty-year-old woman would make such an immature, selfish choice."

Oh, that is fucking *it*. I step out of the room and walk down the hall so as not to wake up Tessa. "You know what, Abigail? You're right—it is selfish. But there's nothing inherently immature about making a selfish choice. It is *hard* to put what you know is right for you first, when you know people you love don't respect your choices. It is *hard* to say 'what I want is worthy.' It is *hard* to say 'I know myself and what I need, even if everyone else thinks otherwise.' Don't tell me this is immature when it took me *months* of thinking about it every damn day to make this choice."

I can run five miles without breaking a sweat, but that rant leaves me winded, and my breathing is like thunder in the silence that follows. I don't know if it's because she's internalizing what I had to say or because she's working on thinking of an appropriate comeback, but I don't want to give her the chance to do the latter before I've said everything I need to say.

"Your mother's not happy you're marrying my father, is she? A man almost twice your age."

"He's not—"

"I said 'almost,' and semantics aren't the point. She's pissed, right? Thinks you're making a mistake? Or at least she's completely freaked out that you're gonna have stepchildren your age? I could tell, at your shower."

Abigail sighs wearily. "What's your point, Cait?"

"My point is that you chose what was right for you over what she thought was right for you, and my father did the same—choosing what was right for his new family over his old one. You chose this wedding date. You put yourselves first. And that's all I'm doing here."

"This is a marriage and a *baby*; you're talking about a *game*."

"You're right, Abigail. I am talking about a game. I don't know what it's like to have a marriage and a baby, but I know what it's like to be part of a team with whom I share something I love. So I can't put myself in your shoes any more than you can put yourself in mine, but I suspect this is the closest we're gonna get. So I'm asking you to try to understand me anyway, or at least not to stop my father from doing so. Because I suspect that deep down, when you're not talking him out of it, he does. He gets it. Just let him."

Another long silence follows, and then she says, "Your father's just outside. Hold on, I'll get him."

I'm not sure if that's a concession or acknowledgement of anything, but it isn't a fight, so I'll take it. "Thanks, Abigail. I really hope you do have a special day tomorrow."

If she's still on the line to hear me, she doesn't acknowledge it.

A minute later, there's a fumbling sound, and then, "Hi, Cait."

Cait, not Caity-Cat. Guess he's already been filled in as to where I'm calling from. "Hi, Dad."

He doesn't follow up the greeting with anything, and I don't know how to either. Do I just wish him a good wedding? Do I say I'm sorry? *Am* I sorry?

"I wish I could've done both," I say finally, knowing it's absolutely the truest thing I could say about it all.

"I wish you could have too," he says, sounding tired. "But…I'm proud of you, sweetheart. I know you've worked hard for this."

He sounds a little choked up, and now I feel it too. "Thanks, Dad."

"It's late over there, isn't it? You should get some sleep."

I glance at my watch. It is getting late—definitely past my usual bedtime—but I hate the idea of him just getting rid of me. "Dad—"

"Just make me proud tomorrow, Caity-Cat," he says. "That'll be the next-best wedding present to you being here."

Slight dagger to the heart, but I'll take it. "Deal. And you…get married well tomorrow. Make sure Matt takes some good pictures."

"I will."

"I love you, Dad."

"I love you, too, Caity-Cat."

• • •

Despite the cathartic conversation, I still wake up with a pit in my stomach. It's hard to think about not being there on my dad's wedding day, and it's just as hard to think of him not being here with me. To know that those stands will be empty of support for me sucks, and I have to remind myself over and over as I get suited up that I play for me and my team. Support is nice but I don't need it.

Support is nice but I don't need it.

Support is nice but I don't need it.

I keep this mantra in mind through our warm-ups and pep talk, and eventually, the potent combination of excitement and anxiety fill my brain until I can't think of anything else. Before I know it, we're lining up on the field, two parallel stripes of forest green and white, and the announcer is calling out the name of our starting lineup.

At the sound of "Number 21, Caitlin Johannssen!" the loudest, most obnoxious hooting and hollering fills the air, and I look up at the stands.

Lizzie. Frankie. And Mase.

In the bleachers.

Seven hours away from Radleigh.

If I weren't already overwhelmed with emotion, this would've done it. I could cry right here on the field, except suddenly I feel Tish's elbow in my side and then Nora yanking me into position to hear the national anthem.

As I listen to the familiar tune, I remember standing on the field the day of our first playoff game, thinking I was gonna play as shitty as I could get away with in a misguided attempt to prove how much I care.

Now I know this is about me doing the opposite, proving staying to play was the right choice. Proving to be worth the trip. Proving that whether or not I deserved the captainship this year, I definitely deserve it next.

I have sixty minutes of playing time to help make us all legends. And as I circle around Mariana, who's going up for the draw, I've never had less doubt.

The first draw control goes to Carolina, which puts on a little bit of a damper, but their power lasts for all of five seconds before Tessa intercepts. I cut around the blue-clad defender on my ass, grab Tessa's feed pass out of the air, and quick-stick it right over the goalie's left shoulder.

Beautiful.

When I take my usual spot on the circle for the next face-off, Mariana jerks her head toward the middle. "Do the draw," she mouths.

My eyebrows shoot up. As the tallest girl on the team, I'm a reasonable choice for doing it, and I've certainly practiced plenty, but it's a position Mariana rarely relinquishes. Losing the first one must've really rattled her. I swap spots with her, nodding when she murmurs "push draw" in my ear, as if I really needed to be told to take advantage of my height. I gain control easily—the other girl's a head shorter—and pass it to Mariana, then set up for an invert. She drives it in, and I'm gratified to see the cradling I've been helping her with at practice has been paying off. There's no opening for her to take a shot, though, so I cut down and catch a high pass. The hole doesn't stay open for long, though, and I dash around the goal, cradling it away from the Carolina girl on my tail, and wrap it low on the underside.

Goal.

The screaming from the stands reaches a fever pitch, and my loud-ass friends are audible above everyone. I blow a kiss in their direction with one hand while accepting a slap five from Tish with the other, then retake my spot in the center.

"Happy wedding day, Dad," I murmur. And then I raise my crosse for the next draw.

chapter twenty-five

We are national. Fucking. Champions.

I'm still blinking at the scoreboard minutes after the game ended, the 10 under Radleigh so beautiful and round next to Carolina's 7. And six of those goals? Those are mine, along with eight draw controls and two assists.

It didn't seem to surprise a single person on the field when I was named Most Outstanding Player, but internally, I'm still reeling from it. I've been clutching the trophy like a lifeline since it was put into my gloved hands, and if I can get away with sleeping with it tonight, I'm gonna do it. Not even sorry.

We're standing around screaming, pouring water on each other and into our mouths, and hugging friends and family when Brady's voice cuts into the crowd. "Johannssen, can you come here for a minute?"

The high from winning quickly mellows as I give Brady a jerky nod and tell the team I'll see them later. He hasn't tried to talk to me since naming Tessa captain, and I'm not looking forward to it now. But at least I know he can't complain about my performance today—not with the trophy still clutched in my hand. "What's up, Coach?"

"Nice arm candy," he says with a smile. "You did great today, Johannssen. You've done great every day."

The unspoken question hangs between us, and he knows me better after two years together than to think I'll ask it.

"I know you want to know why we didn't make you captain. We did talk about it—you were a serious consideration."

"But?"

"But a captain represents the whole team. Makes decisions for the whole team. This year, we just didn't get the feeling you were…in the right frame of mind to solidly do that."

My knuckles whiten around the trophy. "I chose this over going to my father's wedding, Coach. I chose this over *everything.*"

"I know, Cait. I know. And of course the team and I are grateful that you did, but that's not the healthiest balance either. If you came to resent the team for the sacrifices you made…" He doesn't say a word about the game after he announced captain, but my cheeks flame anyway. He knows my natural weaknesses, and they don't account for my "errors" in that game. "The temper on the field, the one-man showmanship when you've got something to prove in apology…it was just too erratic to make you a leader right now."

I want to argue, but I can't; he's pretty much nailed it. "I've been working on all that," I say sheepishly. "And…I get it. I do. But next year, I'm telling you now—I want it. And I'm gonna do whatever it takes to prove to you I deserve it." I pause. "I'm gonna win the Fabe, too. And be named All-American. I know those things aren't remotely in your control, but I just want you to know I'm putting that out into the universe."

Brady chuckles. "I have no doubt you'll achieve all those things, if you want them. And I look forward to seeing you in action."

"It'll be a sight to behold," I promise. "But for now, I'm gonna make one more choice that isn't very leader-ly—I'm gonna ride back up to Radleigh with my friends, so knock me off the attendance list for the bus, please."

He nods. "I guess this is goodbye until the fall, then?"

"It is," I confirm. "Thank you for a great season, Coach."

"Thank *you*," he says. He extends his hand for a shake, and I take it. After a beat, I reluctantly hand over the trophy, too. And then I turn around and run to my waiting friends and a long car ride of cramped legs and battles over music and nonstop sexual innuendo.

I can't wait.

• • •

We eat dinner at Mase's mom's house, where she shocks me by actually giving me a hug—something she has definitely never done before. Only once we're completely stuffed do we begin the long ride back to Radleigh, with frequent stops for Mase to stretch his poor legs. Andi's already gone—her last final was three days ago and she left immediately after—but I go back with Mase to his room anyway. Shamblin's felt far more like home to me these past couple of weeks, and the fact that Mase has an extra-large bed doesn't hurt.

"So proud of you, Caity J.," Lizzie murmurs through a yawn when she drops us off, giving me the squeeziest hug known to mankind. "I knew you were gonna kick some royal ass."

"That's our girl." Frankie squishes me next and kisses my cheek with a smack. "Go give her a night worthy of a world champion," she orders Mase.

After something like seventeen hours with my friends, I'm pretty sure they're past the point of shocking him. He just laughs, and we say good night to them and get out of the car, moaning as we stretch our long limbs in the breezy night air.

"Are you actually in the mood to—"

"No," I cut him off, shaking my head. "I am tired as fuck and all I want is to pass out."

He laughs. "Yeah, that's what I thought. Come on." He takes my bag of gear and twines his fingers in mine, bringing me up to his room.

And okay, maybe we make out in the elevator a little bit.

The second we get inside, I drop onto his bed and moan again at how good it feels to have a mattress under my aching bones. "I really wish this place had a bathtub."

"Can't offer that, but I'm sure you'll have your pick of the showers; pretty much all the other student-coaches are gone for the summer."

"Mmm, in a few minutes." I let my eyelids flutter closed and make myself comfortable on his pillows, and a moment later I feel his weight on the bed as he joins me. His warm, solid arm wraps around my waist and his lips brush my shoulder, and I think that if I died of exhaustion right now, I could actually be okay with it.

"So, I did something I hope you'll be happy about," he says hesitantly. "If not, it's cool—just tell me. But I've been sitting on it a couple of weeks until all your other stuff was settled."

I turn onto my side to face him and prop myself up on my elbow, trying to read his eyes for clues. "Oh?"

"You said you didn't really have plans for the summer yet, and I'm only on board here for the first summer session, so…I called Robbie."

"Robbie?" My eyebrows shoot up. "Stone Creek director Robbie?"

"Yeah." He reaches out and curls a wayward strand of blond around his index finger. "Asked if they might need a couple of extra hands for July."

"And?"

"And…they do. Or maybe he was just being nice because he was excited to hear our names, but either way, there's room for us to work as staff for the month if we want to. I figured this way, you've still got a month to spend some time in San Diego with your dad, maybe get to know Abigail a little before the baby comes. And then, if it sucks as much as you're probably dreading, you get a whole month to blow off steam playing in a pretty low-pressure environment, where you'll basically be the place's biggest rock star. So…what do you think?"

I don't know whether to laugh or cry at the thought of returning to the place that brought us back together and holds so many memories for us from a time that feels like eons ago, when we were very different people. But the one thing I do know is that I absolutely, positively want to go, with the guy lying next to me, the guy who traveled many hours to see me today with two girls with him who were basically strangers, just because he knew how happy it'd make me.

"What about benefits?" I ask, resting my chin on his broad shoulder. "I'm expecting some serious makeout benefits. And I'm definitely going to need a refresher course on those astronomy lessons."

"Astro—*oh,* God, Jo." He cracks up laughing. "You didn't think I actually knew shit about the stars, did you?"

"You didn't?"

"Helllll no. I just wanted to impress you. Rick Foster taught me some of that stuff that first day, and I made up the rest. But apparently it worked."

"Yeah, it worked, you asshole!" I whack him on the chest. "Here I was, thinking you were all brilliant and worldly."

"I'm still brilliant and worldly, just, you know, not about that shit." He grins. "Did I just ruin it? Have I just totally fucked up my plan to lure you with me this summer?"

"Alas, it's gonna take more than a little white lie to run me off this time around," I say. "I'm in. And thank you. For thinking of it, and for today, and for wanting the best for me, even when it isn't always the easiest for you."

He bends his head to kiss me, and though it was probably meant to be a quick peck, I can't resist taking more, sweeping my tongue over his, sliding a hand up his Sixers T-shirt to graze all that smooth skin over hard muscle. He takes my lower lip between his teeth and pulls me closer, throwing a leg over mine, and suddenly, my exhaustion doesn't seem quite as pressing as getting another kind of relief does.

Only problem is that I feel utterly disgusting.

Which gives me an idea.

"How empty do you think those showers really are?"

He cocks his head. "You serious?"

"Bad idea?"

"*Best* idea." He kisses me again, then helps me pull my clothing off my aching body and takes his off too. I barely get a minute to appreciate his gorgeous form before he's wrapping us both in towels, and then he tells me to wait while he makes sure all is clear.

It is.

The hot water feels amazing on my skin, as does Mase slowly kissing every inch of my neck and shoulders. "I bet you could use a massage," he says as he rubs shampoo into my hair.

"Well, I wouldn't say no," I concede, my eyes closing as I relax into the way his fingertips work my scalp.

"Didn't think so." He finishes shampooing, then drops to the floor as I rinse it out, those same strong, able hands working my calf muscles. I shiver as I watch him, and then all thoughts escape my brain as his fingers knead higher and he starts pressing kisses to my inner thigh. I'm reasonably certain that if his hands and mouth come any closer to my body's newest ache, I *will* pass out right there in the shower. But he keeps his distance, focusing on my legs, and he presses a kiss—just one—between them before getting to his feet. Then he turns me around and works his magic on my shoulders and back, sucking gently at my neck as he works the knots everywhere else.

"Mase…fuck." Every touch is so damn good, but the fact that his cock is at full attention and pressing against my ass is starting to blur all his hard work. "I can barely feel my bones anymore."

He nips gently where my neck meets my shoulder. "Good."

"Sure can feel yours, though."

He skates his hands up to squeeze my breasts, which are extra sensitive under the pelting of the hot shower water, then goes back to massaging. "Also good."

"You know you're making me crazy right now."

"This, again, also seems good."

So irritating. "How about this?" I ask, taking one of his hands and guiding it to feel how wet I am, having absolutely nothing to do with the shower. "That good?"

His cock jerks and he takes his hand back, and then the sound of him sucking his finger whispers in my ear. "Very, very good."

He spins me around, pressing my back up against the cold tile wall, and fuses his mouth to mine, enough heat in his kiss to boil the water beating down on us. I dig my nails into his back as I pull him closer, closer, as if it were somehow possible to fuse our bodies together into one electric ball of light. I'm feverish with how badly I want him, how badly I can feel he wants me, and when he boosts me up and pins me to the shower wall at just the right height to enter me, all I can think as I wrap a leg around his waist is *Yes, yes, fuck, yes.*

"This okay?" he breathes.

Are you fucking kidding me? I want to yell back, until I realize he means the fact that he's not wearing a condom. I nod. "Pill."

"Thank fuck," he mutters, echoing my thoughts exactly as he slides his long, thick cock inside me, making both of us gasp against the pressure. It takes a few seconds to find our rhythm against the slick wall, but if there's one benefit to how much we both work out, it's the strength to fuck hard and fast, having nothing to grab onto but each other's bodies. After a minute I'm not even sure who's saying, "Hold on tight, baby" or "Oh, fuck, I'm gonna come," but we hold together and fuck together and come together and by the time my brain can next form a coherent thought, I've collapsed in Mase's arms and I never want to get up.

• • •

When we can finally move, we soap each other up all over again and actually get clean this time, then brush our teeth and throw on T-shirts and boxers before crawling back into bed. I'm entirely out of energy now and halfway to sleep when Mase's velvet voice rumbles in my ear, "In case I haven't said it enough today, I am so damn proud of you, my champion girl."

He's said it about a million times, but this one feels different, and it makes me shiver a little in his arms. "Thank you."

"And you really are into it? The whole Stone Creek idea?"

"I love the idea," I tell him wholeheartedly, turning in his arms to face him. "And I love you for thinking of it. And for a whole lot of other things."

He cups my cheek in his palm as a soft smile curves his mouth. "I love you too, Jo." The smile turns sheepish. "Sorry. Cait."

"I'm not picky," I tease, bringing that hand to my lips for a kiss. "Nothing wrong with a little nostalgia. Especially for things that never really ended."

"So you don't think it's a step back, right? Going there after getting together here?"

It hadn't occurred to me it might be, but now that he's put it out there, I wonder if it should have. Just as easily, though, I dismiss it. "We met there as kids, and we're going back as…well…"

"Kids who know a little better?"

"Something like that." I wrap my fingers around his and squeeze. "We're old, but we're also new, and what's happened in between has made us very different people. And those very different people still seem to think they belong together, so."

That seems to satisfy him, and he touches his forehead to mine. "We can still make out in the gazebo like kids, though, right?"

I tilt up my face, just enough for him to feel the ghost of my breath on his lips when I say, "Like national fucking champions."

acknowledgments

Anyone who's been waiting for this book since *Last Will and Testament* knows it took me over a year to write. There were times I was afraid I would never finish. It's by virtue of the editorial guidance of Katherine Locke, the ass-kicking of Lindsay Smith, and the endless patience and encouragement of Yoni Fisch that I did, and I am endlessly appreciative and awkwardly love-filled.

Massive thanks are due to the early readers and critiquers who took that finished manuscript and made it shine as much as possible—my inimitable West Coast Bae, Candice Montgomery; hair-petter extraordinaire, Sara "s" Taylor Woods; the glorious Jenn Fitzpatrck (whom I will happily pay in Cajun fries anytime); Patricia Riley, to whom I owe approximately everything; and, of course, Maggie Hall, because I can't even belt a dress without begging her for guidance.

Thank you to the fabulous Sarah Henning for going above and beyond with her copyediting, and to Randy Shemanski and Bethany Robison for the valuable bonus sports knowledge. Much gratitude, too, to my secret proofreading weapon, Christina Franke, and World's Greatest Formatter (and Cait's namesake) Cait Greer. None of my books would be complete without their stunning covers, and for this one as for all my others, all my heart-eyed emojis are once again turned on Maggie Hall.

And finally, thanks to everyone whose love, support, knowledge, and readership gets me from one day to the next: the brilliant, kickass, inspiring authors of the Hideaway; my CP loves; the awesome readers in Dahl's Den of Iniquity; my co-mods (yes, I'm gonna keep calling you guys that forever, no matter what); the clans of Yay and WBW; my peppermint-scented archnemesis; the amazing and generous bloggers, reviewers, and readers whose words, graphics, and letters have meant the world to me; and my family, who is definitely not reading this. (Though Sash and B, if you guys are, I love you both, and thank you for not telling me.)

about the author

Dahlia Adler is an Associate Editor of Mathematics by day, a blogger for the B&N Teen Blog by night, and a writer of Contemporary YA and NA at every spare moment in between. She's the author of the Daylight Falls series, *Just Visiting*, and the Radleigh University series, and she lives in New York City with her husband and their overstuffed bookshelves. If you give her a macaron, she just might fall in love with you.

More often than not, you can find her on Twitter as @MissDahlELama, and on her blog, The Daily Dahlia: http://dailydahlia.wordpress.com.

Turn the page for a sneak peek at the first chapter of Book #3 in the Radleigh University series,

out on good
BEHAVIOR

chapter one

I've been betrayed.

To the left of me in our blue-velvet-lined booth at Delta, Lizzie Brandt is actually fucking *giggling* at whatever Connor, her boyfriend of nearly a year—a *year*—is whispering in her ear while she sips from a highball of scotch.

On my right, Cait Johannssen is trash talking about some sort of sports…thing, which is totally typical except that she's doing it with her fingers laced through *her* boyfriend Mase's.

And I…I'm the lone wolf.

Okay, I'm not that lone—Mase brought a couple of friends to the club from the Radleigh University basketball team, and one's left hand is about three inches from learning that I'm au natural under this dress—but still. *Boyfriends*. Serious ones. Who even does that?

"So, Frankie." I jolt to attention at the sound of my name, and realize Connor's spoken it, and now everyone's looking at me. "I hear congratulations are in order."

"For what?"

Cait snorts. "Only you wouldn't even blink at the fact that you're getting a whole freaking exhibit at an art show."

"Oh, right. That." I feel a little blush coming on and take a quick sip of my vodka with cranberry juice. "It's not a big deal. I had stuff up at the last show, too."

"Yeah, but you didn't have your own *exhibit*," Lizzie says firmly, raising her glass in the air and nearly sloshing it over her hand. I'm not sure whether it's her third drink or her fourth, but she has definitely entered the "proud, cheerful drunk" portion of her evening, which is my favorite Lizzie phase. "This is huuuuge. We should have a party at the apartment to celebrate. Let's have a party!"

"We've been back at school for thirty seconds," says Cait, taking a sip from the single light beer she's been working on all night. She's on a hardcore campaign to win the lacrosse captainship that should've been hers this year, and cleaner living is factoring into that in a major way, sadly for the rest of us. "You're already party planning?"

"Hey, I declared a major—"

"Yeah, one you got lucky as fuck accepted a bunch of your random classes toward it," Cait reminds her.

"Whatever—you're just jealous because Cultural Studies is about sixty-nine times cooler than Econ." Lizzie takes another sip of her drink. "Anyway, I declared a major, I have the perfect resume-building part-time job this semester, my brothers are doing great, and I actually still like this one," she says, jutting her thumb in Connor's direction. "Even you're getting laid, Caity J! What's not to celebrate?"

Cait plucks a peanut from the little bowl in front of us and tosses it at Lizzie. It smacks off Lizzie's nose and bounces right into her scotch. "Ew, Cait!"

"My girl's still got it," Mase says fondly, nuzzling her neck.

"Fucking jocks," Lizzie mutters, taking another sip of her drink, peanut and all.

"Hey," Guy-with-his-hand-on-my-thigh chimes in with mock indignation. I'd actually kind of forgotten he was there.

"Yes?" Lizzie asks, blinking.

He doesn't respond, and the rest of us crack up laughing, though Mase quickly cuts himself off to flash a sympathetic smile instead.

"Now that I think about it," says Cait, "a party isn't such a bad idea. Seems like a good excuse to drag Samara out of the room."

The mention of Cait's roommate makes me perk up in my seat. "Samara, huh? Yeah, I'm definitely on board with this party."

"Oh God, stop it," Cait begs, throwing a peanut at me this time. "For the billionth time, Samara is the literal top of the no-touching list."

"Is she even gay?" Mase asks.

"No," Lizzie answers at the same time I say, "Yes."

Connor and Mase look between us, confused. Mase's friend's hand freezes on my thigh. "Wait, are *you*?"

"I don't discriminate by gender or lack thereof," I say, because sometimes, you just know "I'm pansexual" is going to be met with "What's that?" followed by "Isn't that just bi?" and finally "So, you're down for a threesome?"

This guy is definitely *that* guy.

He blinks, and I can already feel him pulling back, but whatever. I turn to the others. "I'm telling you, that girl likes girls. I swear, I will prove it by Spring Break."

"Please, no one take her up on that challenge," Cait pleads.

"Sorry, Cait," says Lizzie, "but you know I need to see how far Frankie's rainbow magic extends. I think we should put money on this one."

"You're *not* putting money on Frankie nailing my roommate."

Connor scratches his scruffy jaw. “That does seem to go a little beyond crass and into the realm of…”

“Lizzie-esque?” Cait fills in.

He smirks and says nothing, lifting his beer to his lips and taking a long drink.

“Why didn’t she come tonight, anyway?” asks Mase.

“She doesn’t have ID,” says Cait. “Doesn’t really drink. Hence a house party would be a way better choice for her, and frankly, I think she could use something, stat. She did *not* come back from South Carolina this summer a happy camper.”

“I can imagine,” I murmur, taking a sip of my own martini. If there’s one thing I definitely remember from my few conversations with Samara last semester, it’s that she and her family—most specifically her Republican politician father—don’t mesh very well. Lizzie’s right that Samara has never said a word to suggest she likes girls, but I’ve historically had pretty stellar gaydar, and it still pings every time I talk to her.

Or maybe I’m just flirting hard enough for both of us. It’s been known to happen.

“So, party? Friday night?” Lizzie suggests. “Tell your friends! I’d tell mine, but, well.” She gestures around the table.

The rest of us try not to snort with laughter and fail. Lizzie hasn’t exactly made herself the best-liked student at Radleigh University—fooling around with a taken fraternity president and hooking up with a TA who nearly loses his job over it aren't really "Miss Popularity" plays—but God bless her, she doesn't seem to mind.

"Sounds good to me," I say cheerfully, imagining seeing Samara again in the comfort of my apartment. Just because I can't touch doesn't mean I can't look.

Just then, a familiar pair of long brown legs walks in, and I down the rest of my martini and stand up. Racquel I'm-Sure-She-Has-a-Last-Name-Somewhere is always good for a dance on the floor, followed by a dance in the women's bathroom, and all this talk of a girl I can't have has gotten me very in the mood for a girl I can. "Speaking of potential party guests, I'll…see you guys in a bit," I say, popping open my glittery clutch for a Tic-Tac.

Lizzie follows my eye line to Racquel and groans. "Oh, great. That's the girl I'm talking about when I say 'the Loud One,'" she says to Connor in what isn't nearly as quiet a whisper as she thinks it is.

"Guess we're staying at my place tonight," he replies as I make my way over to where Racquel is looking pretty damn good in a clingy red dress under which I'm guessing she's wearing as little as I am.

"Count on it," I call back over my shoulder. Samara Kazarian may not be certain about who or what she wants, but I sure as hell am.

www.ingramcontent.com/pod-product-compliance
Lightning Source LLC
Chambersburg PA
CBHW032206190626
46810CB00019B/2019
* 9 7 8 0 9 9 0 9 1 6 8 4 0 *